Hello Darling,
are you working?

Hello Darling, are you working?

Rupert Everett

Illustrations by Frances Crichton Stuart

William Morrow and Company, Inc.
New York

Copyright © 1992 by Rupert Everett

First published in 1992 in Great Britain by Sinclair-Stevenson Limited.

Publishers and author are grateful to acknowledge the use of the following copyright material:
"Maria" (Richard Rogers/Oscar Hammerstein II)
© 1959, Williamson Music International, USA
Reproduced by permission of EMI Music Publishing Ltd, London WC2H OE
"Let It Rock", "Little Queenie" and "Johnny B. Goode"
Words and music by Chuck Berry
© 1959 Are Music Corp. (All Rights Reserved)

It is the policy of William Morrow and Company, Inc., and its imprints and affiliates, recognizing the importance of preserving what has been written, to print the books we publish on acid-free paper, and we exert our best efforts to that end.

Library of Congress Cataloging-in-Publication Data

Everett, Rupert.
    Hello darling, are you working? / Rupert Everett; illustrations by Frances Crichton Stuart.
        p.   cm.
    ISBN 0-688-11786-4
    I. Title
PR6055.V347H44   1992
823'.914—dc20

92-9360
CIP

Printed in the United States of America

First U.S. Edition

1 2 3 4 5 6 7 8 9 10

ACT I

CHAPTER ONE: in which I want doesn't get

By the time he was eight he knew he would never be a Great Actress.

There it was, sticking out in front of him like a sore thumb: his penis – and his first showbiz disappointment – shattering all his dreams.

It was at teatime one day just before Christmas, when he was only six years old, that it first started to sink in. He was in the drawing room of his grandparents' home in Scotland with his mother, Lady Dinah, his father, the Brigadier, and his Aunt Frances who was known as 'the Martyr'.

3

The Brigadier was hidden in the leather depths of an old wing armchair covered, apart from the top of his head, by the *Financial Times*. The Martyr had arrived five minutes earlier from London and she and Lady Dinah were clustered together on the sofa, catching up with each other. They were swathed in balls of wool, sewing boxes and pinking scissors, since the Martyr was knitting an interminable sweater and Lady Dinah was in the process of putting the fringe on her latest lampshade.

The boy was crouched on a footstool in one of his mother's discarded nightdresses, thinking of nothing in particular. During a lull in the two sisters' conversation, the Martyr picked up her knitting and turned to her favourite nephew.

'Ree,' she said, 'what are you hoping to get for Christmas?'

He didn't answer and suddenly there was a huge tension in the room. The *Financial Times* folded with a loud crackle to reveal the shadowy scowl of the Brigadier. Lady Dinah began to concentrate with blind determination on her fringe. The boy pulled his knees up inside his nightdress and lowered his head into the ruff.

'Well, Ree?' continued the Martyr, oblivious to the *faux pas* she had obviously made. 'Have you lost your voice?'

He looked from one parent to the other, imploring them to come to his rescue, but no one spoke. The clock ticked ominously.

'I want a wedding dress,' the little boy finally blurted out. He put his hands to his ears and stood up. 'I want a wedding dress, I WANT A WEDDING DRESS!' he screamed, utterly hysterical.

Lady Dinah raised a slightly accusing eyebrow in the direction of her sister and sighed.

'Darling, I thought we'd discussed all this. I am not, repeat *not*, buying you a wedding dress.' But before she could take hold of her son, who was now stamping and screaming in the middle of the room, the Brigadier had risen, hurling the *Financial Times* to the ground, a gesture for which he was in fact too small – he was only fractionally taller than the armchair – but which carried a certain naive threat.

'Now look here,' he said, lifting up his son by the ruff of his nightdress, 'I thought I'd made myself clear. Boys do *not* ask for

4

wedding dresses for Christmas. Not in this family, anyway. You're going to get a crack over the jaw if I hear any more of this nonsense.' He dropped his small son back on to the floor and returned to his armchair.

Lady Dinah and the Martyr sat in suspended animation but the little boy now had only idea in his head: to run. He bolted out of the door, slamming it behind him, and ran headlong down the long stone corridor, narrowly missing Mrs Mac, the cook, wheeling the tea trolley towards the drawing room.

He didn't stop until he was safely on the other side of the small door between the back stairs and the rest of the house that marked the end of *Their* territory and the beginning of *His*. He raced up the little turret staircase – thirty-eight steps in all – to the nursery tucked beneath the rooftops, through the white wicket gate at the top, and then he was back in his own rule-free world. The austere gloom of the rest of the house was sharply offset by the simple white walls and threadbare beige haircord carpets of the nursery floor. Like a little ghost, skimming by in his pink nightdress, he went straight to the bathroom and locked the door. He hitched up his nightdress and sat down on the big white wooden seat of the lavatory. He put his elbows on his knees and his head in his hands and sat there motionless for several seconds.

In truth, he was not being deliberately subversive. He just didn't understand the reasons why he couldn't cross-dress. Little did he know – and how could he? – that he had been born into the only quarter of British society that would tolerate at all his particular character discrepancy. No word of anger greeted his appearance on his father's grouse moor in another of his mother's nighties.

'He's musical,' everyone would tell each other knowingly, '*very* musical.' But that winter afternoon there seemed no rhyme or reason at all. Silent tears poured down his ruddy little cheeks and finally a small trickle of urine went plip, plip, plip into the bowl.

That was the other thing. The Brigadier had told him last week that he must do it standing up.

'Why?' he whimpered through his tears, 'why?'

A resigned look on his face, he stood up, hitched his nightdress above his stomach and continued to relieve himself, regarding the procedure with great and serious attention. When he had finished he turned round and looked at himself in the mirror above the bath.

There it was, no doubt about it . . . sticking out in front of him.

'But Rhyssie, darling, it's *always* been there,' reasoned the ever-practical Lady Dinah. '*Frankly*, we've always been quite amazed that you've managed to ignore it for all these years.'

But he was inconsolable.

His name was Rhys Waveral. Rhyssie was only the first in a long line of nicknames he was to have throughout his life. He was five years old when he first decided to take to the stage and he dreamed, with a rare clarity for someone of that age, of his future career as a classical actress.

Until he was ten he lived at his grandparents' and every afternoon, alone in their large draughty dining room, dressed in one of his mother's cast-off nightdresses, he would practise curtain calls behind the huge musty velvet curtains. With one hand on the rope, opening and then closing the heavy curtains, and the other holding out the pink nightdress, he would curtsey endlessly to the empty dining-room table. He provided the noise of the cheering crowd himself and then, after about half an hour of curtain calls, he would give a speech before going down to his dressing room at the other end of the dining room. En route he shook hands with the non-existent bustling crowd, blowing a kiss here, posing for a photo there. Then, once settled in his 'dressing room', he would make imaginary telephone calls to his various agents and lawyers around the world.

And Lady Beth Fraser (as he called himself) needed a wedding dress – the one that was on sale in Mrs McRae's in Inverness – because she was engaged to Ian Mac (Mr and Mrs Mac's youngest son) and the date had been set for next spring.

No-one had more agents than the legendary Lady Beth Fraser

but hers was to be a short career, for pretty soon the nightdresses were removed from his cupboard and replaced with grey flannel shirts and shorts, each with a name tape and a number on them.

An era was passing. The last vestiges of Rhys's freedom were evaporating before the long relentless haul of disappointments began. The moment had arrived – life out of the nursery – when all decent middle-class families did the correct thing and sent their children away to grow up. That moment was called Prep School.

'Hello. I'm Lady Beth Fraser,' Rhys informed the headmaster on his first day and paused, his eyes brimming with tears, to look around and acknowledge the adoration of his new fans, but all he acquired was his second nickname: Wavy

That first night in his dormitory he felt totally rejected and he dreamed that when he was grown up he lived in a bed-and-breakfast and it was very nice.

ACT II

CHAPTER TWO: in which you get what you want . . . but
   in the form that you deserve

This was something Rhys's friend, Bob Browser, had said to him
recently and, thinking back to that faraway first night at school,
had he known the expression then, he would have been able to
smile and turn to the other boys to sigh in a world-weary way: 'My
dears, one gets what one wants in the form that one deserves.'

   For Rhys lived, twenty-two years later, in the Hotel Leicester
behind the Champs-Elysées in Paris. It was a small *hotel par-
ticulier* – it had once been the home of a noble family – but
extremely luxurious and not a bit like the bed-and-breakfast Rhys
had dreamed about.

It was not overstated like so many big hotels these days, and not at all commercial. That is to say there were no display cabinets crammed with expensive jewellery, no boutiques, and no conventions for travelling salesmen. And the stairs were Rhys's favourite stairs anywhere. They were beautiful, covered with a blue running carpet with gold edges and flanked by high white walls. They turned corners around the lift shaft – the lift Rhys never took – and on each landing there was an armchair or a sofa where one could rest – or even pass the night, as Rhys occasionally had done, on the Louis Quinze *fauteuil* between the first and second floors.

At the moment this story begins, Rhys was asleep in his room dreaming about an Arthurian knight; a cluttered, stress-filled anxiety dream that recently he had been dreaming every night. And in it he was always Lancelot.

The knight was always standing with two damsels on the horizon of a rocky coastline. Their clothes billowed in the wind coming off the sea and they appeared as a deathly mirage. And that was it. The dream had no story. Nothing remarkable happened. Rhys/Lancelot was forever trying to get to the knight, running as fast as he could and getting nowhere. The knight was always dressed in black and Rhys assumed, in those odd moments when he was so bored he had to resort to dream analysis, that it meant he was searching for death.

A black knight looked deathly serious. He was always deep in conversation with the two barge ladies but Rhys/Lancelot was always too far away to hear what they were saying. Each time he had the impression that something would actually happen, that the dream would start for real, it would finish. He never managed to get close. Sometimes they would seem to be getting closer but, just as he thought he was finally going to reach them, they would shoot back into the distance.

Just another stress dream except that Rhys, at the time this story begins, had nothing in particular to be stressed about.

Or did he?

He woke up and tried to swallow, but his tongue caught on the roof of his mouth. He opened his eyes and found the visibility was low. The movement in both his arms was minimal on the best of mornings due to his great height but on a 'morning after' he could hardly rise from the bed. And last night he had been out. Out for the count, in fact. His left leg was completely dead and he had to push it like a corpse out of bed. *Thlunck!* It fell on the floor.

'Such is the price you pay,' he mumbled to himself as he lurched off the bed towards the bathroom, banging into the wall by the door as he went. Last night he had been out with Peach, his new best friend, and they had been slumped on a banquette in some smoky nightclub until a quarter to seven. The light over the bathroom mirror threw his face into startling relief. A far cry from Roger, his character in the smash-hit American daytime soap opera, *Our Butler*.

He gulped down a glass of water, washing away the toxic waste that coated the inside of his mouth, as the telephone began to ring. He looked at his watch. It said 10.15, Monday 19 October, 1987.

His face showed a much later time on a much later date. He renegotiated the hazardous door between the bedroom and the bathroom and hobbled towards the ringing telephone, hidden amongst his scattered clothes.

'Hello,' he gasped, collapsing on the bed.

'You sound as if you've got TB,' cracked a familiar and sympathetic voice.

'Oh, hello, Daddy,' he said, trying to sound as if he'd been up for hours.

'Well, you're a bloody little fool, aren't you?' They had always been close.

'Why? What's going on, Daddy?'

'*What's going on?*' roared the voice down the other end of the phone, 'what's going *on?* I'll tell you what's going *on*, you bloody little idiot. There's been a crash on the Stock Market, that's what's going *on!* God, you make me angry. You've just gone and landed yourself in it again, that's all . . . .' and he was off on one of his tirades. Throughout his life whenever his father was angry he would go on for hours and Rhys knew it was always best to try and concentrate on something else – 'Turn over and say a Hail Mary' as it said on the leaflet about masturbation at school – for there was no stopping the Brigadier when he was addressing a junior officer.

'That bloody deviant, Gavin Winterton, has just sold all your stock and left you with only half your fortune.'

'Daddy, hold on, could you trot that past me again, please?'

'If anyone's going to trot, it's you. There's been a crash. Don't you read the bloody papers?'

'Not really,' Rhys replied. 'Seriously, Daddy, what does it all mean?' Now he really was beginning to get rather worried.

'It means, you bloody little idiot, that in rough terms (a favourite expression of the Brigadier's) you are down to just under half your capital which, bearing in mind your tax liabilities incurred in that ridiculous television series you made, leaves you with a whacking great overdraft. What are you paying in that bloody stupid hotel? You'd better get out of there pretty damn quick, is all I can say. That . . . that *imbecile* (the Brigadier's voice soared) Winterton sold you out. Anyone with any sense at all held on in there, but not Winterton. Oh no! He had to go and be too damn clever, didn't he? Sold you out at the very bottom of the crash just like all those hysterical idiots in New York. Anyway, you'd better get a bloody move on. Find a job. Get that stupid agent of yours to pull his finger *out* . . .' and with that the Brigadier hung up.

Poor Lady Beth Fraser. What a sorry sight she presented after the conversation with the Brigadier had unnerved her so.

He sat motionless with his head in his hands, luxuriating in the silence. Through his fingers he could see a tiny lump of hash on the dressing table.

'Good idea,' he thought to himself, 'a little joint to blow away the blues.'

As he rolled, several things dawned on him. He had paid his enormous tax bill, which meant he was completely broke. As he licked the sticky side of the cigarette paper something else struck him. How was he going to pay his *hotel bill*? Four months in a large suite would come to quite a lot of money. With increasingly shaking hands he lit the joint and inhaled deeply. The first spliff of the day was always the best.

Not only was he broke but he was also in considerable debt.

He should move into a smaller room, shouldn't he?

But then if he did the hotel would become suspicious and maybe they would ask him to pay up.

Which he couldn't do, so he really ought to sit tight.

Suddenly he felt much better and even began to giggle a little as he tripped over his underpants on the floor and crashed on to the bed.

I know what I'll do, he thought to himself, I'll ask Cherubin.

Cherubin was the *valet d'étage* on his floor. He was a small, slightly chubby and extremely charming Portuguese bit of fluff who spoke French with an unfathomable accent. He and Rhys had become friends shortly after Rhys's arrival at the hotel. One of Rhys's New York friends had sent him some of the most lewd pornographic literature on the market. As a Catholic Rhys was strictly against such things, of course, and he hid them away on top of the cupboard in his room. One afternoon he came back early to the hotel to find what appeared to be a convention of hotel staff in his room. Cherubin and his gang (ten of them in all) had unearthed the porn and were lounging, each with a mag in his hand, all over the room – on the sofa, on the bed, on the floor, even – squealing with pleasure at each new page they turned.

When Rhys arrived back they froze. But he was secretly delighted. He went to his cupboard, took out his overcoat and left again. Nothing was ever said by anyone but from that moment a bond was struck. Rhys had one over on them, and Cherubin became his official spy in the hotel.

'*Mauvaises nouvelles*, Cherub,' Rhys told Cherubin as he came in. Bad news.

'*Quoi? Quelles mauvaises nouvelles*, Monsieur Waveral?'

'I seem to have gone broke overnight.'

'Too much nightclub, Monsieur Wavy.' Misunderstanding, as usual.

'No, Cherub, you don't understand. Now listen, I want you to do something for me. I want you to go down to Reception and find out how much my bill is. Secretly, mind you. I don't want them to know I'm asking.'

'*Oh la, la, la, la, la . . .*' said Cherubin for a while. '*Com-*

ment je peux faire ça? Non, je ne peux pas. Non! Non! Non!'
He waved his little paws in front of him in a gesture of refusal.

'Si, Cherub,' insisted Rhys, 'please. I'm in real trouble. You
have to help. And by the way, if you don't I shall simply have to
report you to the housekeeper about reading all my pornography,
won't I?'

Cherubin blanched slightly. They had never mentioned the
porn scandal. Rhys ploughed straight on. 'It won't be that difficult. You can take Marie Thérèse with you for look-out. Please.
You have no idea of the problem I have. I have to see how much
I owe without the Manager and the rest of them finding out.'

Anything to do with the housekeeper could be relied upon to
set Cherubin ranting and he turned to go and find Marie
Thérèse, muttering all the while about how they had fallen on
the porn, not looked for it, fallen on it.

'Mmmm,' said Rhys, 'just like the men who go to Casualty
with cucumbers and bananas up them with some story about
falling on the fruit bowl.'

Cherubin squealed in delight and disappeared.

Rhys had breakfast. And his bath. But there was no fun any
more. There was a new underlying hum in his subconscious.
His angstometer was up again. The beautiful white panelled
walls of his little sitting room, where he was usually so peaceful,
screamed at him. He found himself beginning to work out how
much he was paying per square metre per hour, and so on. . . .

He put on his jeans, his tie-dye T-shirt and his tennis shoes
(Travel Fox, of course, he was a slave to the rhythm, a victim
strapped on the altar of high fashion), and prepared to hit the
street. Past the telephonist, (normally Marie Claire, sometimes
Josephine depending what time he went out) and the concierges,
Jean, Victor and Monsieur Kohler, who were congregated
together, looking up at him expectantly. He always sang as he
went downstairs to let them know he was coming. They liked to
see who had spent the night with him.

It was not so much that Rhys brought people home in the
Biblical sense – although obviously he was human and he had
erred, as they say – but more that when he had been out he
invariably came home with his friends to wind down. Among

his circle, his room was the favourite after-club wind-down venue due to the fact that there was Room Service and Cherubin to look after them.

Troupes of festive bright-eyed, washed-out people would fall out of taxis in the early hours of the morning in front of the Leicester, to the delight of Fabrice and the other doormen. Peach Delight, Rhys's new best friend, would organise these events, deciding who would be allowed to come and who would not.

'Honey, not *eem*, *ee* in trouble for murder,' she would say to the ever-eager Dorhys.

'Oh, really?' her host would reply sadly. 'Well, if you really think not, Peach darling, but he seemed absolutely charming at the club.'

Peach vetoed Rhys's party invitations with a hand of steel which was probably just as well, since Rhys inevitably got caught up with the wrong set on his travels through the Paris clubs – or the 'wrong' wrong set.

The hotel staff, until now accustomed to the rich and elderly, were mesmerised like rabbits caught in the glare of headlights by the goings on. With their mouths hanging open, they would watch Rhys's party walk through the hall and disappear into the elevator like some extraordinary magician's trick.

'*Mais qu'est-ce qu'ils font*, Cherubin?' they would ask eagerly. What on earth are they *doing*? Cherubin, always a model of discretion, would reply somewhat accusingly, '*Mais, ils boivent du chocolat.*' They're having a hot chocolate. He thought it better not to mention to the others things such as the boy with the lighted blow torch freebasing in the bathroom or the burning cigarettes in the hands of those about to nod off under which he always managed to slip an ashtray at the last minute. Rhys would watch his new friend and valet with a smile as Cherubin moved around the room, filling a coffee cup here, propping up a body there. The air was always thick with smoke, music played and everyone would chat quietly, putting off the evil moment when they would have to touch back down to earth and face the screaming reality of the next morning in the city. Sometimes Rhys would look around his room at seven in the morning and find himself unable to recognise a single face except Peach's.

But when Peach sensed that Rhys had had enough, she would simply move the party on, like a traffic warden, in another caravan of taxis to the next venue, and he would be left to prepare for the mammoth hangover forever brewing in the back of his head.

In the hall everyone said 'Bonjour' and seemed very pleased to see him, or at least they acted as if they were, which was what counted.

'T'as quelquechose à fumer, Rosbeef?' Fabrice, the impertinent doorman who always called him 'Rosbeef', asked him as Rhys strode past him into the street. 'Got something to smoke?' he repeated in a macabre English accent.

'Eh, con,' replied Rhys in his best French. 'Who d'you think I am? Your dealer?' In fact the doorman was Rhys's friend and Rhys didn't mind being asked for drugs, even if he was a well-known soap-opera star.

But he couldn't think about that today. There were far too many other things to worry about.

CHAPTER THREE: in which there is no corner for Rhyssie

He had come to Paris for the first time when he was sixteen. Lady Dinah had convinced herself that going to Paris was essential for any educated Englishman, but the sort of education darling Rhyssie received was 'gathered in the field', as the Brigadier would say, and not in the History of Art classes in which she had enrolled him. Rhys discovered Pigalle and sex shops and remained ignorant of the finer details of the Doric column. . . .

He stayed with a very rich family in Neuilly who, Lady Dinah informed him in quaking tones of wonder, had a Raphael. Neither she nor Rhys quite knew what a Raphael was but Lady

Dinah knew it was a very sensible and good sign. There was a series of rather tawdry Turners in the Waveral family somewhere and it had always given everyone a great sense of security. Rhys fell in love with Paris and decided that one day he would most definitely live there. In the meantime, however, there was much to do. He must shuffle off his family coil. He returned to London to encounter the second of his showbiz disappointments: Drama School.

He had auditioned for all the top-notch places and been turned down. So he went to the only place that would have him, the Centrale Kontiki Academy for the Performing Arts which, in its own way, was also a bastion of the theatrical establishment, only to find that drama school was just like public school. Change the tweed and twills for sequins and stacks and you had the same hypocritical, bureaucratic social bloodbath as you had before. Rhys had always imagined that the acting world would be inhabited by wild, eccentric sex maniacs who lived on their nerves. He had imagined, indeed hoped, that an actor was some-one who used his life as a muscle, exploring it, stretching it, building it up so that it would explode through him, shoot past the footlights and soar into the gods as the pagan sacrifice drifts to heaven on the cloud of incense.

At the Centrale Kontiki, where the portrait of the founder, Madame Kontiki (of all the ridiculous names), hung in the hall, Rhys found they had different ideas as to how to reach the gods. A series of 'Hahahahahahahs' on an upward arpeggio followed by a series of 'Hehehehehehes' on the way down, not to mention a whole load of 'Whoooooooshkas' (dropping from the waist on Whoooosh!, and coming up on ka!), were apparently all you needed to get you to the top.

Rhys couldn't believe his ears, especially when he was told that the most important thing about acting was to learn how to make vegetable soup so that one could prepare it in one's digs on Sundays when there was no show and eat it for the rest of the week. After two years he was out on the ears he couldn't believe.

'It's not that there is no small corner of the British theatre into which your son might fit,' they told Lady Dinah sadly, 'it's just we are unable to imagine where that small corner might possibly be. . . .'

No corner for Rhyssie – or Dorhys as he had now become known – until he met Hennie Schwab. Hennie was huge, both in person and profession. She was the casting director for the largest American TV network, National Syndicated Universe (NSU), and Rhys met her at three o'clock in the morning at the Embassy Club.

He was in the ladies' loo with Adrienne Stuart, a long-legged fragile beauty and Rhys's young bride whom he had married while at drama school, and a friend, Dorinda Carr Smiley, chasing the dragon on a little bit of tinfoil and talking in little whispers, which is very difficult for Hoorays, when suddenly two people entered the next cubicle. Everyone went 'Shhhhhhhhh!' very loudly and went on with what they were doing. It was clearly a very tight squeeze next door because the thin board partition began to quiver as if it were fit to burst. The American (by the sound of things) couple inside laughed and joked regardless while they manoeuvred themselves around the tiny space and, after several minutes of being banged about, the straining partition finally shattered, literally, into smithereens, leaving an enormous hole. In the ensuing silence the three friends peeped through the hole and there on the other side was one of the largest women Rhys had ever seen, sitting on the bowl. Her friend, a slightly overweight man in his forties, had a plastic bag full of cocaine and was shovelling it into the nostrils of his huge partner. In the heat of the moment she had got the stuff all over her big round nose.

The couple looked horrified to see the faces of Adrienne, Rhys and Dorinda looking through the glory hole. For a moment everyone was too shocked to speak. Rhys took his none-too-clean handkerchief out of his pocket and offered it through the hole. In an effort to break the ice he said, 'Would you like to use my handkerchief, madam?' The large woman stared at him for a second and then replied, 'Gee, thanks,' grabbed it and wiped her nose. She continued to gaze at Rhys, ignoring Dorinda's, 'Are you here on holiday?' Finally the fat woman turned to her companion and said, 'If only this dude was an actor and not a junkie he'd be perfect.'

'Can't one be both?' ventured Adrienne but the woman ignored her too and, turning back to Rhys, asked, 'You're not an actor by any chance, are you?'

'Well, actually, I am rather,' said Rhys, suddenly uncomfortable in his surroundings.

'*I don't fucking believe it*. He's the one,' she said to her friend. 'Hey, let's get outta here. I gotta talk to you.' She eased herself off the loo seat and poked her head through the hole. 'By the way,' she continued, 'we never saw each other here. Geddit?'

'Goddit,' replied the three polite Hoorays in unison.

'Gimme your number. I'm gonna call you tomorrow.'

Numbers were duly exchanged through the hole.

The two Americans looked at each other.

'Hal, are you gonna stand there in frozen animation forever or are you gonna give these kids a bit of your blow?'

'Here, kids,' said Hal, proffering the bag obediently.

'Oh, *speedball, yummy!*' enthused Dorinda Carr Smiley referring to one of the most dangerous drug combos: heroin and cocaine mixed.

'So, are ya good?' Hal asked Rhys.

'He's absolutely brilliant,' Adrienne told him.

'*Per-fucking-fect*,' breathed the fat woman. 'So, hi, I'm Hennie Schwab and I'm casting a series. There's a role you might be perfect for. Do you have any film on ya?'

'Well, I'm afraid I haven't actually got my camera on me . . .' began Dorinda.

'No, I mean any film I can show the network on ya?'

The three Hoorays looked puzzled.

'With you in it. . . .' Hennie was exasperated.

'Eh, no,' said Rhys.

'That's too bad. Well, I'm gonna set up a meeting anyway, even if you are brain dead . . . Get yourself a ticket to LA and I'll get you a great job if you're even half good.'

And Hennie Schwab departed from the ladies' loo with Hal in tow.

Adrienne, however, like the ever-practical Lady Dinah, was a Scot and the next day her first thought had been where on earth was Rhys going to find the money for the ticket to Los Angeles?

Rhys's answer was short and to the point: 'Daddy's credit cards.'

They were living for the time being in the basement of the Brigadier and Lady Dinah's bijou cottage in Chelsea. The stairs between the basement and the ground floor had been taken out to make an extra room and the only entry to the basement from the main house was through a trapdoor in the kitchen floor.

There were disadvantages to this, quite apart from the obvious one of living in the same house as one's parents. Prior to his marriage to Adrienne, and even afterwards while she was away in Scotland, Rhys often 'entertained' and each time he did so some sixth sense seemed to alert Lady Dinah to fling open the trapdoor at the crack of dawn and shout, 'Darling, do you want some eggs? Fresh from the country. Perfectly delicious. And, what's more, I've brought you some sweet peas . . .' and her legs would descend through the ceiling, down the ladder. Rhys would be forced hurriedly to disengage himself from another's naked form and leap forward to relieve her of the tray before she could advance any further.

'Thank you, Mummy. I'll be up in a minute.'

For the time being Rhys had lost his key to the basement and his only port of entry was through the Brigadier's front door, for which he had a key meant to be used for emergencies only.

'Where's *your* bloody key?' the Brigadier would snarl on his way to the City in the morning when he came upon his punk son creeping through the kitchen, stealing the milk from the fridge as he went.

'Oh, eh, downstairs. . . .' Rhys would answer evasively.

So one day when Rhys was safe inside the bijou basement, the Brigadier was driven to drastic lengths. He placed a crate of Bollinger across the trapdoor and Rhys was imprisoned for days, since the basement door was also mysteriously locked on the inside and he couldn't get out.

'That'll teach the bloody little idiot a lesson. . . .' the Brigadier muttered to himself as he steamed off to the City.

Mercifully when Rhys and Adrienne returned to the cottage from the Embassy that night nothing barred their way through the trapdoor into the kitchen. Stealthily, they crept up the stairs, giggling, going '*Sshhhhhh!*' at each other very loudly. On the landing Adrienne slipped away from Rhys and tiptoed into the main bedroom at the front of the cottage. Seconds later she tiptoed back.

'This way, Ada, Daddy's in here,' said Rhys, leading the way into the Brigadier's dressing room where they were met by an extraordinary sight.

The air was thick with farts and tucked up beside the Brigadier was his favourite gun dog, responsible for at least half of them – although the Brigadier was a celebrated 'poofer'. Agatha was one of a litter of ten dubbed by the Brigadier the Ten Little Indians. Nine of the puppies had been distributed around the estate leaving only one, whom the Brig had named Agatha Christie.

Agatha began to wag her tail in recognition. Adrienne and Rhys froze as the Brigadier shifted in his sleep and murmured, 'Not tonight, Dinah. It *is* Lent, remember?'

Rhys found an American Express card in the name of Dimbleby Waveral. No Brigadier, which was a relief. Rhys didn't think he could pass himself off as a brigadier, Centrale Kontiki training or not. But as they were creeping out of the room Agatha came bounding after them. Rhys was already half-way down the stairs but Adrienne, poised for descent on the landing, was knocked flying. Rhys heard the resounding crack as her ankle snapped before she fell into his arms. As he carried his uncomplaining wife down to the basement he reflected that only one ticket to Los Angeles would now be required and yet again he would be separated from his wife.

Poor Adrienne. She was always in the wars one way or another. At their wedding reception she had even managed to break her neck.

They had been married in Chelsea Register Office and had returned to Rhys's basement flat in his parents' home for the reception. The theme was Doctors and Nurses. A crowd of drama students and Hooray junkies awaited the happy couple, all dressed up (not to mention tanked) for a serious celebration. Adrienne wore a neck brace with green fur sticking out of the top and Rhys went as a drip.

The drama students drank beer and took speed while the Hoorays smoked smack off tinfoil and drank vodka. The loving couple, being half Hooray and half student, did everything. It was just the beginning of the massive upper-class junk phenomenon and Adrienne's accident would mark one of the first in an ever-escalating series of tragic events which ended in deaths, headlines and bewildered members of the nobility clutching their handbags in Al-Anon meetings.

In the first twenty minutes of their marriage Adrienne was perched safely on the thin metal bar of a fireguard, a cigarette in one hand and a large glass in the other. Her eyes, pinned like a Siamese cat's from the smack, were fixed on something across the room when suddenly, like a giant Redwood, she started to fall backwards into the fireplace. To celebrate the occasion the fire had been lit. It did not occur to Adrienne to move either of her arms and she crashed into the side of the fireplace, breaking her neck and pouring her drink all over herself in the process.

As usual she did not complain. For a while no-one realised that anything had happened. Adrienne had simply disappeared. All that remained in view were her legs sticking straight up from behind the fireguard. The Hoorays went on chasing the dragon, muttering, 'Bloody good, this gear, bloody good,' and the students went on drinking cans of beer and discussing each others' talents. 'I thought you were ace as Trigorin, man, really ace, but your Posthumus pissed, though. You really fucked up there.' 'But you know why?' *Blame, blame, blame, the actors' middle name.* 'Lyall just gave me no direction. . . .'

Rhys, moving like the perfect host from tinfoil to tinsel, found his newly wed wife lying on her back in the fireplace with the fire licking dangerously close. He could easily have left her there, imagining that was where she wanted to be, but something caught his eye. Where her face should have been was the back of her head. He touched her gently to see if she was all right and she said 'Ouch!' – politely.

The Hooray who had been sitting next to her, and had been chatting continuously even though she had long since disappeared, looked down and drawled, 'Oh, look. Adrienne's broken her neck.'

And she had. Very badly. She was rushed to hospital where Rhys found it very hard to make the doctors understand why she was wearing a neck brace already. She underwent a series of rather dangerous operations and was then packed off to Scotland for a rest. The couple were separated for ages and now Adrienne had just returned to London to join her husband.

Only to bid him farewell yet again.

CHAPTER FOUR: in which Rhys becomes Roger

In Los Angeles, Hennie Schwab turned out to be as good as her
word. She presented Rhys to the network as *the* young actor in
England everyone was wild about and the idiots bought it – how
were they to know he'd spent the last year being trapped on and
off in a basement by his own father?

At his screen test in the giant NSU Studios, Dorhys felt lost
and bewildered. Hennie Schwab referred continually to his performance in *The Hole in the Wall* – 'A great off-West End show!'
– and at one point, so carried away was she by her powers of
invention, that she turned to him and said, 'Hey, do that scene
where you strangle the policeman.'

The three NSU execs, identical in their suits, ties and haircuts, together with the director, sat back respectfully in their chairs with expectant smiles on their faces.

They could tell. Hennie Schwab had done it again. This was real Talent.

'The scene where I kill the policeman?' Rhys asked Hennie in despair, tears brimming in his eyes and panic strangling his voice.

'Yeah, or some other . . .' she replied, all smiles.

There was an embarrassing pause. Rhys was too tired to continue. He'd had enough of the charade, let alone having to improvise when he was jet-lagged.

'You . . . er . . . fucking policeman . . .' he began rather lamely, but could not go on. Tears of humiliation started coursing down his cheeks.

'You fucking policeman . . .' he repeated as he put his hands to his eyes to hide the tears. 'How could you *do* this to me?' he screamed at Hennie, unconsciously reaching out his hands in a James Dean 'I got the bullets' gesture. 'If I'd *fucking* known you were going to put me through this when I saw you through the hole in the *fucking* wall, you *bitch*, I'd have told the *fucking* police there and then . . . you *fucking* policeman . . .' His tears turned into hysterical laughter as he saw all the execs' intent, excited faces. 'Your *fucking* nose buried in a *fucking* bag of coke playing with people like me. . . .' He sank to his knees, saying, '*Never again!*'

He was about to get up, collect his coat and leave when he was deafened by the applause from the studio executives.

'My God,' said one, 'you really are something. I really felt I was right there.'

Rhys looked at Hennie Schwab and she winked.

'Now, Rhys, we wanna do an informal little test,' minced the director, all black polo neck and scarves. 'Let me tell you a bit about what we're doing. Our story is called *Our Butler*. Isn't that just the greatest title?' Without pausing for Rhys's response he went on. 'The canvas on which we are painting this delicate human comedy is Beverly Hills: green nature, beautiful pools, houses, cars and the family – Mom, *Dee-ad*, Kimberly and Li'l

Andy. The first episode starts when their old butler, James –
we're talking to Sir Maurice Goodbuns for that role – leaves their
employ to return to England. So the agency sends Roger, a
young breath of fresh air in the lives of the family. You've read
the scripts, Rhys, and I know an actor of your calibre hates to
read so let's do an informal little improv. Hennie will play Mom
and you will be Roger. You are in the kitchen of the family
home and it is your first day. Let's roll a bit of film here, guys.
OK, and. . . .'

Rhys, who never felt spontaneous even under the influence
of drugs, had drawn the line at improvisation a long time ago,
so he found himself now in a state in which, if asked, he would
probably not remember his own name. All he could think about
was his fury with Hennie Schwab who was sitting in her chair
pretending to be knitting. *Knitting*!

'Shall I get Madam her glasses?' he asked. 'I think we're a little
old to be knitting without glasses in this light.'

'Thank you, Roger, but I think I'd like a drink.'

'Of course, Madam, you look as if you need one. What'll it
be? A rum and coke? Or just *coke* straight up?'

'No, Roger!' Hennie looked stricken. 'I'll have a small port,
thank you.'

'Greedy, Madam,' replied Rhys, beginning to enjoy the
improvisation, '*for most people one sailor would be enough.*'

'CUT!' shrieked the polo neck and scarves.

Rhys got the job and so taken with his improvised dialogue was
the studio that every episode ended with the same quip. No
matter what had happened during the preceding half hour, no
matter where; even if Kimberly had been abducted by Medellin
coke barons or *Dee-ad* was in intensive care at Cedars Sinai, at
the end Roger and Mom would always find themselves alone
and he would ask, 'A drink, Madam?' with one eye to the camera
and a frisky smile on his face. She would reply with naughty
knowingness, 'A small port, please, Roger.'

Rhys would then look straight into the camera and say, camply, 'Greedy! For most people one sailor would be enough,' before gazing into freeze-frame as the credits flew up to the tune of 'All the nice girls. . . .'

The show became such a success, moving from syndication to a prime-time network slot, that Rhys, his face gliding from the cover of Vogue to the cover of Time, was voted Most Popular TV Star of 1985. When he appeared on The Johnny Carson Show to celebrate this fact Johnny said, by way of introduction, 'I only need to say five words and you will know at once who my next guest is. He's just an ordinary guy who has taken America by storm but if he offers you a drink, whatever you do, don't say "I'll have a small port."' And at this point the entire studio audience stood up and screamed:

'Gree-deeee! For most people one sailor would be enough.'

Like all dogs, Our Butler had its day and eventually it began to slip irretrievably in the ratings. Finally it was given a graveyard slot on a Tuesday afternoon and the studio decided to replace Rhys with some new blood: vampires.

Rhys promptly upped and went to Paris. He checked into the Leicester and never left.

Now, he had lost all his money and they would surely throw him out. His father was livid, his wife as usual was far away and his fans must never find out. Suddenly he was all alone.

Then he remembered Peach.

CHAPTER FIVE: in which Rhys drowns in unshed tears

Rhys emerged from the hotel and hit the Champs-Elysées. He began to walk towards the Place de la Concorde, a walk he took every day. On every news-stand the headlines blazed about the Stock Exchange crash but Paris seemed to be going on as usual. Water still gurgled out of the drains, directed into little streams by bundles of carpet tied up with string. Rhys always wondered who was responsible for these carpet dams. The concierges' union, perhaps? *Ain't no crash loud enough*, thought Rhys. Not for Paris, anyway. This was the only city he was constantly happy to see and by the time he had traversed the Tuileries and arrived at the Palais Royale he was, as they say in France, *en forme.*

Peach and Rhys lunched every day. They met at the brasserie underneath her apartment and normally she was very late. Sometimes she was so late that by the time she arrived Rhys had already finished his lunch and there was only time for five minutes' chat over his coffee while she ordered. They both invariably ate the same thing: Rhys had sole while Peach, bizarre as it might seem, always ordered *andouillette* (stuffed chitterling sausage). Rhys drank beer and Peach gulped down water with thousands of pills, some vitamins, some not.

Thus, when Rhys arrived at the brasserie (he would never go up to her apartment during the day as she never opened her shutters), he was surprised to find her already there, stuffing a huge dick-shaped sausage into her mouth. That Peach should choose to eat an *andouillette* every day was bizarre because she was not exactly one of your sausage-eating, beer-swilling, pipe-smoking diesels but more of a lychee-nibbling Thai girl. She was thin but stacked like Jessica Rabbit with long black hair hanging over a bleached white face. She had bright Betty Boop lips, shy and questioning in good old *Mutiny on the Bounty* tradition, and soft Eurasian eyes. In effect she was a startling beauty. Rhys had never seen so many men with instant erections turn their heads than when passing the delicious Peach in the street. No matter that once, when she was very stoned, she had shaved off her eyebrows and they had only half grown back – now they were painted. And then she had had a motorbike accident and been seriously scarred.

Peach was like a Chinese doll. But cracked.

She smelled deliciously of expensive scent, her wrists and neck clinked with rare jewels and more often than not she was swathed in giant floor-length furs and very little else. What Peach Delight did to accumulate all this wealth no-one exactly knew, or if they did they didn't discuss it. One thing was certain: she did not work in an office nor did she keep office hours.

'Darling, what happen? You change your dealer?' You always had to speak in the present tense if you wanted Peach to understand your English. Her English was extremely expressive but totally without tense or time.

32

'Hi, honey. I'm really sorry. I have rendezvous with a client. Last night is too much. I lose all my jewellery.'

'How come?' asked Rhys.

'Yeah, howcome,' she agreed without offering any more concrete explanation. 'You look really bad,' she said to change the subject.

'Thanks, dear,' snipped Rhys, 'as it happen things are rather bad at the moment.' He told Peach about the Stock Exchange crisis. She punctuated his story with gasps of 'Too much!', grunts and other polite interpolations but he could tell she wasn't really interested. He wasn't particularly surprised. Last night appeared to have been a heavy one for both of them.

'He leave today, that bitch!' cut in Peach suddenly, looking him straight in the eye.

Rhys went cold and his temples began to pump. 'Why?' was all he could say, though inside he knew.

'He is afraid. Forget him. He go back to New York.'

Silence. Everything seemed to be going wrong today.

'Did he say anything? We were going to Jocelyn's party tonight, weren't we?'

'He don't know what he want. He just want to enjoy.'

'Not us, obviously,' replied Rhys sadly.

As usual they were talking about Pascal. Pascal passed himself off as a Colombian but was in fact Moroccan. He was small with dark, heavily lashed eyes and beautiful cushion-like lips. He had a very muscular body with a tattoo of a syringe hanging off a vein in his arm. He was based in Paris where he lived with his wife, the long-suffering Caroline. Rhys and Peach had both been obsessed with him for some time although strangely enough he had never come between them.

Nor they between him, unfortunately.

Their relationship had been conducted in nightclubs and occasionally in the Leicester. In fact it was with Pascal that Rhys had slept on the Louis Quinze *fauteuil* on the stairs, the closest thing to first base he was ever likely to get. Not that it had been unsatisfactory to Rhys's way of thinking. Often the three of them had reeled back to the Leicester in the early hours to sleep together in Rhys's enormous bed and that was that. They had all had more than their fair share of sex at a very early age and to Rhys it was something of a relief not to be hurling himself yet again into the sexual abyss, but to be standing on the edge with his seat belt firmly fastened. Age!

Now, however, he felt completely defeated. First no money, then no Pascal. He and Peach sat in silence.

Then: 'I feel very *depressing*,' sighed Peach.

'How is your wife? She is in Scotland?'

Rhys tensed. He adored Adrienne but now was not the moment to dwell on her.

'You always pick your moment to ask after her, don't you? She's feeling fairly "depressing" too, I should think, but to be honest I don't really know how she is. I haven't spoken to her for a few days.'

'Howcome?' asked the Peach without much enthusiasm but Rhys was far away and didn't, or wouldn't, reply.

In the street they searched for a taxi. It was raining.

'I think I'm getting a cold,' said Rhys, feeling his glands.

'Unshed tears,' Peach told him as she jumped in her taxi on her way to a rendezvous. 'I take sleeping pill and see you tomorrow.'

Peach seemed to have taken the last taxi in Paris and he walked back through the rain, feeling worse and worse. By the time he arrived at the Leicester, he had more or less seized up altogether. His body ached and he was shivering like a jelly. As he feared he was greeted with endless messages – from the Brigadier, from his accountant, from his mother, even one from his wife.

He went upstairs and took his temperature – he was never far from a thermometer – and was horrified to find he had a fever of 102°. Panic swam up through his veins from his feet. What was happening to him today? Was it flu or something much more macabre? He huddled underneath the always clean and crunchy linen sheets and immediately began to sweat.

This was not flu, he convinced himself.

This was AIDS.

He was not exactly ashamed to say that between the ages of fifteen and twenty-three he had had a great deal of sex. Then one day, when he was sitting in a rented hotel room where he was living with an actress ('another actress' as he told Lady Dinah by mistake), he turned on the TV and his life completely swung around.

The picture came up before the sound and there, in close up, was Douglas, a boy with whom he had found himself in several different positions on several different occasions. Without knowing exactly why (perhaps he was naturally pessimistic and paranoid) alarm bells started ringing inside his head. The sound of his girlfriend running her bath, the room where he was sitting, everything around him flew away and he was left with the voice on the television, calm, authoritative, very BBC, telling him that Douglas was one of the first people in England to have caught the new killer cancer which had already taken its toll among the American homosexual community. It wasn't called AIDS then but Rhys immediately imagined that the man on the television was talking directly to him and he freaked.

Even though it was midnight he called his doctor and insisted on going round to see him. There he was sedated and told the bitter facts. The next day, hung, drawn and quartered, he had a blood test at the clinic (at that time they could only check your white blood cell count which was by no means conclusive) and he felt like he had heard you're supposed to feel when you're drowning. His whole life wobbled before him. Waves of regret, guilt, terror and humiliation choked him. Why had Lady Dinah warned him about 'strange men who take you to their cottage in the woods, pop you up on the kitchen table, give you sweets and then play with your willy'? It had sounded like utter heaven to him at the time but now he realised that this was the moment when he had first deviated from the route. It was followed by all manner of memories, flashing up like signposts on the road to the ultimate destination: the clinic.

As it happened his white cells turned out to be quite chirpy. Two years of celibacy (more or less) followed, he took the HIV test (negative) and slowly but surely his life restarted.

But his system had been overloaded with panic. Some fuse deep inside the computer had burned out and his life would never be the same. Monsters lurked in his dark and paranoid mind and he was never again to enjoy sex as he once had. Sex equalled life had been the equation, but when the computer jammed, sex equalled death. There was no sex safe enough, no test sure enough. . . .

Since then he had taken the AIDS test every six months. Each time he went with his heart in his mouth, the same undiminished terror, the same resolutions. With each test he had been all right but all the time it came closer and closer – first someone he knew of had it, then someone he knew slightly and finally someone he knew well.

Suddenly it was the next day and Rhys found he had slept for eighteen hours. Cherubin arrived with the doctor and almost before he knew it Rhys was tucked up and rammed with suppositories. He couldn't eat and he couldn't move. He was convinced the hotel doctor was just another out of work actor when he told him that he had the same flu as everyone else.

Cherubin was a marvellous nurse. He massaged Rhys's head. He coaxed him into drinking something and he opened the window by just the right amount. Rhys began to feel very relaxed. Then Cherubin suddenly scribbled something frantically on a piece of paper, thrust it into Rhys's hand and rushed out.

He's crazy, thought Rhys as he unwrapped the piece of paper, what does he think he's doing? He's left me his telephone number. Oh God, I hope he hasn't fallen in love with me, that would be too ghastly. And what a long phone number. Too long. It must be his number back in Portugal. Is he leaving? Maybe he's been fired. Oh, no, how terrible! I'd better put it somewhere safe.

He stuffed it under his pillow and tried to go back to sleep but there was something nagging at him. He woke up, grabbed the piece of paper and read again: 70837480.

It was his hotel bill. Nearly seventy thousand pounds. He couldn't bear it.

The telephone rang. 'C'est ton Papa,' Marie Claire downstairs told him. 'NON!' he cried and staggered into the bathroom to vomit.

Right, this was it. He was going straight to the Louis Pasteur Clinic. Everything was out of control.

'Just get a grip on yourself, Dorhys, you're behaving like a twelve-year-old girl,' a voice inside him whispered. 'Go back to bed and grow up.'

Right, he thought, safely back in bed, I must make a plan of action, and he promptly fell into a deep sleep.

The Brigadier rang incessantly. Rhys ignored him and called instead Gavin Winterton, who sounded extremely relaxed.

'Ah, Rhys, my dear, I've been meaning to call you. What a business, eh?'

'I must say it has rather dumped me in it, Give-Gav.'

'I know, old fellow, it's bitten a lot of us right where it hurts.'

'What do you think I should do?' whined Rhys rather helplessly.

'What can any of us do?' returned Gavin smartly.

'You sound very relaxed anyway, Gav.'

''Course I do, old fellow. Remember Ray? He's just come round with something really amazing, just like old times.'

Old times, thought Rhys. 'Ray the Milkman?' he asked. He was always called Ray the Milkman because he delivered and took a cheque on a monthly basis. He had been in prison for several years now and thus Rhys was rather surprised to hear Gavin mention him. '. . . I thought you'd stopped all that.'

'You can never teach an old dog new tricks, Rhys,' sighed the tranquil Gavin.

There was a long pause.

'So that's that?' said Rhys.

'It is really, I'm afraid.'

'I'll see you around then, Give-Gav, try not to get too out of it.'

'I'm going up to Scotland for three months to clean up, so don't you worry. It's the pressure of the whole bloody thing, you know. That's all. Maybe I'll see your missus while I'm up there.'

'Oh, do try not to, Give-Gav,' said Rhys sadly.

Rhys hung up. He had always been rather fond of Give-Gav. They had been friends for fifteen years. Gavin had always been rather hopeless and the most profound discovery in his life had not been work or love or literature but heroin. He worked on the Stock Exchange, which only served further to convince Rhys what a blind eye the Empire-ruling generation of their parents (always so proud of their ability to judge character) invariably turned. More often than not Gavin was completely conked out at his desk by lunchtime ('One too many V&Ts at the board meeting, you know what it's like,' his naïve secretary told passing callers), and Rhys recalled finding him comatose one day.

It was during the reign of Ray the Milkman and his deliveries and however much anxiety this caused to Give-Gav's rapidly declining group of friends, up from Radley and down from Oxford, it came as a welcome surprise to all, including Rhys, when Give-Gav started making a fortune on the money markets. Obviously scag worked much more effectively than alcohol, the stockbroker's usual drug of choice. First half a million, then the other half and then, *bang*, three and a half million. At this point Rhys had made one of his most fundamental mistakes. He had taken his money out of the hands of the Brigadier, a very proficient stockbroker himself, and given it to Give-Gav to deal with. Three-quarters of a million pounds from *Our Butler* and he gave it all away to Gavin. The rest was unfortunately history.

When the fever finally began to subside, Rhys set about calling his agents as part of the great Plan of Action. Rather in the vein of Lady Beth Fraser, he had many agents. One in London. One in Paris. One in Rome and two in the States. Then on top of that he had a press agent in London and another in Los Angeles. He called them all at various times, depending on where they were, and put out his general SOS. By the evening he was utterly exhausted.

A week had gone by since Black Monday, as it had been christened by the press. Instead of his agents calling to tell him he was in demand for everything going, the Brigadier called twice daily. Once he even got through.

'Next plane, you bloody little idiot. I warn you I'll be on the next plane. I'll make sure you get out of that bloody silly place you live in even if I have to come and drag you out of there myself. Next plane. . . .'

'I'll send a horsebox to meet you at the airport, Daddy.' Rhys hung up.

The telephone rang again immediately.

'A Rolls Royce horsebox, Daddy, I swear. Or would you like a Bristol? You like Bristols, don't you?'

'Sure, I love 'em. Listen, kid, you wanna go back to your old profession?' a voice shrieked down the other end of the phone.

Hennie Schwab. How extraordinary!

'What *can* you mean, Hennie? And incidentally, hello darling.'

'Yeah, *incidentally*, d'ya wanna go back to your old profession?' More shrieks of laughter. Rhys was slightly miffed.

'Hennie, are you aware that I have been extremely ill? Glands, sweating, flu and everything. You might at least ask if I'm feeling better, one never knows these days.'

'Listen, hon, it would have to be the immaculate conception. You told me you had been dry for six months.'

'Dry, Hennie, is an expression reserved for drinkers.'

'Exactly, cocksucker. Now listen to what I said.'

'I heard you. Do I want to go back to my old profession – whatever that may be. Incidentally? Well, the answer is no. Not for anything.'

'Not even for a hundred thousand dollars?'

'Certainly for a hundred thousand dollars. When do I start?'

Screams of a demonic dimension along with a good deal of 'Attaboy!', 'Yeah!' and 'I *like that!*' hurtled down the static. Finally she calmed down.

'You English kill me. Right, here's the scoop. My friend, Rikki – you've heard me talk about her, the one we call the Duchess – well, she's crazy for you and she wants to come and see you in Paris next week.'

'And?'

'If she likes the colour of your water she may want to swim.' Hennie's voice had suddenly gone all little girl, which Rhys found intensely irritating.

'Well, tell her to bring a wet suit, the water's cold.'

'Hey, dip 'em, Dorita, and listen. She would like to invite you to spend the weekend with her in Tangiers.'

Now Rhys was getting really angry.

'Why on earth would I want to go to Tangiers?'

'For the hundred thousand dollar lox.'

'Just for the weekend?'

'Just for the weekend.'

'What's she like? I bet she's ugly. Is she ugly, Hennie?'

'Is the Pope Catholic? I have to go. I have a call holding.'

And she hung up.

CHAPTER SIX: in which Rhys returns to his old profession

A sudden August downpour found the young boy sheltering in the lift-shaft of Gloucester Road Tube station. It was almost midnight and he had been there for nearly half an hour. If he had been asked what he was doing that night he would have been hard pushed to say because he didn't really know himself. It was the hunting instinct he had inherited from his father that had drawn him to this particular corner of the jungle but, while his father aimed with certainty at pigeons, woodcock, pheasant and deer, crouched in a drizzling Scottish glen or sitting on a shooting stick in the middle of a field, the boy was not aware of what it was exactly that he was hunting.

He was, after all, only fifteen and on his summer holiday from school. His instinct – which in the future would prove to be a pretty canny asset – had drawn him like a magnet from his father's Belgravia mews to the King's Road, and from there to the Fulham Road. He had wandered aimlessly in the blistering summer heat, watching the people and looking in the pubs and shops. It was the first time they had left him on his own in London. Only for two days, then he would have to take the train to Edinburgh and join the family for the summer stalking trip.

It hadn't rained for ten weeks and so, as the first spots began to come down, he found himself, as if by magic, standing just inside the entrance to Gloucester Road station, waiting. Every so often the lift doors groaned open like the mouth of some high-tech Metropolis monster and somnambulistic zombies poured forth into the rain, screeched, then scattered in their various directions like fieldmice from a bale of hay. The boy watched, charmed, and although his face bore an almost down-cast expression, what he saw presented him with a picture of almost unfathomable beauty.

He was drunk on freedom. He was free from surveillance, ('He *is* fifteen, darling,' 'Yes, but he's still a bloody little idiot'), left for the first time to discover the streets without the mink coat and handbag of his mother click, click, clicking beside him.

They'll never find me now, he thought, whatever happens, whatever tragedy occurs, and he almost laughed out loud.

A brown Rolls Royce, similar to his father's, splashed to a halt beside him on the kerb. The engine was turned off but no-one got out. After a minute the window whirred down. Then nothing. The boy strained to see who was in the car but it was too dark to make out more than a silhouette. The silhouette was motionless. So was the boy. The only thing moving was the rain, beating down on the roof of the Rolls and rising in steam from the hot black street. Suddenly the muscles in the boy's ribcase were shot through with adrenalin as if responding in a new language to an unspoken call.

'This is hunting,' he said to himself.

Finally a gruff East End voice emerged from inside the car. 'Nothing serious, is it? It can't be that bad, eh?'

'It's raining, that's all,' replied the boy.

'Live in Gloucester Road, do you?' the voice asked.

'No, I live in Islington.' Lies.

That seemed to be the end of the conversation. The boy watched the rain. He wanted to scream. After what seemed a lifetime the voice asked, 'What's your name then?'

'Keith,' lied the boy in a voice that was already not his own.

'Need a lift then, Keith?'

'Thanks,' said Keith and climbed in.

Inside the Rolls the noise of the rain on the roof was very loud and the voice laughed. 'Pissing down, eh?'

Not very Rolls Royce language, thought Keith, and turned to look at his new friend. He was big. Enormous! He had a huge head like a bulldog with a mammoth fig-shaped honker sticking out the middle. He had giant murderer's hands. Five or six black hairs were neatly combed across his head and whatever hair he didn't have on top he made up for down below. A matted jungle of wiry black curls sprouted from his shirt like weeds in an ill-organised garden. Glinting in the midst of the forest, like fairy castles, were gold chains, watches and rings.

'What's your name?' asked Keith.

'Jerry,' said Jerry, and started the car. He pulled out into the road and and went round the block, back on to Cromwell Road towards Knightsbridge.

Between the V&A and the Brompton Oratory Keith received his first-ever professional proposition.

'I'll give you twenty-five quid if I can fuck you twice,' said Jerry, very matter of fact. Keith, already on the point of fainting, choked. Twenty-five quid! Nearly three years' pocket money.

'Make it a round thirty,' he heard himself saying. It would seem he was a natural pro.

'All right, then. How old are you, anyway?'

'Sixteen.' Keith lied again.

'You're a sexy little thing, that's for sure.'

'Yeah, so are you,' oozed Keith, warming to his new role. His heart was beating almost uncontrollably and he was gasping for breath, but Jerry didn't notice. The boy was a natural actor.

They drove in silence for several minutes but as the Roller

swung into Park Lane Jerry asked, 'Been at it for long then, eh?'

Keith could see the windows of his Aunt Sylvia's flat. The lights were on. Maybe I should drop by with Jerry, he thought to himself, say Cooeee!

'Ages,' he told Jerry.

'What are you smiling like that for? I can tell you're a strange one.'

'Too right, Jerry, too right.'

'Like it, do you, Keith?'

'Like what?'

'Like it. Do you like what you do?'

'Duck to water.' *Quack, quack*. Keith was flying. Now they were turning up the Edgware Road. 'Where are you taking me, Jerry?'

'To my place in Maida Vale,' said Jerry, slapping his hand on Keith's thigh and squeezing it.

Keith came in his pants.

'*Aaaaaargh* . . . you from London, originally I mean?' was all he could manage. He couldn't believe what was happening. Jerry didn't appear to notice anything.

'Yeah, I'm a London boy all right. I'm in buying and selling,' he said grandly.

And so, it would appear, am I, thought Keithie.

They chatted pleasantly as they drove through the rain, Keith's heart still beating like crazy. In the space of half an hour he had grown up, simply and efficiently, like a butterfly who had deserted its cocoon.

Later, when Jerry stumbled from the car and opened the boot, Keith saw a chauffeur's cap inside. Oh, dear, poor old Jerry. He wasn't in buying and selling at all. He was a chauffeur. It was true that Keith had noticed that his aftershave, lashed on with the extravagance of the Incas, did not exactly represent the higher end of the market. Still, thirty quid was thirty quid and it didn't do to be despondent. One didn't always strike gold one's first time out, but Keith made a mental note. Check the facts.

Jerry now began to act rather cautiously, entering a large panelled hall and making no move to turn on the lights. In the shadow of his place of work, he no longer attempted to play the boss. He stumbled over to the staircase and disappeared into the gloom.

'Hey, wait for me. I can't see a thing,' sang out Keith.

'Sssshhhh! For Christ's sake . . . I mean, over 'ere, Keith, take me 'and, thassit, now up we go. I live right at the top of the 'ouse, see? So I don't 'ear the noise,' added Jerry rather half-heartedly, knowing he was no longer fooling anyone.

Yeah, yeah, thought Keith. This really was a most peculiar sort of cultural exchange, he and Jerry living out their fantasies together, although Jerry's performance was decidedly shallow, it had to be said. Keithie, on the other hand, was a full-blown theatrical fantasist and inhabited his dream with the sureness of a real-life actor.

Jerry suddenly reappeared with a torch. 'Losing your way, were you? Follow me then . . .' and they started up a smaller staircase to the top floor of the house. Jerry, with the beam of his torch darting up the stairs ahead of him, reminded Keith of Fagin. I could be Oliver, he thought and giggled, 'Please, sir, can I have some *more*?'

'Fer Chrissake, shut it. . . .' From above.

Even when they were safely inside his room Jerry still didn't turn on the lights. Instead he went to the window and drew back the curtains.

'Hot weather, eh?' he grunted, and without further ado took off his shirt.

They fulfilled the first half of their bargain in the orange glow of the street lamps outside and Keith began to think he was in a German movie (not that he'd ever seen one). But as it turned out, Jerry had a big mouth, bigger, Keith noticed sadly, than other parts of his body. Instead of moving on to the grisly second act, Jerry fell into an instant coma.

For the first few minutes Keith just lay there looking round the room, taking in Jerry's Teasmade neatly arranged by the bed, a framed photo of a female Jerry – a sister or the mother? He coughed discreetly but to no avail. Jerry was out for the count.

'Jerry,' he hissed, 'Jerry, yoo-hoo?'

Nothing. Jerry began to snore. Keith's arm was trapped by Jerry's weight. Keith tried again, a little more forcefully, 'Jerry!'

and was greeted by great sensaround snores like a washing machine going at full spin. In desperation he screamed, '*Aaaaaaaargh*, Jerry, wake up. I'm trapped!'

Jerry came to as if from a nightmare.

'All right, what's goin' on 'ere?' he shouted, still in the cops and robbers dream he had just left.

'Nothing, Jerry, that's just it. So I think I must be going,' said the young professional.

'Oh, righto,' said Jerry, fumbling for something. Keith looked hopeful. 'Now, let me see, where's me wallet?'

'There, on the table,' said Keith quickly.

'Got eyes in the back of your bleedin' 'ead, you 'ave,' muttered Jerry as he waddled round the bed. 'Still, you're a sexy bugger, I'll say that.'

Outside the rain had stopped and the air was clear and fresh. A wind breezed through the trees and in through the window, blowing Keith's hair across his face. In the dark he looked like a sad Madonna.

Jerry, the great Cockney badger, gulped. 'I'd like to see you again.'

'All right,' said Keith, almost in his normal voice.

'You're a luvly boy.'

'Thanks,' said the luvly boy.

'What about same time next week?'

'I can't.'

'Oh.' Jerry looked sad.

'I could the week after if you want, though, what about the week after?'

'Okey dokey,' Jerry brightened. 'Gloucester Road Tube in two weeks.'

They shook hands. Ludicrous.

'All right. So long, Jerry.'

And Rhyssie disappeared into the fragrant London night.

Rhys spent the night in Hyde Park under a large oak. Somehow the idea of returning to the Brigadier's was unthinkable. Something inside him had changed and the sensible Peter Jones curtains and the flower prints on the walls would have been too oppressive now that he had discovered another world from which he had no desire to return.

The next morning he appeared for his appointment at Dr Mainwaring's dental surgery in Wimpole Street feeling fresh and alive.

'We've done a splendid job on those gnashers of yours, young Waveral,' said Doctor Mainwaring as he examined the inside of Rhys's mouth.

'Do I still have to wear my plate at night?' asked Rhys. 'You said I could stop in September if all went well.'

'Just for the rest of the holidays and then you'll be able to bare your teeth at all and sundry.'

'I fully intend to,' said Rhys out loud, without thinking.

'Come and see me before you go back, won't you?'

'I'm not going back next term.' Both of them were surprised by this news.

'Oh, really?' laughed Doctor Mainwaring, 'and what does your mama think about that?'

'She doesn't know. I've only just decided while you were poking around in my mouth.'

'We'll see, shall we?' smiled the good-natured doctor. 'Goodbye, Waveral.'

'Goodbye, Doctor Mainwaring.' Life suddenly seemed as if it were going to be full of goodbyes. So much the better.

That summer at Waveram, the Waveral family seat in the North, Rhys was thoughtful. Lady Dinah was rather worried.

'Dim,' she addressed the Brigadier one evening when they were sitting in the drawing room after dinner. 'Dimbleby darling, are you listening to me? Don't you think Rhys is awfully quiet these hols?'

'What's that?'

'I – said – don't – you – think – *Rhys is awfully quiet?*' she enunciated as clearly as she could for the Brigadier's would-be deaf ears. He jumped and glared at her.

'Bloody good thing too, if you ask me. Always yapping away like a rabid spaniel. Do tell me, I know I'm frightfully naive, but what exactly is that Indian sari thing that he's taken to wearing in the evenings? I can't imagine what Mac and Mrs Mac can be thinking.'

'Oh, I rather like it.' Lady Dinah was always quick to the defence. 'I was rather wondering if he might lend it to me.'

'Good God, first him, now you. Where on earth did he get it?'

'He bought it when he was staying with that friend of his, what's his name? Brock.'

'Brock!' snorted the Brigadier in disgust.

'Anyway, I think you should have a talk. . . .'

She was not allowed to continue

'Oh, do shut up, woman. Isn't one allowed a moment's peace? You know perfectly well that Rhys and I haven't had a talk in years. He'd fall off his perch if I suggested such a thing.' The Brigadier chortled in amusement at the idea of his son's terror.

Silence. It was the nine thousand and ninety-ninth checkmate in the history of their twenty-five-year cold war. Lady Dinah sighed. She didn't understand her son, but then she didn't understand her husband either. The Brigadier shuffled over to the drinks tray and splashed himself another whisky, shuffled back and settled down to the *Financial Times*. Like an old gun dog trying to settle down, he and the pink paper crackled and crunched until they found the right position. From behind the paper his voice continued in the dreamlike tones which signified that he was off on his favourite journey – to the Market.

'I say, Marks and Sparks are up again. But you know, Dinah, he'll get himself into trouble, that one. Mark my words. He'll be in one of those ghastly two-way mirror scandals.' He turned a page and sighed. 'Why are they all such bloody fools in Hong Kong? Hmmmm?' He ventured a peek round the paper at Lady Dinah but she had gone. Mission accomplished.

He chuckled into his whisky, turning it into a snort. 'Sari at dinner. Whatever next?'

Whatever next came rather sooner than he expected. The Brigadier was fishing. Perfect day for it – not too bright and no wind. The dark brown peat-stained water gurgled against the rocks and the Brigadier was in seventh heaven.

Until a cloud appeared on the horizon. Rhys was approaching on the other bank.

'Oh God, the Maharanee.' The Brigadier froze in a pose of utter concentration which he knew could sometimes be effective in deterring his family from coming anywhere near him. Not Rhys, however.

Bloody hell, moaned Dim to himself. Out loud he barked, 'Yes, what is it? I'm fishing.' As if this were not abundantly clear.

'Want to talk to you,' shouted the nervous little faun on the other bank.

'Fishing. Can't you see? Later. All right?' added the Brigadier, trying to make his voice sound friendly.

'No,' said the stubborn boy, '*Now!*'

'Look, we can't have a conversation on opposite sides of the river with you stamping your bloody little foot. We'll scare all the fish away.'

'I want to leave Floundring. I want to get a job.'

Silence. The Brigadier was flummoxed. Rhys could feel his legs beginning to wobble. Please God, don't let me swoon now.

'Reaaa . . . lly?' said the Brigadier after a considerable pause during which time he worked out without the help of his calculator how much he could save in school fees. The temptation to count on his fingers was agonising but then he would have dropped his rod. He was secretly delighted with the suggestion. He absolutely loathed Floundring Abbey to start with. 'Those ghastly monks,' he would say, 'bloody snobs. If they saw the Duke of Buccleuch in one corner of the room and St Francis of Assisi in the other, St Francis would be the one still waiting for a drink at the close of play, mark my words. . . .' Besides, he wasn't a great believer in education. In his opinion the Army followed by a good war gave the chap all the education he needed to get by.

He laid down his rod and ventured into the river as far as his waders would allow.

'Rhys.' He beamed, warming to his wayward son. 'I'm all for it. You have my one hundred per cent support. Can't speak for your mother, though. She'll be the stick in the mud, I'm afraid. But, you know you'll have to get some suits, old chap. Can't go around in that awful sari thing. 'Part from that, I'm totally for it. Now, leave me alone to fish, there's a good chap. Give me time to sort out the problem of how to handle your mother. . . .'

Rhys didn't know whether to take the Brigadier seriously. He had expected all kinds of resistance. But, as he well knew, once the Brigadier's mind had been made up – as it appeared to have been rather too quickly in this instance – there was no changing it.

Later that afternoon a still quiet and thoughtful Rhys sloped off to the now deserted nursery to use Nanny's telephone. He called his girlfriend, Adrienne, who lived nearby. Nearby for Scotland. Only seventy miles away.

'Hellloooo,' whined Adrienne down the other end, 'I've got a cold sore.' She had a permanently worried little-girl voice which had not really changed since she had been a permanently worried little girl. 'What's going on?'

'I think I'm going to leave Floundring and get a job.'

'But you're only fifteen,' shrieked Ada.

'I'll be sixteen in September. Don't be such an idiot. What are you going to do?'

'I'm going to try after Christmas. It's not worth it before. So what are you going to do?'

'I'm going to become a prostitute.' Dead pan.

'Really? God, how amazing. Who with? Anyone I know?'

'With a chauffeur called Jerry.'

'Maybe he can come and collect us. Get us out of here,' giggled Ada. 'What's he like?'

'Quite large, but otherwise rather good. You'll see him when you get to London.'

'If he still fancies you. Maybe he can give me a job, too? What do you think, Rhyssie?'

'I'm not sure,' replied Rhys. 'I think he only likes botties.'

'I've got a botty,' said Ada, all indignation.

'Yes, but you've got a front one, too, and they abhor that, my dear.'

Rhys and Adrienne thought they were frightfully funny.

'So does that mean we're off then, now that you're a certified gay?' asked Adrienne tentatively after the laughter had died down. But the word gay started them off again.

It was their favourite word. They had been familiar with it as an adjective which could describe a ball, a dress, a mood, in fact anything to do with fun, for as long as they could remember. When Rhys was ten he had saved up and bought himself his first corduroy shirt in Carnaby Street. It had been purple (a colour unheard of in the Brigadier's regiment) and was promptly christened 'Your gay shirt' by Lady Dinah . . . 'Darling, why don't you wear your gay shirt?' or, 'Honestly, that gay shirt really does need a scrub.'

It was only on a day out in Edinburgh that Rhys and Adrienne had discovered that to be 'gay' you did not necessarily need to be having fun. They were in a newsagent's, browsing, and came across a publication called *Gay News*. Imagining it to be a cheaper version of *The Tatler* or *Harpers & Queen*, they thought it would be nice to take it home for Lady Dinah. However, when they looked inside they found that the balls and dresses and moods were of a very different nature to those described in 'Jennifer's Diary'. Moreover they were not allowed to buy it and they had spent the rest of that stormy winter holiday plotting and planning how to get their hands on another copy.

'I think I am a bit gay,' said Rhys after more laughter had died down, 'but it doesn't have to change anything between us. We were together before any of this happened. It doesn't make any difference. I think we should go on as usual.'

'Can I just say . . .' interrupted Adrienne – it was one of her favourite expressions and was generally a signal that she was unsure about something – 'I don't quite understand . . . does that mean you can have boyfriends because it's just your "other part"? Well, what would happen if I were to have them too? Would that be all right? And I suppose since you're allowed boyfriends you can have girlfriends too?' Her little-girl voice was becoming very worried now.

'No, it's not like that at all. It's just that I know there's something else inside me. I don't know what but it doesn't have anything to do with anything and it certainly doesn't relate to you. It's something totally different. When I was in that man's house, Adrienne, it was so strange. I thought I was dreaming. When I was alone in London this time I felt like a completely different person. I want to be different. At any rate different from all the dreary old bores here. Anyway. . . .'

Rhys finished or began many a sentence with 'anyway'. So did Adrienne.

'Anyway,' she sighed, tired already at the prospect of the future, 'it all seems a mite complicated. Are you coming over tomorrow?'

'Yes, I'll be there about tea time.'

'Allright, we can discuss it then. I'm making a stained glass window so I must dash. See you tomorrow.'

CHAPTER SEVEN: in which Rhys and Peach go to the bank
to clean their jewellery

'*C'est quoi, "Grayelle"*, Monsieur Wavy?'

Cherubin was opening the curtains.

'Don't leave yet . . .' said the soap star, barely awake, reaching
out across the empty bed.

'*Non. C'est moi*, Cherubin. *J'arrive*. The other one left about
half an hour ago.'

'Oh, it's you, Cherub. How are you?'

Cherubin was padding about, picking up the clothes off the
floor. '*C'est quoi, "Grayelle"*? What is "*Grayelle*"? You were
shouting about it for half an hour. In your sleep. "*Grayelle!*

Grayelle!" Comme un fou. The housekeeper, that bitch, she told me to come and see what was wrong.'

'*Grail*, Cherub, *grail*. King Arthur and all that.' He had obviously been having that dream again but this time he couldn't remember.

'*Ah, oui*.' At last Cherubin understood. 'Like that terrible TV series that was on last year. *Terrible!*'

Rhys rolled over, a bit miffed. Cherubin found time to watch crap about King Arthur but he had never so much as mentioned a word about *Our Butler* which had been a huge hit in France. Everywhere he went he was hailed, 'Roger! *Notre Bootlair.*'

The telephone rang. The Leicester had strict instructions not to put any calls through before eleven, especially not emergencies. They could wait until the evening, by which time it would be far too late to deal with them. Rhys glanced at his watch. Ten-thirty.

It was Marie Claire.

'Marie Claire,' he began, 'haven't I told you. . . .'

'*Bonjour*, Monsieur Waveral,' she interrupted, 'just to let you know that Madame Peach is on her way up.'

On cue there was a knock on the door.

'Oh heavens, I forgot. It's jewellery day. Cherub, what shall I do?'

Cherubin didn't answer. He was too busy billing and cooing over Peach's new fur coat. '*Alors ça . . . ça, c'est vraiment quelquechose,*' he murmured over and over again.

'You like it, Cherubin?' Peach loved to be admired and as he reclined in bed and looked across the room at her, Rhys thought that she was almost the most beautiful woman he had ever seen. When she saw her friend was still in bed, however, the Peach's face collapsed.

'*Rhysling*, honey, what you do? I book the vault for half past eleven. Please come.' Peach's tone was that of a Vietnamese jungle revolutionary and Rhys jumped out of bed, disappearing swiftly into the bathroom. After all, they were going to be his jewels one day.

Peach had put all her money into furs and jewels. She did not have a bank account and she did not own a house. She was deeply suspicious of '*le system*' and had never had a credit card. Whatever cash she had she put into more furs and more jewels. The furs lived in a fridge at the Porte de Clignacourt and the jewels, rather more conveniently, lived in the rue de Louvre. The jewels she had left to Rhys and the furs to their friend, Pascal. He wished he had the jewels and Rhys was very happy not to have been willed the furs. Once every three or four months Peach took Dorita down to the vault and they sat there for an hour, chatting idly, as they cleaned the jewellery that would one day be his. Security was very strict and it simply did not do to be late on jewellery day.

Five minutes later they were in a taxi and on their way.

'Look at my new ring, honey,' giggled Peach. It was a huge diamond with little sapphires all around it.

'Mmmm, *chouette!*' drooled Rhys. 'You have new client?'

'Yes, honey, he like me a lot.'

'Pascal is back from New York.'

'Howcome?' Peach promptly downed a couple of aspirin.

'He's angry.'

'Why?'

'He had a problem with a client,' Rhys explained.

'Shame!' chanted the two friends in unison. 'He only want to enjoy. . . .' It was the conclusion they always reached about Pascal and they dissolved into laughter.

'Actually, you just missed him,' confessed Rhys after a pause. 'He left just before you arrived.'

'Bitch!' drawled Peach.

'It wasn't my fault. He arrived at the Leicester at six o'clock this morning. He said he didn't want to go home stoned to his wife. I have to say one thing though, Peach. He isn't as nice looking as he was.'

'Poor Caroline,' sighed Peach, referring to Pascal's wife.

'Thank God she doesn't understand French is all I can say,' said Rhys.

'Why?'

'Because if she understood French she'd understand her husband and if she understood Pascal I don't know what she'd do. . . .'

'She'd have sex change,' said Peach matter-of-factly, *'ici, c'est bon, merci. . . .'*

And they climbed out of the taxi.

In the bank all eyes were fixed on Peach. One hundred erections strained in one hundred pairs of pants as our girl teetered on her heels towards the door marked Safe Deposits. Rhys followed at a respectful distance and those who managed to tear their eyes away from Peach's departing rear end beamed at him in recognition.

'Oooooh la la la la la la! C'est Roger de Notre Bootlair. Mine's a small port, Roger!' they called out.

The Superintendent of the Vaults, Madame Carlage, led the two friends through endless hallways and doors. It was rather like being in a luxurious prison, thought Rhys, as yet another door was clunked shut and locked behind them. Madame Carlage, a strapping diesel of a woman, was chatting animatedly as she showed them into the viewing room. Now they really were in Cell Block H. They sat down on the two chairs and faced each other across the little table. Madame Carlage returned with Peach's safe deposit box and left them alone. Peach unlocked the box with her little key. Inside were a variety of smaller jewellers' boxes – from Cartier, from Van Cleef and Arpels, from Aspreys – twenty or thirty altogether. Peach reached in and rummaged about a bit until she came up with an old transistor radio which she placed on the table between them, tuning it to a classical station. Next she produced a little mirror from her bag and a small packet of coke. Meanwhile Rhys unpacked the jewels and the cleaning equipment. To the accompaniment of the slow movement from Ravel's *Piano Concerto*, the two friends were ready to enjoy their picnic. They both did an enormous line, lit a cigarette and luxuriated for a minute before going to work.

'Nobody could ever find us here,' said Rhys.

They began to clean the jewels. Peach used an old toothbrush, dipping it in polish and then scrubbing the metal parts, while Rhys had the more delicate task of cleaning the jewels themselves. To the outsider they looked like a pair of hardened professionals. Which they were. Conversation was cut to a minimum but they did have to decide which piece to sell so that Peach could redecorate her bathroom.

'I think it should be that little green one,' Rhys said finally.

'I can't. It have too much personal value,' replied Peach.

'Why? Who gave it to you?'

'No one. I stole it,' said Peach, matter-of-fact as ever.

'Then why can't you sell it?' Rhys was getting very suspicious. Peach sighed. She picked up the little green ring and started attacking it with the toothbrush. She pushed her hair behind her ears in a vain attempt to stop it falling continually over her face.

'The boy I was with when I steal it . . . he die next day. So I can't really sell.'

'How did he die?' Rhys prepared another line. The coke was good. It made them both feel important.

'He die in his bed in the middle of party at his house. It was horrible.'

'Howcome?'

'Howcome? Howcome? That what they all say to me: Howcome you do nothing, Peach? Howcome no one call the doctor? It was a party. It was very late. We at clubs all night and go to his place after. We take Ecstasy. We take cocaine. We smoke. Everything. We in the kitchen, in the bedroom, we dance, watch TV. At first he OK. Then he lie on his bed and let the party go round and round. Slowly but surely the people sleep, they talk more quiet, when the phone ring the machine answer. The sun try to come through window but these people shut the blinds. It is hot in Paris during this time.'

Peach paused and her hands trembled as she applied the polish with the toothbrush.

'At about five o'clock I am in the kitchen with Henri. You meet him one day, you remember? I say, "Too much, I must go home." I go to the bedroom to say goodbye and my friend is dead. "It's my party and I'll die if I want to." There is big problem after. Everyone go to police for evidence. Big problem for me, you can imagine. Afterwards they find he take heroin as well. He make – how you say? – cardiac. The people, they very nasty. They say, "Oh, Peach, she too stoned to see," but there is nothing. Nothing to see. I don't like drugs from then. I take, yes, more even, but I don't like. Before I think why all this problem with drugs? Drugs are great. You know the last thing you think of is death but death is always very near. In the clubs, in the bars, I don't like any more drugs.'

They worked on in silence, dwelling on Peach's horrific story. Rhys and Peach came from such different backgrounds but now they felt very close. Peach finished her part of the work on the dead boy's ring and handed it to Rhys. '*Voilà*, now you know story of this!'

In return Rhys confided in Peach about his forthcoming ordeal with Rikki.

'I have to meet her tomorrow for lunch,' he said.

'Great!' Peach cheered up enough to tease Rhys. 'Honey, you change a lot. It scare me!'

'I have to pay my bill at the hotel somehow.'

'But I already say to you, you take my place at the rue St Denis and I work from home. It's nice there.'

'It's nice at the Leicester as well, and anyway they'd never forgive me if I left now. Good coke, huh?'

'From my friend Christian from New York. We enjoy. I think I sell this one, what do you think?'

'Oh, I really like that one,' whined Rhyssie.

'Too bad!' said Peach, matter-of-fact to the end. She reached once again for the mirror and her bag of coke.

And she lined up.

CHAPTER EIGHT: in which Mrs Rikki Lancaster stakes her
   claim

Fabrice, the doorman, dug his hands deep into the pockets of
his liveried uniform. There was a harsh chill wind blowing that
day, quite suddenly taking the city from a drizzly, moist autumn
into what was to be an extremely cold winter. The clouds hurtled
across the sky and people ran along the street.

   The street in which the Hotel Leicester was situated ran from
the Champs-Elysées straight to the river and the wind flew down
it at an alarming and deceptive rate. You could be walking down
the Champs-Elysées feeling the cold as well as the wind on your
face but, once you turned the corner towards the Leicester, you

were literally propelled by forces beyond your control down the street, past the hotel and into the river if you weren't careful. And it was days like this that Fabrice and his colleagues particularly enjoyed: hats, bags, brollies and even people would fly down the street towards them.

A peculiar duo appeared on the horizon coming round the corner: a tall, skeletal woman in a mauve and black turban with matching cape followed by a smaller, dumpier version in a sensible tweed two-piece. The discrepancy in their heights would have been comic enough without the aid of a particularly strong gust of wind which interrupted their intense conversation and suddenly blew them, like puppets on wheels, down the street towards the hotel. Capes, bags and coats were caught in the wind and unfurled like the sails on two homeward-bound schooners as they skittered, totally out of control, across the pavement towards the Leicester. Their screams and laughs could be heard like seagulls above the wind and Fabrice, whose penchant was for the Older Woman (*des vraies chiennes*, as he would say), slipped into his French James Dean pose, leaning against the wall of the hotel with his feet and his eyes crossed and a sensitive scowl across his not very James Dean face.

At fifty yards Mauve and Black looked a rather tasty thirty-five but, as the two women screeched to a halt under the awning of the hotel, the compliment that distance pays to faded beauty disintegrated in the cold remorseless light of day, presenting a beaky crow of fifty-five plus.

The two women were in quite a state and leaned against the railings of the hotel, gasping for breath. They were, on closer inspection, quite extraordinary, for on the one hand they looked quite young but on the other they seemed to be timelessly old. The skin on their faces might be translucent and without a wrinkle but it contrasted sharply with the blotchy skin on their knobbly hands. Their eyes were bulging out of their sockets from exertion and the lips of Mauve and Black had dried into into a diabolical sneer. But both women seemed to be the proud owners of perfect teeth.

Fabrice's disappointment clearly showed in his face because when she finally caught her breath, Mauve and Black growled in a resonant California brogue, 'Well, don't just stand there. Take our bags.'

Rhys was trying to take a nap.

After a gram of coke it was a test for anyone's moral fibre but Rhys was finding it even harder than usual on account of the endless telephone calls from his father.

For the first five or six calls Rhys simply hung up. Why on earth had Marie Claire suddenly taken it upon herself to put calls from his family straight through?

On the seventh call it was just impossible to ignore the Brigadier.

'Hello, Daddy, I just got in.' Very breezy. Very polite.

'Bollocks!' boomed the Brigadier, equally polite. 'I've been trying to get hold of you for days but you don't even have the manners to return my calls.'

'I know, I know,' replied Rhys soothingly, 'but you know I just don't feel like talking to anyone at the moment. You know how it is sometimes?'

'Sometimes? What do you mean, sometimes? With you it's all the bloody time. Don't be so bloody airy-fairy. Now, let me spell it out for you once and for all: you-have-got-a-major-problem . . . with me so far?'

'Yes, Daddy, certainly am. . . .'

'And you're doing bloody f-all about it!'

The storm clouds were gathering. Tirade and lightning any minute.

'Mmmmm. Listen, Daddy, I really can't talk. I'm exceptionally late. I have a meeting with a director. Bye.'

'I haven't finished yet, you bloody fibber. You don't have any bloody meeting with a director. You're just kipping.'

'Prove it.'

Silence. Uh-oh. Maybe that was going a little too far.

'It's a marvellous film, really, Daddy. All going to be shot on location in Kabuki or somewhere. Must go. Bye.'

Rhys hung up. Phew! That had taken some nerve. He was in

the process of rolling a well-earned joint when the phone rang again.

'Next plane,' hissed the Brigadier menacingly, and this time it was he who hung up.

Rhys smoked his joint and decided on a walk in the Tuileries. Things were getting rather hot under the collar. Too hot.

'Tuileries,' he barked to himself and slammed the door to his suite. He started off down his favourite stairs in the whole world and stopped short as he realised he'd left the key on the inside of the door. One of his extremely bad moods flashed upon him and he ground his teeth and dug his fingernails into the palms of his hands as he continued downstairs.

Arriving in reception he found his passage blocked by a pile of endless shopping bags blown in with the two ladies.

'Oh God!' He stood there waiting for someone to clear a passage. The two women turned sharply and stared at him with glaring smiles.

'Fans!' barked Rhys again to himself as he began to make his way through the sea of bags. 'My God,' he said to Fabrice in French, 'Wicked Stepmother is here. Has anybody warned Snow White?'

'Or the 101 Dalmatians?' echoed Fabrice and they both started singing in chorus:

> *Cruella de Vil*
> *Cruella de Vil*
> *If she doesn't get you*
> *Some evil thing will*

Outside the wind had died down, to be replaced with mournful Paris drizzle. As he raced along the street, accosted by passing Americans – 'Hey Roger, mine's a small port' – Rhys suddenly realised where he'd seen the original version of the tall woman in mauve and black. Right down – or up – to her turban and her giant earrings she was Patricia Neal in the film of *Breakfast at Tiffany's*.

In the Tuileries he sat for half an hour, hunched in his overcoat, and tried to collect his thoughts. The park was more or less empty and even the hustlers were calling it a day. They would take up where they left off later in the clubs. Rhys knew some, recognised others.

'*Salut*, Rosbeef' some called as they passed, '*T'as vu* Peach? *Tu sors ce soir?*' Had he seen Peach and was he going out tonight?

'*Oui, oui!*' laughed Rhys, beginning to cheer up.

There was such a cross-section of Paris pond life in the Tuileries. Professional bankers rubbed shoulders with professional bonkers. Art dealers in green felt coats slunk around under the dripping trees looking for another good deal. Assorted children shrieked and screamed as they ran about and dogs sniffed one another's bottoms regardless. Mummys and Nannies sipped drinks in the outside bars and the grand palace with its cheeky new pyramid looked coldly on.

'If those walls could speak,' remarked a Yorkshire tourist to her friend.

'Yes, but would they?' replied the friend knowingly, 'the French are very discreet, you know.'

Mrs Rikki Lancaster lay on her bed. Her companion, Miss Schumann, appeared from the bathroom, stripped down to her skirt and bra.

'Have you done your exercises, honey,' she said with calm authority.

'Yes Elida' lied Rikki Lancaster, 'I so want to speak to H.L. I feel very close to him here, you know?'

'I know, dear,' replied Elida, smiling. She sat down on the bed beside her friend and the two women held hands.

'This wretched migraine,' moaned Rikki Lancaster.

'Don't hate it,' piped Elida Schumann, 'you must learn to love it then it will get better. Now how are those breasts feeling?'

'Wonderful. The scars are almost healed. Can you imagine, I thought they'd never go.'

'Well, there were complications dear,' admonished Elida mysteriously.

'I'm never water-skiing again,' declared Rikki Lancaster as usual. 'Come now, Elida, let's talk to the dead.'

'Oh, not *dead*, Rikki. *Never dead*. Just in the silver orchard, I keep telling you,' and Miss Schumann got up, adjusted her enormous bra, and went back to the bathroom.

'Have you had your herbs, dear?' she called through the wall.

'No,' replied Mrs Lancaster, who was staring at the ceiling and seemed to be listening intently.

'Here's your green magma, then,' said her companion, giving her a glass of evil-looking liquid.

'*Mmmmmm!*' said Rikki, clasping it in both her hands and downing it in a dramatic gulp.

Miss Schumann proceeded to move her chair into the middle of the room and brought out from her big black doctor's bag several candles and more crystals of different shapes and sizes. She placed the candles around the chair in a circle and lit them. She hung some of the crystals around her neck – they were on chains – and laid the rest in her lap. Her fingers were covered with crystal rings. Her face bore the expression of someone about to jump off a bridge into the river.

'Shut the curtains, would you, dear?' she said to Mrs Lancaster who was strutting about the room in a state of high excitement.

'Hello, H.L.,' she sang as she closed the drapes. She drew up a chair and sat outside the circle of candles facing her companion.

'I smell ectoplasm strongly,' confided Elida Schumann, 'it's a good sign.'

They both let their heads drop on to their chests as they sat, silent for a few minutes, like a couple of discarded puppets.

After a bit Elida Schumann began to moan.

'*AaaaaaaOoooooooAaaaaaaHhhhh,*' she went, rocking back and forth. She sounded as if she was working up to a mammoth orgasm. Mrs Lancaster had her eyes tight shut, showing in all their glory her gigantic false eyelashes. An expectant smile played around her lips and she kneaded her hands together.

The picture was certainly bizarre.

Especially if you were Cherubin, who arrived at that moment with clean towels for the bathroom. He smothered a little gasp just in time and giggled to himself as he tiptoed over to the sofa where he plumped up the cushions.

'*Elles sont folles, les bonnes femmes!*' he said to himself. They're complete nutters!

He peeped through the door once more on his way out and was horrified to find Elida Schumann writhing around on the floor, pulling on the straps of her bra.

'Hi, babe,' she said in a voice that was definitely not her own but that of an old man.

'Oh, hi, honey!' replied Mrs Lancaster cheerfully, 'there you are. So how's every little thing . . . ?'

Cherubin dropped the towels and ran from the room.

Rhys headed home. Yet again Paris had restored his equilibrium and to celebrate he walked up the middle of the Champs-Elysées in between the traffic.

Back at the hotel, Cherubin was arranging flowers.

'*Ooolalalalalalalala*, Monsieur Wavy. You are very popular. Two bouquets.'

Dorita laughed. 'Who are they from?'

'I have left the cards. . . .' Cherubin waved gaily in the direction of the mantelshelf.

The first card read 'A *demain*. Kiss, kiss, kiss,' and was signed, 'Your Duchess, who is close by.' Rhys groaned. Oh, God, he was really getting into this too deep. He raised his eyes in mute prayer but then he saw the ceiling with its beautiful cornice, so simple . . . and yet so expensive!

So he opened the other card which read: 'Welcome back to the market place. We missed you,' and was signed, '*ta collègue*, Peach.'

'I have a very important lunch tomorrow, Cherub, so I think I'm just going to have a tiny little something on a tray and spring clean my face. What do you think?'

'It's a bit late for spring clean,' said Cherubin.

'Oh no, do you really think so?' said Rhys, clutching his face and pulling up the skin.

'I mean, it's nearly Christmas,' purred Cherubin from behind the flowers.

'Anyway. . . .' said Rhys, disappearing into the bathroom.

Clarins beauty products had been centre stage in the soap sud's life since he was twenty. And now with all those little character-revealing crow's feet won in the battlefield of Life's Rich Tapestry, they had never been more important.

So he slipped into a white towelling Hotel Leicester bathrobe and put Kathleen Ferrier singing Das Lied von der Erde on the stereo. Then he applied a generous helping of a green mask called Doux Peeling to his face and settled down with a large vodka and tonic.

What has become of my life? he thought as he watched Cherubin arranging the flowers. I had a good Catholic education, I'm reasonably good looking, I used to make a good living and now. . . .

After the required interval he returned to the bathroom, rubbed off the green mask and gazed at himself in the mirror. You're absolutely pathetic, he giggled to himself, you'd better pull yourself together for the Duchess tomorrow or you'll be given your UB40 before you can even get your hand up her skirt. The idea of the explanation he would have to give the dole officer as to why he had been fired restored his humour and he lashed on the blue mask with even more abandon than the green.

The phone rang. Rhys whisked out and grabbed it, taking it back into the bathroom with him. There was a loud crash followed by a flood of obscene Portuguese. Rhys opened the bathroom door and there stood Cherubin in the middle of a floral bomb site. The telephone wire was wrapped round and round the foot of the flower stand. Rhys and Cherubin stared at each other for what seemed like eternity. Then Rhys said, 'I think I'll just put on the white mask now,' and, handing Cherubin the telephone, he went back to the bathroom. This time he locked the door. 'The reason you have never made it as an actor is because you are so ridiculously uncoordinated. You are hopeless!' he told himself as he applied the white mask, forgetting first to remove the blue. 'You have no discipline, you have no staying power, at the first sniff of discouragement you cave in, you must take a grip on yourself . . .'

Outside Cherubin gently replaced the receiver on the hysteri-

cal voice erupting out of the telephone: '*You have no discipline!*
You have no bloody staying power! First sniff of criticism and you
cave right in. Got to take a bloody grip on yerself! Next plane
. . . NEXT'

Rhys prepared to get a grip on his face. He scrubbed away at the
white mask wondering why it had turned powder blue. He
cleansed his skin with the green Clarins tonic lotion and then
peeped excitedly into the mirror to inspect the breathtaking results.

And screamed in horror.

His face had come up in a series of huge red blotches.

CHAPTER NINE: in which Rhys lunches with Mrs Rikki
   Lancaster

The next day Rhys woke up early to the sun streaming through
the windows. It was one of those early winter Paris days, very
bright and cold. He dressed quickly and rushed out to St
Clothilde to attend the 8.45 Mass. He wondered if Mary Mag-
dalene went on hooking after she became a saint. He suspected
not. Feeling slightly uneasy, he decided to skip Communion.
At least his face had gone down.

   He talked to his agent in London who, as usual, was discourag-
ing about the work front. 'At the first sign of discouragement
you cave in.'

'But what about that thing in Alabama, Dumpling? *Dumpling*? Are you awake?'

Dumpling Hines. Rhys had been with him for years. Dear Dumpling. There was only one slight problem with him. He couldn't keep awake. He was permanently asleep at the wheel. He fell asleep in plays, at dinner parties, in the gym, in the bath, even on many occasions while talking on the phone. The only place he didn't fall asleep was in bed, where he loved watching television. As a result he was the only person in the world who had seen every single episode of *Our Butler* when they re-ran it at four in the morning.

'Just a second, Rhys, we're just propping him up. There you are, Dumpling. Oh, *Dumpling!*'

Rhys could hear the sound of much scuffling and laughter, not at all the type of thing you expect to hear from a high-powered agent's office.

'Whip me, Flower Fairy,' someone was saying in the background. Another voice could be heard explaining, 'It's Rhys, Dumpling, you were talking to Rhys . . . about Alabama. . . .'

'*In the heat of the day down in Mobile, Alabama, Working on the railroad with a steel driving hammer . . .*' sang Dumpling, who related everything to Chuck Berry. 'Rhys, darling, why didn't someone here tell you? They've decided to go with something much older.'

'Some*one*,' Dumpling, some*one*. One isn't an object. Not yet, anyway.'

'Exactly, darling, someone. They really wanted *someone*. You know what they're like about names, the Americans. They want a movie star. To them you're *Sweet Little Sixteen* even though you are a *Brown-Eyed Handsome Man*. Come in this afternoon and we'll have a chat. Shame about *Love in the Desert* being cancelled. They were really keen on you for that.'

'I can't, Dumpling. I'm in France.'

'Well, what about when you come back? When are you coming back?'

'I'm not, Dumpling, I live here. I have done for almost six months now, remember?'

''Course you do, darling, just lost my trolley for a moment

there. Well, mind how you go. *Go, go, go, little Queenie.* . . .'

'Darling Dumpling, your trolley, as you well know, went missing presumed dead shortly after your birth.' And with that Rhys hung up.

He chose his wardrobe for the lunch carefully. Black trousers and white shirt. Suede shoes – the utter limit in the Brigadier's eyes ('. . . and if that wasn't enough the fellow was wearing suede shoes. Ha ha ha ha! Got his number, what?'). Rhys added a dark blazer and the look was complete. I really do dress rather well, he told himself, I look quite striking.

The doorman, Fabrice, asked him if he was going to a court case to give evidence. Rhys took this rather badly, got as far as the Champs-Elysées and then returned to the Leicester at a slow gallop, emerging for the second time five minutes later dressed all in grey.

'Now you look like a dealer,' said Fabrice but by this time Rhys was too late for a second change.

He had worked up such a sweat bounding up the stairs, changing and bounding down again that all his Clarins Beauty Flash had melted and run down his forehead into his eyes, virtually blinding him. By the time he arrived at the Voltaire, where he was to meet the Duchess for lunch, he looked like he'd been through a car wash.

As he entered the restaurant, his adrenalin began to hiss about his body. She was right, the Peach Delight, when she said that the most exciting part for her was walking down the hotel corridor beforehand. Who would be behind the closed door? What would they look like? Would they be unbelievably ugly or unbelievably cute?

He stepped through the red velvet curtain between the entrance and the restaurant and looked around the packed and delicious-smelling room. At the far end, seated in regal splendour on a banquette, were Mrs Rikki Lancaster and her partner in crime, Miss Elida Schumann. They stuck out from the rest of the room like proverbial sore thumbs. Both were dressed to the hilt, Rikki Lancaster in her hallmark turban and cape and liberally splattered with chunky jewellery, Elida Schumann in a garishly checked tweed suit.

They saw Rhys immediately.

And he saw them.

Not more than a millisecond passed before Rhys, a mathematician of no particular note, made the simple and horrific equation: two and two makes four. It was the 'Wicked Stepmother' from the Leicester. Peach's 'hotel corridor' maxim blanched slightly in the harsh light of reality and Rhys's first instinct was to nip back behind the red velvet curtain, if not to leave then at the very least he needed a drink, fast.

As if sensing this the two women smiled encouragingly as if to say, 'Come on, it won't be that bad' as they beckoned to him. The rings on their fingers glinted in the winter sunshine streaming in through the windows and their hands appeared to Rhys like magical magnets pulling him towards them. He reviewed his Patricia Neal theory en route and decided Mrs Rikki Lancaster was better cast as Edith Sitwell.

Everyone in the restaurant turned as one and smiled as they recognised Roger. He hoped and prayed no-one would shout out 'Mine's a small port' as he tried hard to look suave and debonair. And they didn't. This was a very smart restaurant. Finally he reached the table and shimmied into his seat opposite the two women on the banquette.

'Duchess Rikki?' he asked, remembering what Hennie had said everyone called her, and cocking his right eyebrow in a rakish fashion.

'How did you guess?' asked Mrs Lancaster.

'How did I guess?' replied Rhys with just a hint of panic in his voice. 'I just felt it. Am I late?'

'A little,' laughed Rikki Lancaster gaily, 'but we expect that from you artistes, don't we, Elida?'

'We never know what to expect from an artiste,' admonished Elida Schumann, 'that's why they're artistes.'

'Gosh, I never thought of it like that,' oozed Rhys. 'How interesting.'

'Now before we go any further,' interrupted Rikki Lancaster, 'let me do two things: introduce you to Elida Schumann, my very dear and trusted friend, and give you a glass of champagne. You do like champagne, don't you?'

'Yes, and I think I am going to like Elida Schumann too. Hello,' purred Rhys, shaking hands.

'Hello,' twittered Elida, turning red.

'Why, Elida, I do believe you've coloured,' said Mrs Lancaster, and the two women giggled. Rhys took matters in hand and moved on.

'It's lovely to meet you both at last. I thought Hennie was joking when she told me you were coming.'

'One thing you should know about me . . .' the turban twitched slightly . . . 'is I never joke.'

Ah, thought Rhys, this *was* going to be fun.

'That's right,' piped in Elida, looking lovingly at her friend, 'she's not a joker when it comes to serious things.'

The two women looked at each other solemnly and then, as if to show they were actually blessed with a sparkling sense of humour after all, they pealed suddenly into crickety trills of laughter. Their stretch-fabric faces expanded and their features almost disappeared altogether as their laughing mouths opened wider and wider, revealing rows and rows of bright white shiny teeth.

'Gimme five,' screeched Mrs Lancaster, proffering her hand.

'Gimme ten,' squeaked the other, holding out hers, palm upward.

'Gimme fifteen,' demanded the Duchess and the two women clanked together their baubled trotters.

'And gimme a drink,' pleaded Rhys in desperation.

They drank their champagne together and went 'Mmmm' collectively. Elida Schumann leaned over intimately.

'There's a beautiful warmth in your hands. You will never pass through the Black Forest.'

'Oh, really?' said Dorhys politely. 'Jolly good.'

The two women laughed.

'The poor boy doesn't understand what you are saying, Elida. Elida is a psychic, a channeller, to be precise.'

'Does that mean you know what I'm thinking?' asked Rhys, laughing nervously.

'That depends,' replied Elida, fixing her eyes just above his head. On reflex Rhys turned round, thinking there was someone behind him, and Mrs Lancaster laughed again.

'There's no-one there. I expect Elida is looking at your aura, aren't you, dear?'

'No, I'm looking for the waiter. Twenty minutes for a glass of water!'

'Is this your first trip to Paris?' Rhys asked.

'Heavens no, honey. My husband, Herman Lancaster, or H.L. as he was known, often brought me here. He was a movie producer, you know. A famous producer and he loved France. So I feel like a local girl.' She giggled coquettishly.

'Me too,' said Rhys without thinking. They all laughed. 'I mean Paris does that to one, doesn't it?'

'Yes, dear, . . .' said Mrs Rikki Lancaster, 'we are so pleased to meet you. When Hennie said that you were friends and that we could meet you we were so joyous.'

'Hennie told me a lot about you, too,' lied Rhys.

'Sure, sure. You know something? I know I've seen you some-place before. Not on the TV. For real.'

'How incredible. I feel the same thing,' said Rhys, thinking – yeah – in a nightmare!

'Whooo-eeee!' Suddenly Elida clasped her hands. 'Didn't I tell you, Rikki? Rhys, you are not going to believe this. I did the crystals for her this morning. I'm a crystal therapist, you see. I felt the most incredible heat coming from Rikki's heart and colon and I said to her – well, didn't I, Rikki? – I said. . . .'

At this point Sticky Rikki butted in. 'She said to me, Duchess, someone from your past life is very close. Something that you have been waiting for across the centuries is very close to you. And then when I saw you, Rhys, it was as if I had seen you before. I know we've all seen you on TV but this is different. Really different. I feel we know each other. Do you feel that way too?'

'Do you know, I do feel something strange,' exclaimed Rhys.

'You have a great love in your past life, I can feel it. I'm going to ask around in the silver orchard when we channel tonight.' By now Elida was nearly hysterical. The effect of the two crea-tures was quite heady and luckily for Rhys and his rapidly droop-

74

ing face, the Maître d' arrived with the menus and a few polite but forgettable greetings. Safely tucked behind his menu Rhys peeped out discreetly to take a closer look at his two new friends. The view was slightly impaired by their menus and all he could see was Rikki's turban and Elida's hurricane-resistant bouffant. Today the Duchess's turban was jet black with a huge jewel in the middle like an eye. Elida's hair was also black with a great big curl swooping across the top. Underneath they each sported tied-back, dry-cleaned, steam-pressed foreheads with two pairs of electric eel eyebrows and four heavily bejewelled trotters clasped either side of the menus.

So while the girls shrieked and giggled behind their menus like the witches from *Macbeth* (whoops, the Scottish play, lovey, knock three times, come in and turn around till your next job) Rhys got out his glasses to take a closer look at them.

They ordered a delicious lunch which the two women devoured with the voracity of a pair of vultures. Between them they drank two bottles of wine, Cognac and champagne so with their coffee they lay back somewhat shell-shocked.

'H.L. would have loved you, Rhys,' said Rikki dreamily as she stared into her brandy glass. Elida nodded sagely.

'He had a great understanding of the geography of the soul.'

'That must come in handy,' ventured Rhys.

'Handy? Why it's *essential*, honey. I learned it from him. I really understand people. So does Elida. Of course, she has her art to inform her as well but we can tell a phoney when we see one, can't we, E?'

'Oh, we certainly can,' said Elida and the two women looked at Rhys, who suddenly felt uncomfortable.

'So where are we going exactly? Hennie didn't quite explain. . . .'

'We are going to Tangiers in Morocco, to a ball given by our friend Ashby de la Zouche, and it's going to be *maaarvellous* fun. . . .'

'Good,' said Rhys and then he looked at his watch.

Conquest over, he became bored. He mumbled something about a meeting regarding a film and after endless arrangements, goodbyes and details such as, 'I'll call you tomorrow evening,' he got up.

Then Rikki took his hand and said very deeply and sincerely, 'I can tell you're very sensitive, Rhys. So am I.'

About as sensitive as a Sherman tank in shawls, thought Lancelot, but he said, 'I can tell we are going to be great friends.' He looked directly into her eyes. This was easy-peasy. He had done this same scene countless times on the telly. 'We are great friends, Rikki, and I feel we have been for some time.'

He leaned down and kissed her on both cheeks then walked to the door of the restaurant. He turned round, getting the maximum benefit of the late afternoon sun on his face, and waved. He made a pretend telephone with his hand (little finger and thumb extended over a wrist), held it up to his ear (rather French, actually) and then, at just exactly the right moment, with a swish of his cloak, Lancelot du Lac made his exit.

Severely shaken by the event, Rhys rushed over to Peach's – where she was throwing an impromptu party for four in her bed – and only returned to the Leicester at seven o'clock the next morning in a state of advanced intoxication.

'Hennie? Are you awake?' he screamed. 'Listen, she's here and, oh God, she's brought her friend. If I make it a double contract, does that make it two hundred thousand dollars? What? Yeah, there's another one, she's smaller than the Duchess. What's that got to do with it? One hundred seventy-five thousand? Pay or play? Hennie, what are you talking about . . . ? Hennie?'

But she had hung up.

The phone rang immediately.

'Listen, Hennie, what's wrong with her? Is she up to it?'

'Up to what, you spineless little idiot? Now, look here, I've booked my charter flight to Paris. Aldershot Airlines. Algy Duff-Cox recommended them. Yer mother can't come with me. She's

76

open to the public or some such nonsense. Now listen here, plane arrives at oh-eight hundred hours day after tomorrow and you'd bloody well better be. . . .'

But Rhys had hung up.

CHAPTER TEN: in which Rhys meets the deaf queen

'This is Elida Schumann speaking. Let me pass you Mrs Lan-caster,' sang the telephonic alarm call at the other end. Static hissed and crackled as once again Rhys wondered what on earth he was doing talking on the telephone at such an unearthly hour.

'Hi, darling,' purred the five thousand doves, 'Hennie told me you read scripts from seven a.m. so I wasn't afraid to call so early. Now, we've been to the travel agency to get your ticket and this is the plan. Are you listening, darling?'

What was all this 'darling' all of a sudden?

'Yes, Duchess, I'm all ears,' croaked Rhys.

'Great. So now we are on for Friday. Elida has booked you to fly into London next Thursday afternoon and we have made a reservation for you at Claridges. We will all leave together for Tangiers on Friday morning. How does that sound, darling?'

'Terrifying,' mumbled Rhys into his pillow without thinking. 'I mean I'm terrified of flying,' he corrected hastily, 'but otherwise it sounds fantastic.'

Suddenly there was a piercing shriek down the other end of the phone. Rhys imagined for one marvellous moment that Elida had stabbed the Duchess with a hat pin – but no such luck.

'Rikki has turned her hearing aid up too high,' said the speaking clock, 'here she is again.'

'Hi, baby, sorry about that. Now you are coming, aren't you?'

'Yes, I'm coming,' replied the crestfallen Rhys.

'What? Speak up. This is a terrible line. Turn the volume up, idiot!'

You're screaming, thought Rhys, but out loud shouted '*I'm coming!*'

'Whaaaaat?' shrieked the five thousand doves.

'I'M COOMMMMIIIINNGG!' shrieked the harem and the line went dead.

Poor old Mrs Lancaster. Well, she wouldn't be the first deaf queen in Rhys's life.

Since that rainy night when the boy first met Jerry, the seasons had come and gone, and living in London had considerably changed him. He was at the Centrale Kontiki and he had married Adrienne but every now and then Rhys became – Ollie. Soon after the night with Jerry, Rhys had changed his professional name from Keith to Daniel; Daniel had become Greg and finally Greg was Ollie.

Thus, on a subsequent rainy night, Ollie found himself by a railway siding with a potential client.

'Let's go down that alleyway there,' said Ollie.

'What?'

'Let's go down that alleyway there,' repeated Ollie, slightly ruffled.

'I'm sorry, I'm deaf. What was that?'

'He said why don't you go down the alley together?' chimed in another very clipped Glaswegian voice. Ollie and his client both turned. The third voice seemed to come from a very small queen with no hair and a moustache, dressed in motorcycle leathers. Beyond him in the gloom Ollie could see what seemed like millions more little pint-sized people leaning against the dripping brick wall of the railway embankment. Maybe I've come to the under-fives by mistake, he thought as he towered above them all.

At last his client – older, at least forty-five – seemed to have got the gist and with a long sigh of realisation, reminiscent of a buffalo, he set off with Rhys.

'Do you come here often,' asked Ollie.

'What?'

'He wants to know if ye come here often,' echoed the Glasgow queen who was following them. Ollie and his trophy turned again but still the older one couldn't – or wouldn't – hear. The leather queen flashed Ollie a sympathetic glance.

Ollie stopped at a suitable niche in the Victorian brickwork but the deaf queen didn't.

'Psst, over here, mate,' said Ollie but the deaf queen trundled on regardless.

'Over here,' sang the leather queen, trying to be helpful, but even that didn't work. Ollie was beginning to have quite enough of the leather queen chorus and the next time he raised his manicured eyebrows to share another moment of disbelief with our hero, Pollie merely stared back coldly.

Finally ensconced in the niche, Ollie noticed that out of the fog all the rest of the pint-sized queens were gathering. It was like a very macabre version of *The Wizard of Oz*. Rhys tapped his feet together three times and said, 'I want to go home, I want to go home,' but nothing happened. The deaf queen didn't seem to notice, nor did he seem to mind that a non-paying audience was assembling. So they got down to business.

The odd drop of rain splashed against the siding. The mist

hovered. The occasional Tube train clattered past, its lights throwing the munchkins into terrifying relief against the black walls. The city – London – seemed far away and the only continuous noise was the scraping of boots against bricks and cobbles punctuated by the odd rasping cough.

Nearing conclusion, Ollie said politely, 'I'm coming.'

But the deaf queen was miles away. 'Whaaat?' he asked.

'I'm coming,' repeated the drama student, recently married and slightly embarrassed.

'What you say?' asked the other.

'*He's coming!*' chanted the chorus of munchkins, 'HE'S COMING!'

It seemed that Rhys and Adrienne were destined to remain apart. Whatever spirit of adventure she had had before breaking her neck at their wedding, Adrienne lost straight after, and for the rest of her marriage her neck, amongst other things, was to give her considerable discomfort. So she remained for much of the time at her father's home in Scotland while her buccaneer husband roamed the world in search of he knew not what.

It would be wrong to say that theirs was an altogether unsatisfactory marriage because they drew a certain strength from each other even though they rarely met. They had, after all, known each other almost since birth and would, when asked, explain that they had spent more than enough time together already, twenty years in fact. Now they were on sabbatical.

They spoke on the telephone often and Rhys went to Scotland once every six months. They both fully expected to be reunited one day but for now their aims in life were incompatible. Adrienne had a horror of the outside world and had lost her footing on each and every visit into it. Rhys also had a horror of it but his was a Catholic one and so, like the moth that flies in ever-decreasing circles around a candle, he flitted around the world with his heart in his mouth, wondering if he would ever make it home.

Rhys's homosexuality, a subject for snickering among their

family's acquaintances, was of very little consequence to them. Like life, it was a passing phase. Adrienne had watched it arrive in his eyes very early on in the calm and comfort of the nursery, and she had nurtured it and surveyed it in her own little lost way all through their childhood. When the couple first had sex it was beside them as they lay together, like their child, something they both knew would need to be protected. After Adrienne broke her neck and returned to Scotland it was literally burning in his eyes. She could see it like a butterfly, flitting behind his pupils, catching the sun and glinting like pieces of glass in the river.

With an unusually deep intuition for a little lost girl, Adrienne knew there were two things she could do with Rhys's homosexuality. She could put it in a jar, watch it flap around and die and then slam it in the middle of a crusty old bound copy of *Punch* and forget about it. Or she could take it in her shaking hands – shaking, lest they should hurt it – tiptoe to the window and throw it as far as she could out into nature.

Adrienne was not a Catholic.

And so she watched from the window with deep relief to be inside as her beautiful butterfly husband flitted and flapped around the world. Sometimes she would listen with pleasure as she heard from friends of some latest tomfoolery he had committed. Other times she would wait like the wives of soldiers fighting far away in some dangerous war, powerless to help, but still hoping.

She had her spies too, of course – trusted friends or colleagues who could tell her of his exact predicament.

One of these spies was Marie Claire, the switchboard operator at the Hotel Leicester.

'*Bonjour*, Marie Claire. *Ici* Madame Waveral. How are you?'

'Aaaah! Madame Waveral. *Ça me fait plaisir de vous avoir. Comment allez vous?*'

'All right, but I'm a bit worried about Rhys.'

'Aaaah, all the family as well,' said Marie Claire confidentially. 'All the family. The Brigadier, he is phoning every day but I tell him: don't worry, Monsieur Wavy, your son he look very handsome at the moment. You know when things go bad, he look bad too.'

The two women laughed.

'I thought maybe I'd come over tomorrow to see how things are,' ventured Adrienne, 'but then I don't want to waste money. We're very short of money, you see.'

'Oh, ah know, but dat ees why de Brigadier want to zee eess son. I zink to elp, non?' Marie Claire always became very French at the mention of money.

'I'm afraid you don't really know the Brigadier, Marie Claire. But he looks all right, then, my husband?'

'He looking marvellous. I pass you him now.'

The line went dead for a few moments and then Rhys's voice suddenly shouted, 'Marie Claire, this is beyond a joke!' and the line went dead again.

Adrienne went 'Hellooooo, Helloooo?' a few times in her little-girl voice and then hung up. Rhys was in what she called a Brigadier mood and she couldn't deal with that. She wrapped her woollen shawl closer around her – Scotland was icy in October – and padded slowly back to her studio in the turret where she was making a stained glass window featuring St Francis of Assisi.

CHAPTER ELEVEN: in which Rhys receives a little pocket
   money

Rhys was in pandemonium. It was already Wednesday and he
was leaving for London the next day. Had he been secretly
hoping to be relieved of this terrible quest by a call from Dumpling with news of a job – or was it just a case of good old
first-night nerves on the eve of an opening night?

   Luckily for him Peach was taking the situation firmly in hand.

   'Once only, honey. Do the deed only once during the entire
weekend or else she won't respect you.'

   Cherubin, who was doing the packing, was furious at not
having been kept in the picture. '*Une fois quoi*, Madame Peach?'

he asked, red in the face with fury. But the two friends were ignoring him.

'I get you some pills. *Tiens*! Take before you do it.' Peach handed Rhys four Ecstasy capsules.

'But where shall I put them?' whined the wimp of the year.

'*Dans ton cul*,' snapped Cherubin. Up your. . . .

'Mmmm, perfect. *Geniale*,' giggled Peach as she lit an enormous spliff and then handed it to Cherubin. 'Honey, you can't wear these clothes. You have nothing more suitable?'

'Suitable for what?' cried Cherubin, taking a long draw on the joint and promptly having a coughing fit.

'I'll have to get something in London when I get there.'

The telephone rang. It was the manager.

'Monsieur Waveral, your father is arriving tomorrow. Where shall we put him?'

'He can stay in my room but make sure he pays something towards the bill, OK?'

'He said he wants the smallest single room so I hope your room is all right for him. Where will you both sleep?'

'Oh, I shan't be here. I shall be in Tangiers.'

Suddenly there were peals of laughter from Cherubin in the corner.

'I must go,' Rhys explained to the manager, 'Cherubin is having a turn,' and he hung up.

'*Qu'est ce que ce passe là?*' Rhys demanded.

'I find this in your baggage,' explained Peach, handing Rhys a loo brush in its container.

'It's for fishing out those cachets from *ton cul*, after,' screeched Cherubin through sobs of joy. '*Une fois seulement*, only one time, Monsieur Wavy, only after the cachet. But what are you going to do, Monsieur Waveral? I don't like, I don't like at all!' and with that he left the two friends alone.

'What this, darling?' Peach was holding up a little china jar of cream whose label had come off.

'Oh, thank God you reminded me,' said Rhys, snatching the jar from her, 'it's my La Prairie Eye cream. Didn't you know I was the La Prairie Eye queen? It helps me fight against the tinkle-wrinkles and what's more . . .' he picked up the Ecstasy

86

Peach had given him '. . . where better to hide my E?' He slipped the pills into the cream.

'Now you have Vitamin E cream,' said Peach, clapping her hands in glee and then quickly hiding them behind her back. She hated her hands. They were huge and distinctly unfeminine. . . .

'Now where's my passport?' said Rhys. 'Darling, did I ever show you my new passport photo? It makes me look like Montgomery Clift with measles. . . .'

Rhys was petrified of flying. On a long haul he would take scores of Valium but the flight from Paris to London was so short he didn't have time to get down to any serious pill-popping. There was, however, plenty of time for several strong vodkas and as usual Rhys left the plane lurching like a giraffe that had been shot with a tranquilliser.

It was bad enough that he had to fly but he was also returning to 'the centre of negativity' as he called London. He had not been back since he had left for France. The only thing he was remotely looking forward to was seeing his mother, whom he had telephoned and invited to dinner.

Sitting in the taxi riding into the city he watched listlessly as the same old roads went by.

The Hogarth roundabout.

Good heavens, what had happened to the Cherry Blossom factory? Whoosh – gone! And the ballet school, with darling old Margot Fonteyn's studio next door – or was it Rudi's? Who knew? Who cared?

Past West Kensington Tube and into the Cromwell Road.

In fact it wasn't at all distant. It was as if he had never been away. Landmarks shimmered in the autumn twilight. The V&A. The Brompton Oratory. Knightsbridge and, of course, Harrods. Rhys opened his window and the air smelt of bonfires. He closed his eyes and luxuriated in nostalgia.

When he arrived at Claridges he found that the Duchess had

reserved a very impressive suite for him, filled with flowers, champagne on ice.

'What has become of me?' Rhys giggled to himself as he uncorked the bottle. He looked at his watch and saw it was six o'clock. Just time for a nap before dinner with Lady Dinah and Anita Blumenthal, his theatrical lesbian friend.

'Darling, I thought you said you had no money. What on earth are you doing in a room of these proportions?' Lady Dinah marched in at approximately thirty miles an hour, glancing here and there like a fox sniffing the wind, doubtless looking for something that needed mending. As usual she was dressed very simply in a green tartan knee-length skirt, matching green tights, black patent court shoes and a bright orange blouse.

Rhys stared in horror. 'Mummy, what on earth are you doing in a fluorescent orange blouse? You look as if someone has turned up the colour too high on the TV.'

Lady Dinah was fielding well. 'For one thing it's not orange, it's tangerine. A perfectly lovely tangerine. And for another I *like it*, so I don't care what you think. Miss Polenska, my seamstress in the village, made it. Now, do stop larking about and tell me what you're doing over here? Have you got a lovely job or something?'

'Yes, I have rather. I've become a prostitute.'

Peals of laughter erupted from Lady Dinah. 'Oh, darling, you are awful. No, thanks awfully, Rhyssie, no champagne. Do they have any cider? I'm on an absolute cider fetish. Now, come on, what *are* you doing? Really?'

'I've told you. I've become a prostitute.'

'Enough. Don't bore me. There's the door bell. Shall I go? Who's coming?'

Questions were banged out with military regularity. As always Rhys found himself in a complete daze after fifteen seconds with his mother. But at least she hadn't mentioned his father.

'Anita Blumenthal,' he said quickly, watching her accelerate to forty-five miles an hour as she went to the door.

'Oh, *goody*! The one you always say is a lesbian. I shall watch for signs this time. I know you're pulling my leg. Anita, my dear, do come in. How amusing to see you here.'

'Hello, Lady Dinah, how are you?' replied Anita, who had her hair piled high in a Victorian style and was sporting a pale pink jogging suit. Lady Dinah eyed it like a magpie about to swoop.

'Perfectly well, thanks. Now where did you get that track suit? It's exactly what I want for sewing in the study in the winter.'

'Harvey Nichols.' Anita hugged Rhys. 'How are you, darling, and what are you doing here?'

'Oh, it's *too* boring, he's become a prostitute,' said Lady Dinah as she settled down in an armchair and reached into her John Lewis bag for her tapestry.

'You don't mind if I get on with this, do you, darling? Any news of the cider? Now, Anita, are you working?'

'No, Lady Dinah. It's an awful year for everyone. Have you got anything, Rhys?'

'Absolutely fuck all. In fact I'm going to chuck it in. Shall we go down and have dinner? I'm absolutely starving.'

Lady Dinah began to put away the tapestry she had just got out. 'What about my cider?' she asked plaintively.

'We can have it downstairs, Mummy, it'll be much quicker.'

Their entrance into the dining room at Claridges – pink and tangerine with Rhys in between – caused quite a stir. They settled into a cosy corner table and the two women proceeded to cross-question Rhys.

'I've *told* you, I've become a prostitute,' he insisted.

'Well, what do you mean exactly?' asked Lady Dinah. She could never be quite sure if he was pulling her leg or not.

'I mean that this woman, Mrs Rikki Lancaster, is taking me to a party in Tangiers for the weekend and paying me a hundred thousand dollars.'

'And what do you have to *do?*' asked the two women together, leaning forward.

'Nothing, I hope,' said the boy.

Lady Dinah took a gulp of cider. 'I don't know. What do you think, Anita? Is he telling the truth?'

'I don't know either but there's someone very strange waving at us over at the top of those stairs. Who is it, Rhys?'

'Darling, I've absolutely no idea. I haven't got my glasses on. Hang on a min.'

'Don't worry, Anita, it's just some ghastly American fans of Rhys. My dear, we're quite used to it by now. Ever since he did *Our Gardener*. My goodness, though, aren't they dressed up?' Lady Dinah laughed, thoroughly enjoying herself.

'*Our Butler*, Mummy, do try to remember. *Oh my God!* It's her. It's the Duchess!'

'Duchess who?'

'Mummy, don't you ever listen to me? I've just told you. Mrs Rikki Lancaster.'

'Yes, but you didn't say she was a Duchess.'

'She isn't. . . .'

'Well, whatever she is it's riveting. Is she coming over?' said her Ladyship, gulping down more cider.

'Which one is she? There seem to be so many,' shrieked Anita.

Rhys concentrated on silent prayer as Rikki's party advanced upon them. She and Elida had arrived with another party of ageing Californian ex-pat matrons. Their collective age would have read like a transatlantic telephone number and now, as if drawn by some silent command from their leader, they were moving across the floor to the Waveral table.

Rikki's appearance defied description. Rhys stared at her, completely transfixed, trying to work out what on earth she was wearing. It was as if the entire Paris Collections had been hung on a naked Christmas tree, topped with a black chiffon turban covered in tiny gold stars. This particular turban was exceptionally tight so that Rikki's eyes were pulled upwards and outwards giving her face a distinctly Oriental slant.

She waved in an intimate fashion in Rhys's direction but then it seemed as if his prayers had been answered. She stopped with her party at a large table in the middle of the dining room laid for at least fifteen people.

'The night of the living dead,' said Rhys, thinking out loud.

Everyone in the dining room stopped eating and listened while Elida barked out the placement when, horror of horrors, the Duchess of Lancaster suddenly began to wend her way over to the Waveral family table.

Rhys stood up to receive her.

'Golly, he's never done that before. I think it's rather good, for him, don't you, Anita?' Lady Dinah thought she was muttering this in an aside but in fact she was screaming to be heard over Elida's voice.

'Rikki! What a surprise. Can I introduce my mother, Lady Dinah Waveral, and my great friend, Anita Blumenthal. This is Mrs Rikki Lancaster.'

Lady Dinah beamed and held out her hand but the Duchess responded only with a faint smile.

'*Mother*,' she repeated, staring at Lady Dinah in disbelief, 'Rhys Waveral's *mother?*'

'Spot on,' replied Lady Dinah, 'he does have one, you know. Don't tell me I don't look old enough. May we offer you a glass of cider? My dear, *do* sit down. Here, let me take your cape. . . .' Lady Dinah's empire-ruling stare bored right through Rikki's forehead and out the back of her star-spangled turban as she wrenched Mrs Rikki Lancaster's fur cape from her shoulders. Hennie had never told her she'd have to meet his mother!

The Duchess decided it was time she started running her own show.

'Rhys, *darling*,' This time the 'darling' was a blatant take off of Lady Dinah's drawl. 'I forgot to tell you. Tomorrow morning, the car will arrive at 8.15. I'm sorry it's so early but the sooner we leave the. . . .' She gurgled with innuendo.

'The sooner we get back,' agreed Rhys without thinking.

'No,' corrected Anita sternly, 'the sooner you get there,' and everyone laughed.

'Now where is it you're going, all of you?' asked her Ladyship.

'Tangierssssssss,' cooed the five thousand doves. 'Now, Rhys,' she whispered, drawing him aside, 'here you are, fifty thousand dollars in cash as agreed. Elida will give you the rest later . . . after . . . you know. Oh, and by the way, we bought you some clothes. Don't be angry. We've asked for them to be delivered to your room. You'll find them after dinner. I see you got the watch . . . so, bye darling.' She kissed him possessively on the cheek with a glance at Lady Dinah who was watching them with beady eyes. 'Come and have a drink at our table later. Bye everyone.' And she hobbled back to join her party.

'*Rhyssie*. . . .' began Lady Dinah in the tone of voice that brooked no argument whatsoever, 'did I just see that Lancaster woman give you a little pocket money?'

'Just a little, Mummy, nothing to worry about. . . .'

'Hand it over now, there's a good boy. You know what you're like with loose cash.' Lady Dinah grabbed the envelope out of her son's hands and clicked it shut inside her own perfectly sensible black patent bag. 'I'll take it to the bank for you tomorrow.'

They ordered their food and when it arrived the conversation changed, much to Rhys's relief.

'Peter Moody's back in hospital.' said Anita.

'What's he got, poor thing?' Lady Dinah was always eager to discuss illness.

'Cancer all over. He was perfectly all right up until about five months ago and then suddenly. . . .'

'He's been unwell for much longer than that, I reckon,' said Rhys. 'It's strange because he's always been such a health fanatic. Has he got any money?'

'That's just the problem,' explained Anita, 'he's in real trouble there. He hasn't paid his mortgage for two years, apparently, and they're kicking up a huge fuss. We're going to have a whip-round for him, Rhys.'

'Is it really cancer or does he have AIDS?' asked Lady Dinah.

'Oh, no, it's not AIDS,' replied Anita, quick to the defence. 'It's certainly cancer.'

'What's the difference?' said Rhys, annoyed, 'he's dying either way. That's the main thing.'

'Not necessarily,' said Anita. 'Biro's doing a wonderful job with the crystals.'

Rhys suddenly felt his temper going.

'Oh, don't be so ridiculous, Anita. Peter's dying. Biro and her stupid crystals aren't going to make any difference. Come on, let's go.'

Back upstairs in Rhys's suite they were greeted by an ominous looking suitcase in the middle of the floor. Lady Dinah and Anita fell about unpacking it like two schoolchildren, shrieking with glee at each new unsuitable piece of clothing. Everything was at least two sizes too big.

'Well, your uncle can have it for Christmas,' said the ever-practical Lady Dinah. 'Look at all this silk underwear. Have you ever seen anything so ghastly? If I saw a man in this I'd think he was queer.'

Anita and Rhys sniggered quietly. Lady Dinah was always good for a laugh.

'I really must go to bed now, my darlings,' yawned Rhys. 'I must be bright-eyed and fresh for my client tomorrow.'

He walked them down to the foyer and out into the street to wait for a taxi. Lady Dinah took his arm. 'You're not really being a prostitute, are you, darling?'

'No. Not really,' replied Rhys uncertainly. 'Will you . . . will you be seeing Adrienne when you get back to Scotland? If you are would you give her . . . you know, would you give her my love and everything?'

'Oh, yes, of course I'll tell her I've seen you,' breezed Lady Dinah, 'but I doubt she'll take it in. She's having the most awful trouble with her stained glass window. Apparently she made St Francis look like a Martian with antennae and things and the Moncrieff-Derwents, who commissioned the thing – five years ago, I might add – are highly upset. Ah, here comes my taxi. . . .'

'The Moncrieff-Derwents have always been highly upset,' commented Rhys as he opened the door for his mother.

'And highly upsetting to boot, if you ask me. Anita, can I drop you off? Goodbye, darling boy. Have a marvellous time in – where is it you're going? Tangiers? Your father hit me with a golf club in Tangiers. By mistake, of course. I was standing too near as he swung, or something.'

And on that note the taxi disappeared into the night.

CHAPTER TWELVE: in which Rhys becomes Dorhys and
   has his first Macrobiotic Tea

That night, alone in his glamorous suite at Claridges, Rhys felt
low, and thought of death. Peter Moody was dying. So was
another friend, of something quite different. And in Paris
another. None of it seemed to make any sense. None of it even
seemed to be real. Each time these tragedies crossed his mind
they hit him with a new force. A blast of hackle-raising adrenalin
would shoot through his body, thrusting equal doses of panic
and fear into his system.

   Blood (so fragile and intricate), under the bridge, as they say,
thought Rhys, subdued by a whisky and a joint which Anita had

left. He took the telephone, ridiculously overstated like the rest of the room, and dialled Peter Moody's number. It surprised him that he could remember it after all these years.

'Peter, it's Rhys,' he said immediately when it was picked up after a few rings.

'Peter's asleep. Who is this?' said a woman's voice he did not recognise.

'It's Rhys Waveral. I'm a friend of his. I was just calling to find out how he was,' replied Dorhys, the familiar adrenalin pumping through him again. There was a marginal pause before the voice replied cautiously, 'You know he's not well at the moment?'

'Yes. Yes, I did. I wanted to know how he was, that's all. How is he?'

'He's starting a new course of chemotherapy tomorrow. It's quite exhausting so he decided to get an early night.'

Another small pause.

'I'm so sorry,' was all the soap star, so used to playing scenes of this nature on TV, could think of to say.

'Yeah,' said the voice, loosening up a bit and taking a drag on a cigarette, 'yeah, it's been really rough for him. And all this chemotherapy stuff has really taken it out of him. Why don't you call next week? Give him a bit of time to calm down from tomorrow. I know he'd like to talk to you. We were laughing about you just the other day. Oh, by the way, I'm Mary. I'm helping out for a while.'

'Hi.'

'Hi,' she replied.

'What were you saying about me?' asked Rhys, not really wanting to know so much as wanting to keep talking.

'He was saying that you played a hymn called *Soul of our Saviour* instead of *Mad About the Boy* one night in *Blithe Spirit* in Derby. It was very funny.' Mary laughed.

'I don't know why they were all so thrown,' he replied. 'Same difference, really. *Soul of my Saviour* and *Mad About the Boy*. Interchangeable, I'd say.'

They both laughed.

'Anyway, tell him I called, will you? And that I'll call again soon.'

'OK. By the way, you know there's a whip-round for him? You've been sent a letter. See what you can do, eh?'

Rhys didn't ask for any more details. 'All right. Nice to talk to you. Bye.'

And he hung up.

Rhys remembered well the first time he had met Peter Moody.

It was the time when he and Adrienne were living in the basement of the Brigadier's cottage in Chelsea. The telephone was ringing.

'It's for you,' murmured Adrienne in her sleep, but neither she nor Rhys moved. This was partly due to the fact that their bed was so small that it always took a good three minutes to untangle themselves from one another before they could move. Finally Rhys stumbled away from his inert wife and waded through the debris of the night before in search of the mauve hand-painted phone.

'Daaahling!' gasped a familiar voice. It was Dorinda Carr Smiley.

'What?' croaked Rhys.

'You've got to come over. The most terrible thing has just happened.' And she hung up without another word.

Rhys stared around the sordid sitting room. Somehow, they had completely gone to seed, he and Adrienne. Half-filled coffee cups, dating back weeks, rubbed shoulders with dog-eared magazines and dirty clothes. Rhys was at drama school and the couple had followed the example set by their peers (and most of them were indeed peers), and had sunk into a more or less permanent haze of hash and heroin.

Rhys tottered back to the bedroom, debating all the while whether to ignore Dorinda's call and flop back into bed for the rest of the day when he remembered something quite ghastly. A whole group of Kontiki students had arranged to come round to the cottage and rehearse act two from an incredibly irritating play called *Hobson's Choice* at ten o'clock and it was already nine-thirty. Rhys about-turned and went into the bathroom, gathering clothes as he went along – a smelly T-shirt wrapped around the handle of a saucepan, trousers left by the loo looking as if the wearer had been sucked down the bowl from inside them. Everything smelt and what was more, when he looked at himself in the mirror, he too was a pretty frightening sight. Short cropped blond hair merging into a grey face. Little matchstick arms and legs, weighed down even by a flimsy T-shirt.

'Oh God,' he groaned, 'I've got to get a job. This is all going too far.'

It was a mere budgie's flight from the Brigadier's to Dorinda's flat in Fulham which Rhys had, in fact, visited as recently as the night before. Dorinda answered the door with a tinfoil pipe in her mouth, waving another piece of foil in her hand.

'*Darling!*' she gasped again, 'you are an absolute *brick.*'

She walked back into her flat, tottering along on extremely high heels, her ubiquitous Gucci bag slung over her shoulder. Nothing much appeared to have changed from the night before. Veronica – or *Vronica* as Dorinda pronounced it – and Tony, her lodgers and partners in crime, were decomposing on Dorinda's large, once beige, sofa. The mess was double that of Rhys and Adrienne's flat.

But the young Empire Rulers of Today didn't care. If they could no longer afford staff, well, so much the worse for the staff. Tidying up was rarely done. The kitchen sink was full of baked-bean encrusted plates and the empty tins were lying scattered all over the floor.

'We haven't been to bed. Tony and Vronica have been *marvellous.*'

'Why? What's happened?' asked Rhys, taking the tinfoil pipe from his friend.

'Careful with that. It's really good stuff,' she warned, eyeing the brown, oil-like evil lurking on the tinfoil. Rhys settled down in his usual place on the beige sofa to listen to Dorinda's tale of woe – and to enjoy the sudden rush starting at the back of his neck.

'Roddy S-C has left me,' wailed Dorinda, unloading fifteen

packets of Rothman's King Size out of her handbag on to the floor.

Rhys wondered what the problem was. Roddy Summers-Cox was an exquisitely beautiful Hooray with short-cropped, dyed white hair and a short-cropped dyed white brain to match.

'No! How *awful!*' Rhys tried to sound suitably sympathetic.

Dorinda prattled on. 'Well, you know Joan who always goes to the Embassy? The one who looks like Joan Crawford? Well, she's actually a man called John from Bromley, can you imagine? I was at the Village gambling last night when R S-C suddenly arrived. I said *"Daaahling*, you seem to be in an awful state" and he went and told me – *just* as I was beginning to win – that he was having an affair with her. Can you *imagine?'* she repeated.

'Yes. Rather clearly as a matter of fact,' said Rhys. He had known Joan for some time and of course he had always had his suspicions about Roddy S-C. 'Cuckolded, my dear Dorinda. Whatever would your poor dead father say? Ditched for a trans-sexual!'

'Not even . . . ' snorted Dorinda.

'Apparently he's got a whopper,' said Tony and he and Vronica started to giggle.

'Maybe this is the time to remind you you are a month overdue with your rent, Tony,' giggled Dorinda, apparently enjoying the situation just as much as he was. She leaned back on the cushions, her pinned eyes luxuriating in all the drama.

'The whole thing's the limit,' she said in a kind of dream.

'Adrienne's got a boyfriend, too,' said Rhys.

'No!' Dorinda's head jerked up. *'Darling,* I *am* sorry.'

'Don't be. He's rather sweet actually, he's called Perky.'

'Perky Burton Sinclair?' asked Vronica.

'No, he's in Australia at the moment, working on an outback,' said Tony.

'In the outback,' corrected Rhys. 'No, this Perky is from Bexhill. He's a musician.'

'Sounds like the outback to me.' Tony snorted with laughter.

Rhys stayed until about four o'clock. When he left he walked in the warm spring afternoon towards his home. How things had changed since that summer night when he had met Jerry. Now he found himself walking in the direction of that encounter, towards Gloucester Road. His mother had been right. She had accused him of lacking the moral fibre required to stomach the diversions and deviations of the metropolis and here he was, on the verge of junkydom, a walking skeleton. It was not exactly how he had planned his life and neither drug abuse nor the hustling scene were as glamorous as they had appeared at the start. His friends had no clue as to his professional activities (with the exception of his wife), and the double life he had so relished at the outset was now beginning to divide his whole character. He had begun to feel that his character was nothing more than the splinters of a china cup thrown against the wall in a fit of pique. Some of the pieces had gone missing and Rhys now seriously doubted his ability to reform his personality.

'Oh, well,' he thought, 'something will turn up.' He was an eternal optimist.

Sure enough, something did turn up. Rhys became aware of someone following him down the street. He stopped to look in a shop window, and the someone stopped a little further back. Rhys promptly struck his 'business as usual' pose and within minutes the fish was hooked and landed.

'Hello,' said the man, tall and hawk-like.

Rhys feigned surprise. 'Hello,' he replied.

'Are you shopping?' asked the man, who Rhys imagined to be in his mid-thirties.

'No, not really. Are you?' he answered challengingly and the man laughed.

'No, I'm just going home for tea. Would you like a cup? I live nearby.'

Well, he wasn't bad as punters went, thought Rhys, even though he did smell of rather nancyish cucumber moisturiser. So Rhys accepted the invitation.

Peter Moody's flat was in a very ancient conversion in Redcliffe Square. They climbed two flights of a shoddily carpeted staircase and went into his flat which was all grey, but quite swish.

'Got any chocolate?' asked Rhys once they were seated at the kitchen table.

'Good Lord, no,' replied Peter Moody, 'death to the colon. I'm macrobiotic.'

'What's that?' asked the little innocent who had come across nothing more than fast food with the drama students and Hooray junkies he knew.

'Brown rice, vegetables, you know,' said Peter Moody, moving closer to Rhys along the table. This was the moment Rhys always dreaded.

'Do you fancy me, then?' he asked.

'Well, you're a little scrawny but yes, I do, in a way.'

In a way, thought Rhys. Oh dear, this doesn't give me much bargaining power. 'Well, it'll cost you fifteen quid, scrawny or not.'

Peter Moody just threw back his head in laughter.

'It's not that funny. . . .' said Rhys when his new friend – and rapidly turning enemy – showed no signs of stopping.

'Oh, come on,' Peter said finally. 'I'm sorry, it's just that this hasn't happened to me before. Though I suppose I have suddenly fallen into the punter age group. But I'm frightfully sorry. You see, I've only got five quid on me.'

Rhys was beginning to feel distinctly peeved.

'Well, I'm sorry, too, but you've missed the spring sales by one month. This is the new stock. Fifteen quid.'

'*New stock?*' guffawed Peter Moody. 'What are you on, anyway? To look as you do. . . .'

'Nothing,' replied Rhys. This wasn't going so well.

'Let me look at your pupils,' said Peter, taking Rhys's head in his hands. 'Yes, just as I thought. Pinned.'

'Look, I didn't come here for social work, fuckhead!'

'What you need is a good healthy meal. You'd probably snap if I had sex with you. So it looks as though we're going to have to leave it until I've taken some money out of my Post Office savings book.'

And with that Rhys was served his first macrobiotic tea.

From that moment on the two met often and struck up a peculiar friendship. Peter recognised Rhys's predicament all too well and, as he too was an actor, Rhys learned all sorts of things from him. Not necessarily about the techniques of acting but certainly about the actor's life. Peter was always crooning away on the phone to other actors, comparing the latest slights they had suffered, licking their wounds, shrieking with laughter. The proverbial Post Office savings book was often referred to but the foray to the Post Office was never actually made and the friendship remained platonic.

It was an auspicious moment for Rhys, who was rechristened Dorhys by Peter, because it gave him another slant on life and Peter's obsessive attention to health threw his own utter disregard for it into question.

But now, in the end, it was Peter Moody who was dying.

CHAPTER THIRTEEN: in which Rhys skates on
exceedingly thin ice and meets The Crazy Gang

The next day various different strands of Rhys's past life were
gathered together at the airport. And, unbeknownst to most
of them, they were all heading for the same destination.
Rhys, a champion skater on thin ice, was once again unwitt-
ingly throwing himself headlong into an extremely bizarre
situation.

He got out of the car feeling very strange in his new clothes.
Corduroy trousers from Cerruti, navy blazer over a sensible pale
blue shirt and oversized Hush Puppy-type shoes were all very
different from the T-shirt, jeans and baseball cap he usually wore

to go to airports. He was extremely nervous about the flight –
on Air Maroc! – and even more nervous about the three days
with the Duchess and all it would entail. He had half decided
to find a way of backing gracefully out of the gory bits but he
knew that would mean he could then wave goodbye to the other
fifty thousand dollars and he needed it so. Not that he'd ever see
the first fifty thousand again if his mother had anything to do
with it.

He remembered Elida's instructions and headed towards the
Air Maroc desk. There, at the first-class check-in, stood Mrs
Rikki Lancaster and her entourage: a motley crew of waxworks
together with a three-foot-high Roddy McDowell juvenile looka-
like wearing dark glasses in their midst. Needless to say they all
turned in his direction as he approached the desk. Elida and
the Duchess broke rank and came towards him with their arms
outstretched.

'*Baaaaby!*' cried the Duchess as she kissed him on both cheeks
with her little painted budgie's beak.

'Welcome to the trip,' said Elida.

'I want you to meet the rest of the group,' Rikki told him,
'they're all crazy.'

So Rhys immediately dubbed them the Crazy Gang.

'Ha!' roared Rikki, 'did you hear what he just called you?
Without even meeting you – the Crazy Gang. You're delicious,
really delicious.'

'Yes, he is. He is delicious,' echoed the Speaking Clock. Rhys
laughed and made the obligatory protest – 'I wish I was' and all
that.

'Now,' said the Duchess, drawing herself up to her full height
and clasping a large crystal round her neck, 'let me introduce
you to the group. This is Thelma Romanelli.' She pointed at a
pear-shaped woman who only came up to Rhys's navel. He
looked down on the top of her head which appeared to him to
be a floating cowpat.

'You gotta have eyes in ya dick to see this chick,' said Thelma
with a cackle and Rhys laughed. Before he could reply Rikki had
moved him on to another woman. This one was considerably
younger than the rest, no more than thirty or so.

'This is our little cherry from Fort Lauderdale, Penny. She's very shy, aren't you, Pen?'

Poor Penny blushed. 'Just quiet, that's all, Mrs Lancaster. Hello.'

'Hello,' replied our hero.

'Penny looks after my darling son. Where is Ethan? Ethan, come say hello to Rhys. You two are going to get on. I can feel it. Ethan is very direct. Ethan, take off those glasses and come say hi to Roger from *Our Butler*. Come on, now.'

It looked suspiciously as if Ethan was trying very hard to escape and Poor Penny was barring his way with her body. He had his head against her chest and was pummelling her stomach as if it were a punch-bag. Elida took the situation firmly in hand, grabbed him by the ear, and swung him round to face Rhys.

Rhys must have looked horrified because Rikki turned to him, saying, 'I know what you're thinking, she's a bit too old to have such a young son but the fact of the matter is H. L. and me, our love was death-defying and I bore fruit when we thought the harvest was over. . . . Say hello, Ethan, this is Rhys Waveral.'

'Faggot!' said the little boy simply.

The Crazy Gang shrieked together as if on cue, '*Ethan, where did you learn a word like that?*'

The check-in clerk at Air Maroc leaned forward as if he too wondered where Ethan had got it from.

'Venice. Where d'ya think? I feel like shit. Can we go to the shop now?'

'Yes, we can,' said Rikki, looking perplexed, 'but only if you behave yourself and say hello to Rhys in the proper fashion.'

'Hello to Rhys in the proper fashion,' repeated the brat with an evil grin.

The Crazy Gang obviously found this highly amusing and were all over Ethan, cooing and stroking.

'OK,' said Elida, the Tour Guide, 'I'm going to check us all in. Rhys, may I have your passport please.'

But Rhys was not paying attention. There were two people at the other end of the hall waving at him. He rummaged in his pockets and finally found an old pair of broken glasses. He put them on and gasped in horror.

'Oh, *no*! It's just not my day.'

Two women were waving frantically and pushing their over-laden trolleys towards Rhys. One of them was small and round. The other was taller – but just as round. As they drew closer Rhys could see that they were laughing hysterically.

At him!

'The Empress has got new clothes,' shrieked the smaller one, eyeing Rhys's navy blazer and matching navy suede shoes.

'What have you come as?' asked the other one, who was Welsh.

'Up for Jane Bond or something, are you?' and they collapsed again. Rhys glanced round, embarrassed. Sure enough Rikki's Crazy Gang had dropped everything to stand and watch the spectacle.

'Fans.' Rhys tried to explain them away with a helpless shrug. 'What can you do?'

'Have a drink,' replied the two girls, brandishing a bottle of brandy at the Crazy Gang who looked a bit aghast.

'Madge and Olwyn, how nice to see you,' said Rhys with a very thin smile. 'Listen, everybody, this is Madge and Olwyn, otherwise known as "Pepsi" and "Shirlee". They're – eh – hair-dressers, you know, in the cinema. . . .'

The Crazy Gang perked up. There was much moo-ing and gurgling and touching of bobs and bouffants. They eyed the two drunken girls in a new light.

'Hello,' said everyone to each other.

'"Pepsi" and "Shirlee" and I have worked together millions of times, haven't we, girls?'

'We've played together more . . .' insinuated Shirl the Whirl with a snigger . . . 'haven't we, *Dorhys*?' and she offered the bottle around again.

Rhys laughed unconvincingly. 'Where are you going?' he asked, trying to keep a smile on his face.

'Tangiers,' sang out the two girls, 'where are *you* going?'

'Tangiers,' replied our hero with very little of the smile left intact.

'Cheer up, have a drink, we're not the only ones going.

There's a whole film crew there already. All friends of yours. You're just off for a filthy weekend, are you?'

Rhys nearly died. 'No, I'm not, actually. I'm going with my friend, Rikki, here. We're going to a fancy-dress ball, isn't that right, Rikki?'

'Oh yes,' said Rikki. 'My great friend, Ashby de la Zouche, you know Ashby? The famous decorator? He's giving an Exotic Fruit Ball. You must both come.'

'Oh, what a shame, they'd love to but they'll be working, they won't be able to come,' said Rhys firmly.

'Oh, yes, we will,' chirped the girls equally firmly, 'we could even help you all with your hair if you like.'

The Crazy Gang looked thrilled. Rhys less so.

'Will there be prizes?' 'Shirlee' asked innocently, looking at Rhys. He could tell she was already beginning to get suspicious. 'Because if the theme is exotic fruit, I know who's going to win.'

'Yes, I'm sure you do, "Shirlee". You've always been a bit of a clairvoyant, haven't you? Now, don't you think you should check in all these heavy bags? The flight's leaving in forty minutes. It would be too awful if you were to miss it, both of you,' Rhys said as sweetly as he could. Which wasn't very.

'You're up to something, Rhys Waveral. I can smell it,' said Madge.

'Nothing, darling, *absolutely nothing*,' replied Rhys firmly.

'Oh, well. We're bound to find out in Tangiers. We're off now. See you on the plane.'

And off they all tripped to check in.

In a far corner of the terminal was a small sign, barely visible, saying Aldershot Airways. It almost seemed to be apologising for itself.

In front of it, in a navy overcoat, brolly, briefcase and the *Financial Times* all firmly in place, ruddy of cheek and drooping of jaw – and standing to attention in front of a coachload of Japanese girls – was the Brigadier.

With absolutely no idea that his son was but a hundred yards away.

The Brigadier was scowling furiously. 'Bloody Japs!' he muttered at regular intervals. The Burma Campaign still lay heavy on his heart. He had been standing at attention for almost an hour now and there was still thirty minutes to go before check-in time.

Finally the desk opened and the Brigadier cleared his throat.

'General Duff-Cox gave me your name,' he said patronisingly as he handed over his ticket.

'What izzit then?' The young check-in clerk grinned at him cheekily.

'What is what?' asked the Brigadier.

'Me name. If Gerry Long Cock gave ya me name, what izzit?'

The Brigadier looked completely baffled. He tried again. He was determined to exercise patience. These illiterate halfwits, fat on the Welfare State, could take an age to get to the point.

'General . . . Duff . . . Cox . . . gave me . . . your name.'

'Looks like he gave you 'is ticket as well, mister. This ticket's already been used.'

'No, no, no, you don't understand, you blithering. . . . I mean, the general hasn't used this ticket. He sold it to me. Everything is perfectly in order.'

'Nah, guv'nor, it's you who bloody don't understand. This is a used ticket. Geddit? It's not valid. Know what that means, Colonel Blimp?'

'Brigadier Waveral.' As usual, any attempt at a joke passed away above the Brigadier's head.

'Well, Brigadier Waveral, in words of one syllable, this is . . . a . . . used . . . tick . . . et and the flight is full so could you please stand aside and let me check in the passengers. And the next time you want to pull a fast one, don't try it on 'ere. Now, push it, Grandad. Next!'

Poor Brigadier! He never had any luck. As it happened, he always had been slightly suspicious of Duff-Cox and now, sure enough, here he was up shit creek without the proverbial paddle.

There was only one thing left for him to do. At exorbitant cost he was forced to buy a ticket at Air France. There was a flight leaving almost immediately.

He boarded by the skin of his teeth and sank, exhausted, into his seat. He sat clutching his briefcase and brolly with the *Financial Times* on his lap to disguise the fact that he hadn't been able to work out how to do up his seat belt.

'Bloody Japanese design,' he muttered, and then looked round to see another two hundred Japanese students were on the same flight.

CHAPTER FOURTEEN: in which the Brigadier meets
   Peach Delight and dances until dawn

The Brigadier had always liked to be seen as cosmopolitan. He
often thought he was giving the impression of unbelievable *mon-
danité*. At dinner parties up in Scotland he would talk about
'Monte' and 'The Jockey Club', 'the Italian Riviera' and 'the
Raj, don't you know?'

   These conversations invariably ended in a row between him
and Lady Dinah because, much to his eternal fury, she could
never resist an opportunity to pick holes in his stories. In front
of their assembled guests, she would say things like, 'I don't know
why you call him that. You never really knew him. Oh, you

mean Monte Carlo? Well, you've never been there either.'

At this point the Brigadier, who was, if the truth be known, a bit of a poseur, would bare his yellowing teeth like a rat, furious to be shown up in front of his guests. He would hurl abuse down the table while the guests tried to force down another morsel of half-cooked venison. Each new tirade would begin with another of his famous family phrases – 'You are *soooo* . . . *oooo* stupid . . .' while Lady Dinah would sit unruffled at the end of the table. After all, life with the Brigadier had been tough and she rather enjoyed these rare moments of revenge. She would continue to fire embarrassing questions at her inebriated husband until he was reduced to such an apoplectic rage that he could no longer pronounce his words and had to sit there moving his lips silently like a rabid fox until there was nothing left for him to do but stumble off to bed.

Paris, of course, was a place he had talked about often – the races, the restaurants, the rowdy nights – but in fact he had only been there twice: once on D-Day and once shortly after. As he was driven through the outskirts of Paris towards the Hotel Leicester his mood improved now that he was finally free of the two hundred Japanese. Then he remembered how 'The bloody French, let us down at Dunkirk' and he muttered away to himself while the taxi driver shook his head in despair. But as they circled the Etoile he recalled the time at the end of the war when he and his closest friend, Colonel Raleighe-Smith, had both contracted syphilis in a week-long attack on the Left Bank.

By the time he arrived at the hotel he was in a thoroughly good mood. The idea of confronting his wretched son filled his mouth with saliva like the thought of a really good meal.

The taxi fare was extortionate and by the time the manager of the Leicester had explained to him that Rhys had departed the night before, the Brigadier's mood had plummeted as quickly as his son's tended to do.

As he was taken up to the third floor to Rhys's room he was unaware of the many pairs of eyes peering out at him from every nook and cranny as the staff of the hotel, in their eternal quest to unravel the mystery of their most eccentric client's life story, watched silently.

'*Come il est distingué!*' they breathed to one another as the Brigadier marched past, brolly folded under his arm, barking questions at the Director of Reservations. *So distinguished!*

'How much? My good man, are you listening? Do you understand English? How much is my son's room?'

Cherubin greeted them outside the door to Rhys's suite with the letter Rhys had written to his father.

'*Bonjour*, Monsieur Waveral, *je suis Cherubin*,' he said, and curtseyed absent-mindedly. The Manager looked at him severely for a moment and then they all went in.

'Christ almighty, this must be costing an arm and a leg!' shouted the Brigadier as if it were the Manager's fault. Poor Monsieur Dubois looked a bit flustered and laughed nervously.

'If you should need anything, don't hesitate to ask,' he replied and beat a hasty retreat, leaving Cherubin with the Brigadier. By now the Brigadier was fuming round the apartment like an old car. Cherubin hastily slipped a few drops of liquid Valium into a Badoit and handed it to Rhys's father.

'Monsieur Rhys always drink this,' he said in his best English.

The Brigadier downed it in one gulp and looked cynically at the Portuguese queen.

'Water?' He snorted. 'Well, I suppose there's always a first time. Stupid little idiot.'

And with that he sat down and promptly dozed off.

'*Ah zoopose dere's always a first tahm, sdoopid leetle idio,*' mimicked Cherubin as he drew the curtains. He put Rhys's letter on the Brigadier's lap and quietly left the room. He was going to be late for the meeting in the fourth-floor laundry cupboard if he was not careful. It was the place where the staff of the Leicester congregated to gossip. Everybody wanted the scoop on the Brigadier and Marie Claire was making tortilla.

When the Brigadier woke up it was late afternoon. The autumn sun glowed through the white flowery curtains and for a moment he too became enchanted by the calm dignity of his son's new home. He sat staring into space for several minutes and was only aroused from his empty dream by the almost silent click of the outside door and the sound of feet moving through the other room. They stopped for a second, continued, and then there was a small knock on the door.

The Brigadier cleared his throat and, forgetting to fold down his hair which was sticking up towards the ceiling, said, '*Entrez*'. The fact that he made it sound like 'in tray' did not deter an exquisite creature from entering the room.

What he saw as the door opened, silhouetted in the late afternoon sun, brought blood flooding to his '*massif central*', as he called it, and drained it at the same time from his face.

Peach.

In a tiny mini-dress, with her hair falling down over her face and a shy yet inviting look in her eyes.

'I hope I not disturbing, sir,' she said in a husky whisper.

'Not at all,' replied the Brig, clearing his throat.

'I looking for Rhys,' she lied. 'We have dinner appointment.' She began to ease her way into the room.

'Oh, so he's stood you up as well, has he, young lady? He is a stupid bloody fool.' As the Brigadier began to get up he noticed that his trousers were undone and thought better of it, folding his hands over his stomach. 'This *is* Paris,' he chortled to himself.

'I am the boy's father,' he said instead. 'Dim. Dim Waveral at your service.'

'You Rhys father?' said the Peach, who was a very good actress. She giggled and moved closer to him. 'I Peach. I friend of Rhys.'

'Peach. That's a cracking name, I must say. Listen, if that idiot has let you down you must allow me to make up for his disgrace by inviting you to dinner myself. What do you say? We could go to Maxim's, eh?'

'Where?' replied the poor girl. It was a long time since anyone had been to Maxim's.

'Maxim's,' said the Brigadier smoothly, 'old stomping ground of mine.'

'But first you must do something about your hair,' said the pro as, ever so discreetly, she touched the Brigadier's upstanding head.

'What marvellous hands you've got,' said the Brigadier in an effort to flirt, 'good strong hands. I bet you could handle a hunter over a few five-bar gates.' Peach withdrew them. She didn't quite understand what the Brigadier was saying since she was not exactly accustomed to horsey talk of this nature.

So she put on her puzzled look.

'You are a hunter?' she enquired.

'Oh yes, but are you a five-bar gate?' roared the Brigadier, overcome by his own humour.

'He joking about me,' thought the Peach as she went to the fridge and dropped some Ecstasy powder into a glass of Badoit.

'Rhys always drink this before going out,' she said as she offered the delirious Brigadier the glass.

'Ha! Water again, I suppose. Don't try to pull the wool over my eyes, Little Missy, I know Rhys is a heavy party-goer,' laughed too-Dim-for-words.

'I know,' agreed the tranquil Peach. 'Drink.'

'And afterwards I shall show you a marvellous evening, little girl,' drooled the Brigadier.

Peach had everything organised.

She took the Brigadier to a small place, dark and delicious, where she came with many a wayward friend, and she listened with rapt attention as he told her about the Burma campaign, the War and finally the D-Day jamboree with Colonel Raleighe-Smith. He explained in laborious detail how he and the Colonel had both had the same prostitute at the same time . . . 'One in the back door, one in the front, so to speak. One was looking the Colonel smack in the face and one couldn't help giggling a bit. . . .'

Peach loved to watch Ecstasy take control and soon she was aware of the Brigadier's hand creeping slowly but surely across the table towards her breast. They both pretended not to notice when it finally landed like a freckled squid and started squeezing lightly.

The Brigadier went on talking and she went on listening. Actually she was rather enjoying herself.

'What do you want . . . *exactly?*' she asked.

It was the same question she always asked and she was invariably rewarded with a good reaction. It was the pause she left between 'want' and 'exactly' that filled the phrase with innuendo and certainly the Brigadier, who was transpiring slightly and exhaling breath in loud bursts through his mouth (as one tends to do on Ecstasy), was in seventh heaven.

'Why don't we go to a nightclub?' he suggested. 'I say, this wine is most awfully good. I feel ready for anything.' *Chortle, chortle, chortle.*

'How about a five-bar gate?' asked Peach.

'Is that a good place? I don't know any more. In my day it used to be Castel but whatever you feel like, little girl. I feel as if I'm in a very strange dream. Now, let me get the bill.'

Which was very expensive. Under normal circumstances the Brigadier's face woud have contorted into all manner of grimaces at the sight of it but tonight he was all smiles.

'Very good, very good,' he told the waiter as he parted with the largest sum he had ever paid for a dinner *à deux*. If he was ever forced to take Lady Dinah out they ate at the Aberdeen Steak House.

'Now come along, young lady,' and he stood up. And sat down again. And stood up.

'Bit wobbly on the old pins,' he remarked, exhaling more deep breaths. 'I must say, I really do feel top whack.'

And they left the restaurant, his hand still firmly clasped to Peach's left breast.

In the taxi Peach had a bit of a struggle to extricate herself from the Brigadier's vice-like grip, but she managed to do so without causing offence while the Brigadier looked dreamily out of the window at the Place de la Concorde. 'Lovely . . . firm,' he murmured, presumably referring to Peach's breast.

'My husband like me to lift weights,' she told him.

'Where are we going?' asked the Brigadier.

'To a nightclub, as you suggest, to see friend of Rhys and mine.'

'Oh, really? Will he be there?'

'No, he away at this time. Here, take this pill. It good for your head,' and she passed him an Ecstasy, taking one herself at the same time.

He didn't offer any objection. 'Yes, I am getting a bit of a headache, Little Missy. How clever of you to know without asking.' He continued looking dreamily out of the window as the truth drug raced around his mind and his hand started the long slow crawl along the seat. . . .

'Marvellous chap, isn't he?' he said finally after several minutes' silence.

'Who?' asked Peach who was miles away, busy fixing her lipstick.

'My boy, Rhys. He's a marvellous chap in some ways. He's a super actor, you know. It's just he never really had much of a chance. *Our Butler* didn't show him up to half his real ability. We've got them all, you know. On that wretched Vidiamo contraption. Never even seen them because Mr Mac has absolutely no idea about electrics. He can mend a plug, yes, or maybe Dinah's hairdryer, but a Videomax, no. Aboslutely not. He's rather a splendid chap actually. You'd like him. No nonsense there, Missy.'

Peach wasn't really listening. She had long since lost the thread of the Brigadier's ramblings and anyway, it was always better to have good make-up than good chat in her opinion.

'Here we are, Dim. Come on.'

'Ready, Little Missy,' said Dim, reaching for her breast again as if it were her hand. They were drawn up outside a little door with crowds of men and women outside. Punks. Queens. Fashion victims. The complete melting pot. A little flashing neon sign told the Brig that they were at *The Golden*.

'Oh, I say, this looks absolutely marvellous,' beamed the Brigadier as he hopped out. In truth he had not been so happy since he was at school, a memory so far back in the recesses of his mind that only the jerk of a chemical rush could unloosen it and allow him to feel free again.

'Good evening,' he said to everyone in sight, proferring his free hand, 'I'm Dim Waveral. I'm Rhys's father.'

It said something for Rhys – though he would have been hard pressed to say what exactly – that most of the crowd accepted the introduction without question and exchanged names happily with the Brigadier as if it were perfectly normal for an old Blimp to enter their midst and expect them to accept him as one of their own. Rhys was a popular man in Paris with a reputation for startling eccentricity and everyone laughed to see his father with his hand still firmly clasped to Peach's breast.

'*C'est le papa de Rosbeef*! Rosbeef's father. Can you imagine? Isn't it wonderful?' they said to one another.

Once inside the club, nursing a huge whisky, the Brigadier held forth as if he were at a hunt ball. The fact that he was actually at an after-hours gay club seemed to have bypassed him completely. He had the divine Peach by his side, which was all that mattered, and his hand had left her breast and was now exploring her bottom. He couldn't believe his luck until she said, 'Ah, here is my husband. Here is Pascal. Pascal, *viens ici!*'

The Brigadier removed his hand from Peach's rear end like lightning but she took it and placed it this time quite firmly on her crotch. 'Don't worry,' she said, 'he not jealous.'

Little did the poor old Brig realise that the small, dark, muscular man coming towards him was not only Peach's beloved, but also his own son's.

Peach was suddenly all animation. 'Hi, honey!' she cried, waving her champagne tequila around like a sparkler. '*Mmmm*, you look very good. *Very* professional. You meet Rhys's father, honey? Dim, this is my colleague, Pascal. Good friend of your son.'

'You said he was your husband,' said the Brigadier nervously. 'Hello. What have you got in that little bottle? Smelling salts?'

'No, poppers. Do you want some?'

'Smelling salts are just the ticket, I'd say. It *is* awfully close in here.'

He took the bottle and opened it. 'Smells of swimming pools,' he said and took a good snort. 'Crippen! Young lady, would you like to dance?'

'Yes, Dim,' said Peach who was very cross with Pascal. He was too much. He only want to enjoy. They eased their way on to the dance floor which was packed with writhing bodies and the Brigadier took the Peach in his arms and waltzed her around as if they were at the Four Hundred, totally oblivious to the loud acid music that was blasting in his ears.

118

She put her cheek on his shoulder and he put his hand almost up her bum, and they danced until half past five in the morning.

CHAPTER FIFTEEN: in which Rhys contemplates a sex
   change, the Waveral women plan a surprise visit and the
   Brigadier steps through the looking glass

While the Brigadier was trundling through the outskirts of Paris
in his overpriced taxi, his young son was almost being sick all
over the Duchess's foot just over Gibraltar.

   His usual two Valium and endless swigs from 'Pepsi's' and 'Shirlee's' brandy bottle had rendered him speechless. He was slumped
over his seat. Not a very good start, yet the Crazy Gang seemed
to take it all in their stride. After all, stars were meant to be
hellraisers and they cackled and crooned over Rhys's inert body
like gremlins, thoroughly enjoying themselves. Rikki was massaging his neck. Her fingers felt like acupuncturist's needles

digging into his skin. Elida was perched precariously on the arm of his seat, swinging an enormous crystal from side to side as if she were dousing for water. Thelma Romanelli, also pissed as a newt, was singing the *Star-Spangled Banner* at full tilt.

Ethan and his Nanny-Penny had been banished to Economy to play gin with 'Pepsi' and 'Shirlee'.

When they arrived in Casablanca Rhys wondered through his haze whether it might not be a good thing to make a run for it there and then, book himself into one of those lovely clinics he had heard about, have a quick sex change and then try again.

But just as he was warming to the idea all chance of escape flew briskly out the window when he ran into yet another old acquaintance in the transfer lounge.

Dawnford Vernon.

There was a legend in the theatrical world once upon a time that Dawnford Vernon was the patron saint of all actors. Rather like St Thérèse of Lisieux, who appeared to every soldier about to die in the Somme, Dawnford Vernon would appear to any actor about to do absolutely anything. If you were working on location in Fiji, Dawnford would miraculously appear from behind a palm tree. Always dressed the same in black polo neck, black hat and black trousers, whether in Rangoon or Mongolia (he was always on location when not collecting his laundry in Paris), he would lurch up and discuss the most recent first night he had miraculously managed to attend. He himself normally played spies.

'Dawnford, how nice to see you,' said Rhys with all the energy he could muster, which wasn't much.

'Rhys, dear boy, are we working on the same production?'

'I doubt it,' answered Rhys, glancing at the Duchess. 'What are you working on and where?'

'Oh, I'm doing a little something in this *Love in the Desert* thing. You know, the NSU mini-series. Simply everyone's in it. Can't understand it if you're not. Too expensive, eh?'

'No, unfortunately Dumpling told me it had been cancelled,' said Rhys sadly. He began to plummet into depression. What was he going to do about Dumpling? Would he ever work again?

Rikki and the Crazy Gang had appeared at his side during

this brief reverie and there was nothing else for it but to make introductions. Yet again.

The Crazy Gang were thrilled to hear about the mini-series and that it was being shot in Tangiers to boot. They promptly invited Dawnford to Ashby de la Zouche's party that weekend. Needless to say Dawnford, who would go anywhere there was free toilet roll and a few actors, accepted with alacrity and, before Rhys could stop him, said he would extend the invitation to the entire cast which would include such showbiz bastions as Sir Maurice Goodbuns, the Duke of Darling-Darling, Little Beige Riding Hood and Harry Bellows-Forth. At each name poor Rhys's face dropped another inch. Everybody he had ever met appeared to be in Tangiers that weekend.

How right he was.

They reboarded the plane, flew the last leg to Tangiers and, once there, piled into three taxis: one for them and two for the Crazy Gang's hat boxes.

Adrienne edged her 1952 Austin Seven gingerly round the corner away from the park gates and drove extremely slowly up the hill towards the village. Her face bore an expression of sheer terror. She hated driving. There was nothing else for it, however. She had run out of money and this meant a visit to Lady Dinah, miles away over the mountains. Lady Dinah couldn't help becoming irritated by her daughter-in-law's sheer uselessness.

It was the day of the opening to the public of the Winter Garden at Waveram and Lady Dinah was already on the front steps with Mrs Mac and the entire Mac family when Adrienne arrived. Adrienne hobbled out of the car, her neck almost at right angles to her body. The three-hour drive had really unnerved her and she shook like a leaf as she kissed her mother-in-law and the Mac family.

'We've got three hundred spastics coming to the garden opening today,' boomed Lady Dinah as they entered the house, 'isn't that rather a good show?'

'Three hundred and one,' corrected Adrienne, catching sight of herself in the long mirror over the hall fireplace.

As Adrienne well knew, conversations with her Ladyship were always liable to be cut short by her sudden departure to do something with no explanation whatsoever. Today was to be no exception. They walked into the library and Lady Dinah settled herself in the armchair she had had moved to the window so she could monitor the proceedings in the Winter Garden. From her bag, *click, click*, she took a small pair of binoculars and began to look out. She loved to watch the people in her garden. Adrienne, always nervous at the best of times, now became doubly agitated at being ignored.

'Well, how *are* you, my girly?' asked Lady Dinah in a somewhat uninterested tone.

'Fine, thanks,' said Adrienne in the saddest of her little-girl voices. Lady Dinah didn't notice. Or didn't want to.

'I saw your terrible husband at Claridges. He was off to Tangiers on some ghastly mission or other and guess what?' Here she put down her binos and started rummaging around in her bag. 'Yes, guess what, awfully amusing. Here it is. Fifty thousand dollars. He gave it to me to keep safe.' Lady Dinah was rewriting history at fifty words a second. 'I expect he thinks I've put it in the bank for him, but no. . . .' She flapped the notes at Adrienne. 'How extraordinary,' said Adrienne who had suddenly come up in a hot flush, 'because I was actually coming to see you on a begging errand.'

'You amaze me,' murmured Lady Dinah, returning to the binoculars.

'Yes,' breathed Adrienne, warming to her story, 'you see I desperately need some money, to pay the bills and to get some materials for my new stained glass window. And Rhys hasn't sent any for ages,' she finished lamely.

Lady Dinah's grip on the fifty thousand suddenly tightened.

'There's the heating bills for our part of the house,' Adrienne continued helplessly, her voice almost disappearing with emotion, 'the telephone bill, Rhys's last dry cleaning bill even. I just can't pay them.'

'Darling, you know you're screaming,' clipped Lady Dinah.

'Can't you just overdraw a little at the bank, just until Rhys gets something? Oh! *Do* look, here are my spastics,' and with that she raced from the room before Ada could get another word in.

Thirty seconds later she could be seen in a completely different outfit – husky and green wellies – cantering across the lawn towards a large group at the other end. Adrienne thought she might as well have a cigarette and sat watching her mother-in-law through the window. Suddenly she missed her husband terribly. Life was so complicated on your own – unless you were Lady Dinah, in which case you battled through regardless. Hers had not been an easy lot, thought Adrienne. First the Brigadier. Then Rhys. Always alone, even when she wasn't. Adrienne smiled as she watched her mother-in-law gesticulating wildly, pointing out this tree here and that bush there.

Suddenly she had an idea. She jumped up, ran out of the library, through the hall and into the garden to join the party. Her Ladyship spotted her coming and raised her arms, shouting to the poor spastics.

'Ah! No garden is complete without one's daughter-in-law. Can I introduce you all to my son's wife, Adrienne Waveral.'

'Hellllooooo,' whined Adrienne to the group, panting slightly. She looked twice as strange as they did in her black tights, big brown jersey, tartan scarf and beret.

'I've had an idea,' she said as the group moved towards the next bush.

'Now this is my flowering oleander,' Lady Dinah told them. '*Flow-er-ing ol-ean-der,*' she repeated, as if it would make any more sense. 'It is in fact the only one in this part of Scotland. *Ohn-lee one.*' She was in an extremely good mood.

'Why don't we pay Rhys a surprise visit while he's in Tangiers,' said Adrienne.

'We've had an enormous problem with the fir garden this year. *EEE-nor-mous.* A little parasite . . . *par-a-site* . . . has been eating all our twigs and prickles and we're rather at a loss as to what to do. They're all being treated but we're frightfully nervous. My grandmother planted the fir wood and there are over one hundred species of tree here. One *hun-dred,*' she mouthed and made ritualistic signs with her hands which went away above everyone's heads.

'We could use what's left over from that money. Come on, it would be a shriek!'

'I must say, that is rather a funny idea,' said Lady Dinah acknowledging Adrienne for the first time. 'You know Dim's trying to track him down and has gone off in entirely the wrong direction.' She turned back to the children. 'Now, this way, spastics, we're going to the walled garden,' and she marched them all off.

'I didn't tell Dim Rhyssie wasn't going to be in Paris simply because he didn't ask me,' she went on, 'so he'll arrive to find Rhys has gone to Tangiers and then he'll have to follow him there. I don't expect Aldershot Airlines do a Paris–Casablanca trip, do you?' At that both women roared with laughter. 'So we two could give the whole lot of them a ghastly surprise. Is that what you're suggesting, girly?'

Adrienne flushed. She hadn't actually thought any further than the idea itself. The reality of it was a little daunting.

'Yes, I suppose I am,' she replied uncertainly. 'And there's the money I wanted too, remember?' she added, but Lady Dinah had gone back to her group.

'Now *this*,' she said dramatically, 'is the walled garden.'

Fabrice, on late-night duty on the door at the Leicester, was very surprised when three taxis full of Rhys's friends drew up at the front of the hotel at six o'clock in the morning. As they all piled out he tried to explain to them that Rhys had left the day before.

Peach explained. 'On est avec le père de Rosbeef, Brigadier Dim. I introduce you. Dim, cheri, viens ici un instant.'

'What's that, young thing?' roared the Briagdier who was by now on his third Ecstasy.

'Say hello to Fabrice, he friend of Rhys.'

'Hello to Fabrice,' greeted the Brig, 'he friend of Rhys.'

Poor Fabrice was rather embarrassed. The Brigadier was in orbit and yet again his flies were undone. They finally got him

126

up to Rhys's room where he passed out, leaving Peach and the Colleagues – Pascal, Victor, Jean-Claude *et al* – to wind down until the early hours of the morning.

Downstairs Fabrice recovered with a secret cup of coffee with Marie Claire and Cherubin.

'What a family!'

'Do you suppose it's a family tradition to come home at six in the morning with fifteen people?'

'*Je ne sais rien,*' said Cherubin, 'but the father, he is not *gentil* like the son.'

Peach got rid of the Colleagues before the Brigadier woke up. She knew that the shock might be too much. Before they left, however, she did grab the opportunity to take a Polaroid of them sprawled all over Rhys's bed surrounding the Brig as he slept with his mouth wide open, snoring like a cow.

Rhys va adorer ça, she said to herself as she climbed on top of the huge wardrobe in her high heels to get the best shot. She rarely slept, the Peach, so once she was alone with the Brigadier she sat filing her nails, watching over him. She could not find much in his face that resembled his son. Dim had spent too much of his time in a bad temper, she decided, and it showed on his face. Rhys's face, she thought, as she Hoovered up a pick-me-up line of coke, was much more gentle, more vulnerable. She thought of him now and laughed out loud.

And woke up the Brigadier.

'Morning, Little Missy. What's on the agenda today then?'

These clients are too much, thought the Peach. One evening and they think they own you.

'That was a marvellous night. Really top level. Can't remember a thing about it, though. Did we go to the house of one of Rhys's friends?'

'We go to house of all Rhys friends,' laughed Peach.

'I tell you what I'm going to do, young lady, I'm going to take you out for a delicious lunch and then we're going to go shopping together. How about that?' said Dim, jumping out of bed.

'I have to see my friend half past four. You come?'

'Splendid! I'll shave.'

Lunch was at the Tour d'Argent and shopping was at Christian

Lacroix, where the Peach was a much-loved client. The Brigadier settled himself in a chair and watched as the divine Peach changed from one glorious mini frock into another. Ecstasy raged in his body and with the arrival of each new frock he announced, 'I feel marvellous,' and bought it.

He waited obediently in the taxi while Peach went in to collect some things from her apartment. She came out with two enormous carrier bags.

'La Hutte,' she said to the driver. 'We go to see my friend Jean Luc. He friend to Rhys too. He nice.'

The taxi trundled across the cobbled streets. It was a dreary day but the Brigadier was in a sort of dream. Something had unlocked inside him and for the first time in ages he felt his habitual anger lift from him like a fog that disperses as the sun comes up.

Suddenly he loved life very much. He slapped Peach on the thigh as though she were a racehorse.

'Where is Loot or whatever it's called? Look at your marvellous strong hands. You'd have no trouble handling a hunter over a five-bar gate. . . .'

'On the outside of Paris. Very dangerous area. Not good for Jean Luc but he have no money.' Peach hid her hands quickly before he could grab one. She hated them.

The smart Haussmann streets gave way to weaving autoroutes and finally to sky-rise blocks. This was something the Brigadier had never seen, not even with the intrepid Colonel Raleighe-Smith. Finally they stopped outside a desolate block. There were children of all shapes, sizes and colours playing ferociously in the wind. Urban poetry. Some of them seemed to recognise Peach.

'Oo la la, c'est la Barbie Doll,' and they started nudging her and asking for money. They were only small but quite intimidating to the Brigadier. Peach was unimpressed and walked right through them saying, 'Va t'en foutre,' but the children persisted. All of a sudden Peach put down her carrier bags and removed her big round handbag from one of them. Instead of getting out her purse, which was what the delinquents thought she was going to do, she took her bag firmly by the straps with both hands and without warning began to bang the children really hard on the heads, shouting obscenities at them.

When she'd finished she shouted, 'Come on, Dim, let's go before their brothers come.'

They walked up three flights of stairs where the walls were sprayed with graffiti. The Brigadier had never been in a place like this before and clasped Peach's hand for reassurance. On the third floor they went down a passage past a long line of front doors, some proud and polished, others unkempt and dismal. At the very last one Peach took out a key and let them into the apartment.

It was a small room that Dimbleby Waveral found himself in, and a far cry from the understated opulence of Waveram. In fact Dim had never been through a front door that led just to one room. It was rather a sad room, too. In one corner there was a bed, in another a makeshift kitchen, but very little else. A week's washing-up lay in the sink.

And on the bed sitting in a sort of lotus position was a very thin middle-aged man with no hair and strangely bright eyes, wearing a pair of striped pyjamas.

'Salut toi!' greeted Peach as she swished over and kissed her friend on the lips.

'Salut, ma poulette, comment vas tu?' he replied.

'Je te présente Dim, le père de Rosbeef. Dim – Jean Luc. Jean Luc – Dim.'

'Very nice to meet you,' blasted the Brigadier who, whenever he became nervous, spoke at double his usual volume.

'You are the father of Rhys? Excuse me for the mess. Peach does not tell me of this visit.'

'Couldn't matter less, old chap. Like a bit of a scrum myself. My wife is forever tidying. You aren't married, judging by all this mess?'

'No, I am not.'

'Peach was unloading the contents of the two carrier bags and handing the Brigadier fruit, magazines, loo roll and chocolate which he put on the table by the bed.

'Tiens,' she said, 'je t'ai acheté Gai Pied,' and she passed the magazine to Dim.

'Your son is my friend,' the man continued. 'We were on holidays with Peach this year. He very nice with me. And Peach, too.' The two friends laughed together.

'Goodness gracious!' boomed the Bridgadier, whose attention had been momentarily distracted by *Gai Pied*, 'there's a chap in here with his balls all trussed up with string. Just like a roast. Here, you'd better take it before I have a heart attack. I suppose you're a *Gai Pied*, aren't you?' The Brigadier found the whole thing terribly amusing and was beginning to chortle away again like a pot with its lid boiling over on the stove.

'Please, Dim, where are your manners?' laughed Peach.

'I don't know, young thing, everything seems to be most unruly in my head but one might as well be direct, no?' *Chortle, chortle, chortle.*

'I was a *Gai Pied*, like you say. Now I am not so gay.' The man was laughing too but in a strange way.

'Probably for the best, you know,' confided the Brigadier, 'they're never very happy. I knew one once who got in the most frightful mess, dressing up in his wife's evening dresses and such like. In the end he hanged himself with one of her bra straps.' The Brigadier found this almost unbearably funny. 'She never had a clue, funnily enough, during their twelve years of marriage. She stayed in the country during the week and he went up to London. He was in my firm. It was only when she found his pipe and tobacco in one of her evening bags that the penny finally dropped. And then of course all hell broke loose. Apparently he'd been famous in the Bayswater Road for years when he'd hitch-hike or something. All way above my head. . . .' Mirth got the better of him and he began to shake with howls of laughter. So did the other two. They had no idea what he was on about but he was such an eccentric sight, sitting there in the untidy bed-sit in his navy overcoat.

'I'm having a marvellous time,' said the Brigadier, after the laughter had died down a bit. 'Thank you for inviting me in to your house. It really is very decent of you. If you're ever in Scotland you must look us up, just fly to Edinburgh and we'll send Mr Mac to collect you, but I'd rather you didn't mention to Dinah that you're a reformed pansy. She gets awfully nervy about it all for some reason.'

'Don't worry,' said Jean Luc, still with the strangest smile as if he were thinking of a joke even better than the Brigadier's drag story. 'Anyway, I'm not a reformed pansy like you say. I'm a dying pansy.'

He looked the Brigadier straight in the eye but the Brigadier thought this even funnier than his own joke and roared with laughter.

'Oh, this is frightfully good, frightfully good. Dying pansy, eh? What have you got, *greenfly?*'

'No. AIDS,' replied the man in the lotus position.

There was silence. The sound of the street rebels below wafted up through the half-open window. Jean Luc and Peach watched the Brigadier who sat suddenly turned to stone inside his overcoat.

Poor old Brigadier. He could hear nothing but his heartbeat and the Ecstasy splashing around in his head, washing his vision with exotic colour. He was in shock yet he knew, even in his state of suspended animation, that he had crossed a frontier and had landed, via some inexplicable route, in his worst fantasy: his son's world. That dark and dangerous area where in his dreams everyone was a cross-dresser at the very least. In fact here he was now, Brigadier Dim Waveral of the Duke of Altrincham's Fusiliers, sitting in one of the squats he had oh-so accurately imagined opposite – horror of horrors (one of his favourite expressions) – an AIDS victim.

Yet thanks to the drug coursing like a racehorse through his veins, the realisation of this nightmare was somehow altogether different in reality to how he had imagined it.

And suddenly he felt very sorry. Sorry for his lack of delicacy. Sorry for the poor man opposite him. Sorry, in fact, for his son's world into which he'd fallen like Alice in Wonderland.

And like his son, who had struggled unsuccessfully to come up with something different to say to the girl looking after Peter Moody, the Brigadier found himself searching for the right words – and failing.

'I'm most terribly sorry,' he said after a long pause. 'I don't really know awfully much about this sort of thing or I wouldn't have gone on so. Have you been . . . er . . . unwell . . . long, if I may ask?'

'One year only.'

'And how old are you? If that's not too frightfully rude?'

'Thirty,' replied Jean Luc, the man who Dim had thought was at least fifty. 'The same age as *Rosbeef, en fait.*'

'*Roast beef*? Oh, I see, you mean Rhys?'

There is a moment in the whirligig that is known as the Ecstasy trip when the taker, still high but exhausted after a long night of dancing and brain cell destruction, can become emotional like a pre-menstrual woman. The slightest thing can touch him more deeply than it usually would and a genuine sadness can be brought out like a boil to erupt and render the victim speechless with grief. That moment had arrived for the Brigadier.

'I know you're both going to think this is frightfully wet but I'm afraid I'm going to cry.'

And there he sat, the old soldier in the navy overcoat, weeping as the Thai girl and her dying friend looked on. The children screamed away in the street below and jets screamed across the sky up above. Urban poetry.

As the Brigadier gave no indication that he was going to stop Peach made tea while Jean Luc put on a record. The two friends sat chatting quietly, occasionally reaching out to stroke the Brigadier on the back or pat him on his bald patch which was now crimson. Eventually, as the sun sank behind the twin tower blocks across the road, the Brigadier produced an enormous red and white spotted handkerchief and blew his nose long and hard, like the funnel of an old departing steamer, which in a way he was.

'I'm really most awfully sorry to make such an extraordinary spectacle of myself. I really don't know what's come over me today. I do feel quite peculiar. Your news is sad to me, old man. What terrific bad luck! And you, young lady, how terribly sweet of you to bring him so many wonderful presents. You are all so . . . so . . . different to how I imagined, I don't know how to explain it.'

'You live in palace in Scotland,' replied Peach gently. 'You see nothing. You know nothing of our problems. Come on, let's go. I have client waiting.' She glanced at her watch. '*Chéri*,' she turned to Jean Luc, '*à la prochaine . . . Mercredi, je crois?*' See you Wednesday, darling.

Jean Luc got up and put his arms round his friend, then walked her to the door. The Brigadier lingered a moment, then reached into his overcoat, where there were many secret compartments, and took out his wallet, a thick, black alligator-skin affair with platinum corners. He removed a large sheaf of bills and thrust them underneath the pillow on the bed. Then he joined the divine Peach and shook hands with his new-found friend, promising to return when next in Paris, inviting him again to Waveram. As he and Peach left the building, the Brigadier barged ahead through the wall of youths on the street, waving his umbrella at them.

'Out of the way, you ridiculous hoodlums, no time for riff-raff like you.'

Peach dropped him off at the Leicester and went on to her rendezvous. 'I'll call you tomorrow,' she told him firmly.

But alone in the hotel, the sadness swept over him once again and he picked up the telephone and called Scotland.

In the library at Waveram, a celebration was well under way. Lady Dinah, her daughter-in-law and the entire Mac family were reeling round the room, plastered on cider, the in house drink that year. The garden opening had been a huge success. Three hundred and twenty pounds had been taken which would go towards the rainforests, Lady Dinah's pet charity. And this year it would actually get there. Normally, the Brigadier placed himself strategically at the garden gates to pocket the winnings.

Last year he had disappeared into Edinburgh and placed all the money on a horse which promptly fell at the first fence.

They were also celebrating Lady Dinah's and Adrienne's imminent departure to Tangiers. Mr Mac was going to drive them to the airport in half an hour to take the London plane. From London they would fly to Casablanca the following morning, and then on to Tangiers. Adrienne was already quite green at the thought of travelling. She cursed herself for having suggested the trip in the first place. It would mean venturing into the Outside World, something she hadn't done for several years. She had tried really hard to fall down the stairs leading from the turret with a tray of glasses in her hands. Unfortunately her fall had been broken by Mrs Mac, a veritable ox of a woman, who was coming upstairs at the time. There was nothing else for it. In the absence of any last-minute accident which would require her to be laid up for a while, Adrienne would just have to go through with it. At least she would see Rhys again.

The telephone rang, trying to make itself heard above the din.

'Hellooo,' tinkled Lady Dinah in a passable imitation of Adrienne. 'Darling! Where on earth are you?' She put her hand over the receiver. 'It's Dim. What? What on earth is the matter? You sound as if you've got the most stinking cold. You're *what*? *Crying*? Oh, for God's sake, that's not very like you, Dim. Oh, darling, *do* pull yourself together. Have a rest or something. I *know* he's not there. He's in Tangiers. No, darling, do listen. Tangiers. You know, where you clubbed me on the golf course that time. Well, go there again if you're so desperate to find him.' She winked at Adrienne. Adrienne turned even greener. God, there was going to be a family reunion and she'd left all her Valium and anti-depressants at home. And her passport.

'AND MY PASSPORT!' she screamed victoriously. Everyone jumped. Lady Dinah put her hand over the telephone and said sharply, 'Girly, please keep your voice down to a shriek, will you? I'm on a trunk call to a sobbing baboon here. What's the problem?'

Adrienne's face bore a decidedly crazed expression.

'Dinah,' she said breathlessly, holding on to her mother-in-law's cashmere cardi and kneading it between her fingers,

'Dinah, can I just say . . . I can't go. I can't go! *I can't go!*' Her eyes were popping. '*I don't have my passport.*'

'Oh, *what* a bore. Well, we'll just have to drive over to Ankerham to collect it and take the last shuttle. Now, let me deal with one lunatic at a time, girly. Dim? *Dim?* Are you still there? What's that? You feel released? Well, kindly arrest yourself. No, of course I can't come with you to Tangiers, I'm up to my eyeballs with weeding. You are aware, I suppose, that the garden is open this weekend and every Saturday for a month. We had three hundred spastics, which was rather a good show, wasn't it? *Three hundred spastics!* Dim, you're raving. I can't go on with this conversation. I've got Adrienne. My dear, I tell you, she looks like she's just sat on a thistle. What? Well, go on your own. He's in the Saunders Hotel. I didn't tell you because you didn't ask, you silly idiot. I mean, if you *listened* to me a bit more I might bother telling you things. Well, we'll see you when you get there. I mean, when you get back. Back here.'

Lady Dinah hung up and turned triumphantly to her daughter-in-law who was sitting in a heap, crushed and exhausted.

'Come on, girly, pull yourself together. We're off! I must say, this amuses me, this amuses me most frightfully!'

ACT III

CHAPTER SIXTEEN: in which Rhys discovers Morocco and
Sir Maurice Goodbuns goes methoding

The Saunders Hotel had been a well-known watering hole for
all sorts of strange deviants throughout the century. Anyone who
found themselves in disgrace back in Blighty, with not enough
money to go to America and live comfortably, inevitably landed
up at the Saunders. Banished Hooray homosexual bombshells
rubbed shoulders with drug-dabbling American heiresses. They
arrived in the Thirties and found that they were actually near
enough for some quite good pieces of furniture to be sent on
to them and bang, hey presto, there they were, set up for
next to nothing in their own teensy palaces. Much better off,

in fact, than they had been in Mummy's flat back in Mayfair.

'Good morning, Mr de la Zouche,' said the lift operator.

Ashby de la Zouche prided himself on his resemblance to Yves Saint Laurent. It was probably the root of all his problems. It was true that the likeness was uncanny: light blond hair, neatly done, with the smallest wave. Black glasses, black tie and grey suit. At a distance. On closer inspection he was much older, not only than Saint Laurent but than everyone. The blond hair was a wig, as fake as the blond eyelashes. His lips were like two thin snakes, constantly rippling, then suddenly pulling together to form a sun-dried sphincter. A king-sized Peter Stuyvesant dangled permanently from his mouth, teetering over with ash, and he talked Southern. The fact that he came from Pittsburgh counted for nothing. He had grown rich in the decoration trade, he came from the South; that was his story and he stuck to it.

He was slightly breathless as he paced down the enormously long hotel corridor, a cigarette blazing behind him more like Liberty than Saint Laurent. The truth was he hated Rikki Lancaster. She too had spent more than a brief spell in Pittsburgh. But when he heard that she was coming with Roger from *Our Butler*, well, that changed everything. Ashby de la Zouche had cassettes of every episode of *Our Butler* and had watched them naked back in New York, while masturbating and dreaming of playing Roger's under-butler.

Now he knocked excitedly on Rikki's door, at the same time hurriedly wiping the shine from his cheeks with an enormous white silk handkerchief.

'It's open,' called a voice from inside.

So in he walked.

The Crazy Gang were all in their slumberwear. Thelma was wearing a giant baby blue towelling dressing gown with a towel wound round her head. In fact everyone sported a turban. Rikki and Elida were in twin pink little girly nighties and their white towelling turbans made them look like a pair of cockatoos. Penny was wearing a fluffy baby pink dressing gown firmly fastened to the neck. Ethan sat in his dark glasses with his Walkman plugged into his ears.

But Rhys – the poor sacrificial lamb – was considerably less camouflaged than the rest on account of the fact that he was undergoing his first crystal massage. He was lying in his shorts on a towel in the middle of the floor with Elida Schumann crouching over him, swinging the mysterious crystals.

Ashby de la Zouche was quite taken aback by the scene which confronted him. 'Ah hope ahm not disturbin'?' He coughed.

'*Ashby!*' cried Rikki and Elida simultaneously, dropping crystals, magazines and towels on poor Rhys in their rush to get to de la Zouche. 'What a pleasure to see you. We didn't imagine we'd get a glimpse of His Holiness until the ball tomorrow night. Do tell, how are the preparations coming along?'

'Everything is going jus' fahn, Rikki, jus' fahn. An who is this?'

Ashby brushed past them towards Rhys's semi-naked body, quickly changing his spectacles as he did so.

'Oh, excuse me, Ashby, this is our dear friend, Rhys. Rhys, say hello to Ashby.'

Poor Dorhys! Poor *Dorita*! First the terror of the crystal therapy session with exclusive views up ladies nighties. And now Ashby!

'How do you do? I'm Rhys Waveral.' He stood up and shook hands. Ashby's lips trembled as he glanced up and down our hero's body.

Which was not bad. Not bad at all.

'Well,' was all he could say on a huge exhalation of breath, 'have ah got a costoom for you. You are an angel, Rhys Waveral. Ah, Aaashby Montgomery de la Zouche, ahm y'all's number one faaan. An with mah costoom y'all are goin' to win the prize with your pants down.' With this he nudged poor Dorita in the ribs, laughing. 'Not literally, of course. As for the rest of you scamps . . . why, if it isn't Thelma Romanelli!'

'Sure is, cocksucker,' quacked Thelma.

'As ah was sayin' . . . as for the rest of you scamps, ah want you down in the souk straightaway to buy your costooms. The theme is Exotic Fruit and ahm sure y'all will find ample inspiration.'

'It is always a pleasure to see you, Ashby,' repeated Rikki rather unnecessarily.

'As for you, Roger,' he went on, lighting yet another enormous

Peter Stuyvesant with an equally enormous gold lighter, 'as for you, ah want you to come to my house for a fittin' at seven o'clock. Is that understood?'

Who does she think she is, thought Rhys as he said out loud, 'Yes, that would be lovely,' or something equally obsequious.

And with that de la Zouche disappeared in a puff of blue-grey smoke, perfumed by Stuyvesant. The Crazy Gang maintained a respectful silence for a while until Thelma broke it with, 'Don't bend over to pick up the soap in the shower, buster, or you're gonna have one nasty shock,' and she cackled.

Rhys liked Thelma. 'Darling, he'd need a wedge to get anything in there. I'm afraid it's been out of order for years.' He knew she'd like that. Now both of them were cackling.

'What are you two little gremlins laughing about?' purred Rikki as she came and sat on Rhys's knee.

'Just passing the time of day,' said Thelma.

'Isn't it strange,' Rikki continued, leaning intimately against Rhys's chest, how close we all feel to Rhys despite only having known him a few days? I love you, Rhys.'

'I love you too, Rikki,' Remember, only once, he heard Peach's voice say.

'Who was that faggot that just left?' Ethan had just emerged from his Walkman.

'His name is Ashby de la Zouche and he is not a faggot. Who taught you that word, anyway?'

'Thelma,' replied the ghastly Ethan. 'Can we go to the souk now, please?'

'I never taught you that word, you odious little fart. I called you it. Now, don't you go spreading vicious lies like that.' With that Thelma left the room to change, rapping Ethan on the head as she went.

It seemed that the rest of the Crazy Gang were not exactly crazy to leave the hotel. Their rooms were all in a row with interconnecting doors. Trays laden with enormous club sandwiches were wheeled in by unsuspecting Moroccan waiters who were then commandeered for other duties such as finding pillows, fetching extra TV sets and setting up ironing boards. Rikki, it appeared, had no intention of setting foot in the souk and she and Elida settled down to munch on their club sandwiches and tune in to a cable TV channel.

Rhys took the opportunity to nip quietly into his room which, needless to say, was next to Rikki's with a connecting door. He lay down on his bed for a few minutes' rest

In vain.

'OK, faggot, my mother says you have to take me to the souk,' blasted Ethan, charging into the room in his dark glasses, now sporting a cowboy hat as well.

'What did you say?' asked Rhys with menacing politeness, holding down an inward desire to leap on the boy and hammer him into more of a lump than he already was.

'Are you deaf as well?' said Ethan.

'As well as what?' asked Rhys. The boy fell silent. 'You know,' said Dorita, 'for a fat little pig you're very rude, aren't you? Why is that?'

'*Why is that? Why is that?*' mimicked the brat. Rhys was just about give in to his animal instinct and pounce on him when luckily the situation was saved by the arrival of the Nanny-Penny.

'Sorry to disturb you, Rhys. Would you mind awfully coming down with us to the souk? Rikki feels it wouldn't be wise for us to go alone. We might be kidnapped.'

'I very much doubt that anyone would want to kidnap Ethan although I live in hope – but yes, Penny, I will come with you. I'll meet you both downstairs in two minutes.'

'But no later,' said Ethan and reeled out of the room like a midget American cop who had just completed a bust.

'Sorry,' smiled Poor Penny as she followed.

As the little party of three left the Saunders, the rain started to spit down. It was not at all how Rhys had imagined Tangiers. This particular corner of the desert was not strapped with bedouin tents, camels and mirages. It was more like the south coast of darling old Blighty. Short green grass covered sloping downs. It was only the houses that gave the game away. They were one-storey affairs, whitewashed, with tiny windows. The Atlantic waves lashed the beach which receded into the South Downs which, in turn, led to ill-organised suburbs. One was called the Old Mountain, another the New Mountain and so on. The Saunders was located at one corner of the old walled city and it was into this labyrinth the intrepid trio now ventured. Local Arabs scurried about the maze of tiny streets and alleyways, quite oblivions to the rain.

'It all seems very pagan to me,' said Penny, clutching Ethan's hand. When Rhys didn't reply she continued, 'You see, I've just been converted to Catholicism.'

'Oh, really?' This was rather interesting, thought Rhys. 'How's that?'

'Yeah, she never stops, night and day,' said Ethan.

'Nor do you,' retorted Penny.

'I'm Catholic myself,' said Rhys. 'It's a very practical religion, that's the thing nobody ever realises about it.'

'I've got this booklet of the latest prophet, a priest in Yugoslavia. It's really inspiring. You must read it,' Penny told him. Rhys noticed that she had begun to flush slightly as they started to discuss religion. Converts, he thought, always the same. Take it all terribly seriously.

'I normally say a rosary about teatime. Do you want to join me? A whole group of us used to do it when we were on pilgrimage to Medjugorje. I sort of got into the habit. It really helps.'

Rhys, who had forgotten to breathe he was so horrified, gagged slightly. He recovered quickly. 'Yes, that would be lovely and I'd adore to read the latest prophesies,' he managed to reply.

Secretly he was thinking: this is *typical*. I've been sent this ghastly pink-lipped convert just to make this whole terrible experience even worse. It's going to be a well-earned hundred grand, that's for sure. Still, there's no harm in a rosary before taking the plunge, so to speak. In fact, I might even embark on a novena straight away. . . .

He was dreaming away when suddenly at the end of the alleyway he noticed a beggar who looked incredibly familiar.

'I've seen that one before,' he said out loud. The beggar was very old with vivid blue eyes in a tangle of deep lines. As the party approached he held out his hand and said in a sing-song voice, 'Alms. Alms for the poor.'

'Goodness, it's Sir Maurice Goodbuns,' said Rhys, instantly recognising the famous voice of the theatre, 'Sir Maurice, what on earth are you doing here? Times can't be that bad?'

The tramp looked up and said, 'Ah, Waveral, yes, I'm methoding, you know. How nice to see you. We haven't met since that mini-series (Sir Maurice pronounced it mini*cerice*) in India.' The old man got up, brushed himself down, and shook hands with Penny. 'Good day. Maurice Goodbuns, pleased to meet you. There's rather an amusing little teashop around this corner. Shall we adjourn there for some refreshment? On me, of course. I'm fat on per diem.'

The trio followed Sir Maurice, who was dressed in a white dress and turban. Even the disgusting Ethan seemed taken aback. Just a little. They turned several corners and found themselves in a deserted alleyway with one small ominous opening in the wall into which Sir Maurice disappeared like the White Rabbit, leaving the others to follow. Inside was a long narrow cellar with a television at one end and five or six men wearing identical clothing to Sir Maurice. This was obviously his local because he was greeted by everyone in the room. Once they were settled at a dark little table Sir Maurice continued.

'My dear, methoding does take it out of one. Have you ever tried, Waveral?'

'No, I haven't really. Just get on and do it, I say.'

'So right, so right, I fear. However, Brad Bingham –' Sir Maurice rolled his r's to death – 'who I must say is most terribly congenial – he's our lead, y'know? – he absolutely swears by it and since I had a week off and Giles has gone trekking round the desert, or whatever it is one does in these parts, I thought I might give it a crack. Ah, Abdul, four of your mint teas, if you please.'

'Straight away, Goodbuns, sir,' replied the grinning snake of a man who had slithered up to the table.

Dorita was finally enjoying himself. Whatever he might say to the contrary – and often did – he was always happy chewing the cud with a few old thesps. Preferably old, in fact, since he inevitably became nervous with anyone his own age. The bar also suited him down to the ground because when he flexed his sniffer dog nostrils, he scented one of his favourite smells: Moroccan black hash.

'Vernon told me you were here. We had dinner last night. I must say the fellow quite exhausts me. Do you know he has been to all my first nights since *Bricusse-cusse?* Quite extraordinary dedication. But enough about me – what did you think of my last picture?' and Sir Maurice, who would have his little joke, burst into a fit of girlish giggles.

'I was going to be in this mini-series but my agent told me it had been cancelled. I suppose that was when they got Bongham or whatever it's called.'

'Who is your agent?' asked Sir Maurice with a sidelong glance.

'Dumpling Hines, unfortunately.'

'Isn't he the one who always falls asleep? Nathalie Norwich was a client of his. I remember when we were doing *Bats in the Belfry* Hines was in the front row sucking a lollipop. Rather rude behaviour for an agent to begin with but then he passed out mid-lick, apparently. Then, suddenly, in the middle of the "Streets of Fire" speech there was the most awful kerfuffle and it was him, Hines, bright green, eyeballs popping out of their sockets, head rocking, with this thing sticking out of his mouth. He'd choked on it. He had the grace to come backstage afterwards and apologise but as he was leaving he clasped my hand and said, "Bye bye, Johnny, bye bye Johnny B. Goode". Fellow's raving mad! Who on earth do you suppose he thought I was? Maybe you should change agents. Go to mine.'

Suddenly Rhys had had enough.

'We must be going in a minute. Penny and Ethan here have got to buy their costumes for a ball tomorrow night, haven't you?' said Rhys, looking meaningfully at Penny.

'If you two faggots could stop talking, we could.' Ethan had clearly recovered some of his form.

'Goodness *gracious!*' breathed Sir Maurice in excitement. He loved talking dirty. 'You're very young to be talking in such an uncompromising fashion.'

'Yeah, and you're very old to be still talking at all.'

Sir Maurice was stumped for a second but then carried on regardless. 'Are you talking about the infernal Budleigh Salterton and his infernal ball?'

'I think he's calling himself Ashby de la Zouche now, but yes, are you going?'

'Unfortunately, yes. He's asked us all. Harry Bellows-Forth, Wally, Bob Browser. All of us except Bingham who won't come because he says it's out of character.'

The two men laughed. 'Well, must be dashing then,' said Goodbuns and got up to go. 'Can't tell you how nice it is to see you again, Waveral. Chin up and see you tomorrow night. Is your wife here? Darling creature!'

'No, she isn't. She doesn't really travel.'

'Pity,' said Sir Maurice and with that he darted out of the bar with alarming alacrity for someone of his great age, disappearing into the warren of rainy alleyways filled with other methoding beggars.

CHAPTER SEVENTEEN: in which Adrienne's neck goes
into spasm and Rhys is fitted for a fruit plate

On the way back from the souk the rain turned into a downpour
and they raced back to the Saunders where, standing in the lobby
beside a stretcher guarded by a nurse, they came upon:

Lady Dinah!

When he saw her Rhys turned white as a sheet and immediately imagined that the Brigadier had snuffed it, a thought that
had, at certain moments in the past, given him extreme pleasure.
Now, suddenly, he was dead scared. As he crossed the lobby of
the old colonial hotel, dodging Moroccan waiters and bellboys,
his mind flashed back.

'I'll send a horsebox to the airport to collect you, Daddy.' He was breathless when he reached his mother's side.

'What's going on?' he asked without preamble.

'I don't know where to begin. The whole thing's been such a disaster,' replied Lady Dinah, wiping her brow with a tattered Kleenex.

'It's Daddy, isn't it?' said Rhys, eyeing the stretcher warily as if he expected the Brigadier's mouldy remains to be lurking under the sheet. 'He's dead, isn't he?'

'Oh, no,' chuckled Lady Dinah, 'no such luck, I'm afraid. No, it's much more mundane than that.' Rhys was aware of Penny and Ethan looming behind him. Oh, Christ, he thought, they're going to tell the Duchess my whole family's here.

'So who's this?' he snapped, pointing at the stretcher. Someone's entire body lay underneath the sheet. However, as he looked closer he could see it wasn't a corpse because it was breathing in little short gasps.

'It's me, I'm afraid,' said the smallest, worriedest voice. *Adrienne!*

'Oh my God!' said Rhys, thinking he was going to faint. Suddenly Ethan's voice piped up.

'Hey, faggot, we're going up to the rooms.'

Rhys didn't move for a second. Vomit was perilously poised at tonsil level and he had to breathe deeply before attempting to swallow.

'Thank you, Ethan and Penny, I'll be with you in a minute. I've just met some friends.' He turned back to Lady Dinah. 'Now, what are you doing here, Mummy? Is this some kind of a joke or something?'

'Well, yes, darling, I suppose it is and it's all gone hideously wrong. All thanks to her.' This last sentence was spat out with uncharacteristic venom.

'I can't help it if my neck goes into spasm, Dinah,' whined Adrienne, close to hysteria. This had obviously been a bone of contention between them for some time.

'Of course you can, you stupid girl!' snapped Lady Dinah. 'Rhys, this is what happened. We decided to play a joke on you and come and visit. Since you left me with all that lovely money

150

we thought we might as well use some of it. But then Adrienne started to get more and more hysterical, like an ill-mannered guttersnipe with absolutely no control.' Lady Dinah's voice was losing control as she recounted her story of doom.

'I *did* have self-control,' screamed Adrienne from under the sheet.

'Of course you didn't, you fibber, you deliberately put your neck into spasm! Luckily there was a doctor on the plane, Rhys, with morphine and things like that, otherwise I would have been forced to throw her out of the window. The sheer *embarrassment*. . . .' Lady Dinah seemed unable to continue and began to sob silently. And judging by the strange movements under the sheet she wasn't the only one.

'And now look what's happened,' continued Lady Dinah once she'd recovered. 'Thanks to your stupid neck Rhys is furious. Aren't you?' she demanded, turning sharply on her son.

But Rhys was miles away. 'You paid with what money, exactly?'

'Yours,' squeaked both voices.

'Oh.' Rhys was suddenly at a loss, then, 'OH!' It was all too much but he didn't have time to dwell on this latest disaster for too long because suddenly whoops and shrieks erupted from the other end of the lobby and by now Rhys knew they were the kind that heralded the arrival of people he knew. This time it was 'Pepsi' and 'Shirlee' again, wheeling the huge make-up trolleys that were matching accessories to everyone in their profession. Things were beginning to move rather fast.

'Rita, *Yoo-hoo*, over here,' they screamed together as they began to wheel their trolleys towards the group.

'Oh, do look, it's those girls,' said Lady Dinah through her tears, 'Poppy and Sherry, look, Adrienne.'

'I can't,' replied the wayward daughter-in-law, 'my neck's in spasm, in case you'd forgotten.'

But Lady Dinah was off, anger and misery lifted like a fog as she charged across the lobby.

'Poppy and Sherry, do you remember me? Dinah Waveral. We met in India on that mini-series Rhys was in.'

'Oh!' shrieked the two girls and they ran to hug Lady Dinah, letting go of their trolleys which careered off untended across the lobby, running down as many Moroccan waiters and bellboys as they could.

'Can I go to my room now?' asked Adrienne of anyone who would listen.

Rhys knelt down beside the stretcher. 'Ada, this really is the most awkward moment for you to arrive here. I'm on an errand of a most delicate nature. I was trying to save our squandered fortune and really, you are the last person I need.'

'Oh, don't you start. Just get me to my room and you won't hear another word.'

'Did you make reservations?'

'Yes, but it was a double room which means we have to share and if we share the rest of my body will go into spasm. Here's the key.' A tiny hand appeared from under the shroud dangling the key.

'Quick, do take me up before "Pepsi" and "Shirlee" get there. I really can't face seeing them.'

As Rhys and the nurse pushed the stretcher into the lift, 'Pepsi', 'Shirlee' and Lady Dinah began an elephant stampede towards them.

'I'll be down in a minute, I'm just taking Adrienne to her room, *I'll be down in a minute!*' He was beginning to scream.

Fifteen minutes later he had tucked Adrienne up in bed. The nurse gave her a tranquilliser and left the couple alone. The room was large and Rhys wondered how much he was paying for it, let alone how much he was paying for the nurse.

'Do you think we should get a divorce?' asked Adrienne suddenly in a detached, dreamlike voice.

Rhys, who had been arranging her clothes in a large tallboy, stopped and looked round. He wanted to protest, say, 'Whatever made you ask something like that. . . .' but somehow he couldn't.

It was true, after all, that they were always far apart and maybe it wasn't only physically.

'I don't know,' he replied quietly. 'Do you want one?'

'Not especially,' she answered, 'but I do think things have to come to some sort of conclusion in life and this . . . I don't really know what to call it . . . this marriage is like a constantly floating bit of pollen. It's stupid to go on like this, don't you think?'

Rhys didn't reply.

After a bit she asked with a giggle, 'Are you back on the game, then?'

'Yes, I'm afraid I am rather. We have no money, Adrienne. My hotel bill was a fortune and then Hennie came up with the Duchess and here I am.'

'It's funny how everything works out different to how you imagine, isn't it?' said Ada, settling down in bed.

'Hysterical!' replied her husband.

'For example, do you realise that this is the first trip I've been on since we were married? I always thought I'd be forever travelling, isn't that funny? Really, it's not me at all. I hate going away. It makes me very nervy.'

'Me too, actually,' said Rhys. 'I can't stop myself from moving about like a lunatic but I don't enjoy it at all. I'm always frightfully nervous inside.'

Adrienne was beginning to drop off. 'Nobody knows you're nervous, though, except me. They all think you're too relaxed and I think that's much better. With me, it's the opposite. They see me coming a mile off and they know that I'm so nervy that if they touch me they will get the most enormous . . .'

The sentence ground to halt. Rhys looked at his wife. She was very beautiful, lying in state in her funeral bed.

'. . . electric shock,' she finished.

He turned off the light and she became a tomb. The light was blue and silver and she could have been Joan of Arc or someone, lying there, killed battling through Life's Rich Tapestry. Maybe it was time to let go, thought Rhys. Because there was no going back. The path had grown over and he could only slash his way on through the undergrowth and take responsibility for the route he had chosen, even if he had chosen it unconsciously. He went over to the window and closed the curtains. The walled city was spread out below in the rain and he felt like a formless spirit in a dream. Life was the dream, in fact. Nothing was so unrealistic as the truth. Nothing was so baffling as the sequence of events in life. He understood his dreams far better than he could ever comprehend what happened in his real life. He tiptoed over to the door, puzzling all the while about the meaning of life, and as he was about to slip out his wife said in the dreamy voice of someone far away:

'You get what you want in the form that you deserve.'

Rhys closed the door. Firmly.

Rhys wandered down the long corridors, through a pass door, up a staff stairway and on to his own floor of the hotel. Events were beginning to overhwelm him. He thought of poor Jean Luc, a prisoner in a bedsit in the depressing suburbs of Paris, and of Peter Moody, radiating to death in a London hospital, but it didn't help to quell his own sense of utter hopelessness. In fact it merely added to it.

In his room he lay down and was just drifting into a dream when the telephone rang.

'Mr de la Zouche's car is downstairs, sir.'

Hell! He had forgotten all about the fitting at the de la Zouche mansion. Wearily he got up and headed downstairs again, this time taking the lift. He braced himself for 'Pepsi' and 'Shirlee', not to mention his mother, as the lift doors slid open, but they were nowhere to be seen in the lobby. So much the better.

Outside the hotel a large black Mercedes with tinted windows was waiting. He made an 'is this for me?' sign to the driver, a young, rather camp-looking Moroccan, who didn't reply, so Rhys got in. They drove past the old walled town and began to climb into the suburbs. The rain still splashed down and cyclists swerved to avoid the deluge of water thrown up by the speeding limo.

'Where on earth am I going?' Rhys asked himself for about the eighteen thousandth time that decade. 'The more I move around the more hemmed in I become.' As the car climbed the winding road the shantyish suburbs changed almost to country. Finally they drew to a halt by a long white wall with a single door in it. The driver opened the car door for Dorita and rang the bell. Before long a similarly swish Moroccan boy appeared, to open the small door and beckon Rhys inside. The driver did not follow.

Rhys found himself in an enormous courtyard filled with sweet-scented bushes and trees. The boy beckoned silently for him to follow. Had Ashby had their tongues removed so that they could not gossip, wondered Rhys as he walked beneath overhanging white jasmine trees towards another white wall. Very wise! Through the other door the boy beckoned yet again and Rhys found himself in yet another courtyard, this time surrounded by a cloister. He was beginning to feel like Alice in Wonderland.

Round the cloister and through another door and finally into the house. The boy seated him on an enormous sofa in an equally enormous hall, all white with a log fire burning in the chimney. And here Rhys waited.

And waited. The sound of the rain had a hypnotic effect and, exhausted as he was, he soon found himself drifting off.

'Mah deah boy, excuse me for the delay!' Ashby suddenly appeared out of nowhere clad only in a pair of shorts. 'Do forgive mah dreadful state of undress but ah've come dahrectly from a fittin',' he explained, noticing Rhys noticing.

'That's quite all right,' said the ever professional Dorita, 'you've a great body.'

'Hours of slavin', pummelin' an' dietin', mah deah, but more of that later. Now, follow me.'

They walked through the hall and up a long flight of stairs – everything was on a Cecil B. de Mille scale at Ashby's – and into a huge bedroom with a bed that could have slept sixteen, and probably frequently did, thought Rhys. It was swamped by a vast mosquito net, as were the windows. Three little old Moroccans wearing fez hats with tape measures round their necks sat cross-legged in a corner amidst acres of fabric. White silk. Gold and silver lamé. Sackcloth, velvet. . . .

De la Zouche turned dramatically in the middle of the room, Stuyvesant ablaze, and announced with great importance, 'Mah deah, y'all are going as the "Fruit Plate".'

'I beg your pardon?' replied the perplexed soap star.

'The Fruit Plate. Don't you think that's droll? Y'all do know that this is an Exotic Fruit Ball, don't you?' He looked rather accusing here so Rhys said, 'Oh, yes, awfully good idea. And what are you coming as, if I might ask?'

'Oh, guess, guess. . . .' screeched poor, demented Ashby de la Zouche.

'Preserved plum?' parried Dorita.

'Y'all are very naughty. Very naughty indeed. No. I am to be *Frutta di Bosca*. Blackberries and blueberries to the uninitiated. What d'ya think? Ain't that *kooky*?'

'Very,' laughed Dorita politely, 'but not very exotic.'

'You and me and . . . Wilbur, another young man ah know, will represent the fruit trolley. You and Wilbur as the Fruit Plates, me, the divine *Frutta di Bosca*. We shall all be wheeled in on a great float disguised as a trolley and then the competition will begin. What d'ya think?' he asked again, as if the look of absolute horror on Dorita's face was not enough of an answer.

'We'll cause as much of a sensation as Lady Caroline Lamb,' said Rhys.

'Oh, my Lord, ah don't think ah've asked her. . . .' said Ashby.

'I mean it sounds marvellous,' said Rhys in desperation. All he could think of was how in heaven's name was he going to explain all this to the group of his thespian friends who would be gathered beneath the float?

'No time to lose. Ahm sure Rikki Lancaster will be champing at her bit to get back in her saddle. Now, Mr Maroun, bring on the Fruit Plate.'

And so Dorita was strapped into an enormous plate into which he had to climb like a tutu. Then he was squeezed into a jacket of giant peaches, pears, strawberries and cherries. As if that wasn't enough he was fitted with a hat like a court jester's in the shape of a banana. Ashby, Mr Maroun and his assistant stood back, speechless in admiration, as poor Rhys tottered around, lurching from side to side like a giraffe in the throes of death.

'Oh, it's too kooky. Mr Maroun, where is the Polaroid camera?'

'Here it is, Mr de la Zouche,' and Ashby snapped away a roll of pictures, gasping and groaning with ecstasy at each one.

'These will *definitely* be going into *Women's Wear Daily*,' he said confidentially.

'Oh yes, *rather!*' said Rhys. Oh, no, definitely not, thought Dorita, there goes my last chance at career recuperation.

It took him almost as long to get out of the costume as it had taken to get into it. Afterwards they had a beer in the sitting room, Ashby still in bis black underpants and matching glasses.

'Herman Lancaster was a great friend,' Ashby confided, 'and when he left Rikki he called me and said, "What shall I give her?" He was talking money, of course. I said, mah dear Herman, give her a round-the-world boat ticket with a hotel reservation for the longest possible time in each port, that's what she needs. *And so did the rest of us.*'

'Poor Rikki,' said Rhys rather hopelessly.

'Poor, thanks to Herman's generosity, is hardly the right adjective. Tacky Rikki. Hellish Rikki. Things like that are better to mah mind. Still, ahm being awfully naughty, aren't ah? She is your friend, after all, isn't she?' Ashby was all caring smiles. Rows of perfect teeth, like the pipes of an organ, glistened in the light of the fire. He moved a little closer and a heavily bejewelled hand flopped down on the back of the sofa in the vicinity of Rhys's neck.

Rhys's hackles rose.

'You'd better leave before ah fall in love, young man,' said Ashby, all moist eyes.

'Righto,' said Rhys, and got up.

'We have all tomorrow night to get to know each other better, after all,' Ashby went on, leading Dorita back through the courtyard. 'There'll be the band, champagne, intoxication, everything. What d'ya think?'

'Er, you don't by any chance know where I could score some hash, do you?' asked Rhys, grasping at what he thought was the ideal opening for such a request.

Ashby's reaction was sudden and ratlike. 'You're not some kind of junky, are you?' he asked suspiciously.

'No, not a bit, I only like to have a smoke sometimes.' Rhys smiled boyishly to show what a hick he really was. There was a rather tense pause during which Ashby seemed to be analysing him from behind the Saint Laurents, then he smiled and even laughed a little.

'Then smoke you shall, mah child,' and with that he opened the little door on to the road, blew a kiss, whispered, 'Goodnight, sweet prince,' and was gone.

CHAPTER EIGHTEEN: in which Sir Maurice Goodbuns gives a dinner party

Back at the hotel Rhys found a message from Lady Dinah.

'Have gone to Poopie and Cheroo's hotel to have my hair done. Speak later.'

She was never one to get the hang of names which was strange since she attached so much importance to them. 'Don't any of your friends have surnames?' she would ask her son. He would tell her their surnames and then she would forget.

With a heavy heart, longing for a smoke, our hero climbed into the lift. Nothing much seemed to have happened since he had left four hours earlier. The Crazy Gang were all still sitting around in their nightdresses, eating enormous club sandwiches. The television was still blaring. Two chambermaids had set up camp in one corner of the room where they were busy ironing and making tea on a tiny gas ring that had appeared out of nowhere. The hotel hairdresser also appeared to have been pressganged into service and was busy wrestling with Thelma Romanelli's beehive. The sound of endless chitter-chatter greeted Rhys like that of sparrows on a telegraph pole, and he had the impression he was entering a harem.

The telephone rang.

'Hellooo,' said the Duchess, smiling. 'Rhys, darling, it's for you. It's that darling Dawnford Vernon. Dawnford, darling . . .' she went on, without handing Dorita the phone, 'how are you? Really? Really? Oh, good, I think we'd love to. Yes, we would. That'd be lovely. Let me hand you over to the darling boy. Rhys, speak to Dawnford. We're all going to have dinner with them. Sir Maurice Goodbuns is going to be there. I *adore* him.'

Rhys took the phone and said in the least strained voice he could muster, 'Dawnford, what's going on?'

'Rhys, darling, Goodbuns came back from the souk and suggested we gave a dinner in your honour. He said he felt absolutely ghastly that you were pipped at the post by Brad Bingham for the role and that to show solidarity we should all go out to dinner. So we'll quite a party – me, Goodbuns, Wally, Bob Browser, Little Beige Riding Hood – why did you name her that, by the way?'

'It's a long story. I can't tell you now, Dawnford.'

'Well, anyway, Little Beige – and who else? Oh yes, Bellows-Forth, and "Pepsi" and "Shirlee" and of course your delightful harem. We're going to send a car for you because the restaurant Goodbuns has chosen is rather hard to find. Nine o'clock, all right?'

'Yes, Dawnford, perfect,' said Rhys, feeling heavy fatigue in every pore, and he replaced the receiver. The Crazy Gang seemed to be very excited at the thought of the dinner and were suddenly spurred into action. Hairdryers blew, powder puffs puffed, nails were buffed and varnished and Dorita excused himself. Penny clinched him at the door and said in breathless tones, like a spy, 'I couldn't find you at five o'clock to say the rosary so I went ahead alone. I'm sorry but we can try tomorrow, if you like? Meanwhile here are the prophecies I was telling you about. They have been approved by the Pope. They're awfully inspiring.' And with that she thrust a little pamphlet into Rhys's hand and rushed away.

As soon as Rhys opened the door to his own room the telephone began to ring.

It was Lady Dinah.

'Hello, dear boy, I gather we are dining this evening.'

'No, we most certainly are not. I can't have you there with Rikki. She'll recognise you as my mother from the other night and there'll be one hell of a hoo-ha.'

'Oh, no, she won't, not with my new hairdo that Poopie has given me. It's bright blonde, darling. You won't recognise me yourself. It's too amusing. I'm staying in Cheroo's room while I'm here. I don't ever want to see that remedial wife of yours again. *There!* Anyway, I'll see you later. By the way, I've told P and S that I don't want to be known as your Ma so we're calling me Betty. Got that? *Betty!* Bye.' And she hung up before Rhys could get in another word.

The Crazy Gang were going full throttle as they assembled in the lobby to take the Goodbuns limo to the restaurant. Even Ethan seemed to be in an affable mood and offered Rhys a cigarette as they were waiting.

'Ethan!' screeched Rikki, who was dressed in sequins from head to toe, 'I've told you before about smoking.' She swooped down on him like a vulture and grabbed the packet of cigarettes just as Rhys was about to take one. Thelma came to his rescue with a menthol king-size.

The car arrived and they all squeezed in. Thelma Romanelli got in the front on account of her size. Rikki and Elida collapsed together like a folding table – a heap of bones. Ethan was sitting on Penny's knee 'Careful, Ethan', 'Watch it, Penny', 'Rhys, can I rest my arm on your shoulder?'

'Certainly, Rikki.'

Ethan was sitting on Penny's knee and set about practising his boxing moves on her tits. They had to be black and blue already but she appeared to take it all in her stride. All part and parcel of being a convert, thought Rhys, as he watched the nauseating child pummel away at his nanny's breasts. There is a future queen of England if ever there was one.

The car finally set off with everyone in good spirits, mostly at the prospect of meeting Sir Maurice Goodbuns in the flesh. Rhys knew that by now he was skimming far too close to the wind but there was nothing he could do except watch it work itself through – like a fever. His mother. 'Pepsi' and 'Shirlee'. Dawnford Vernon. Little Beige. Bellows-Forth and Wally. Not to mention Bob Browser – all together with the Waxworks. His wife, comatose in spasm in some distant corridor, and finally God, a burning reminder in the shape of Penny.

Still, he thought, as the car wove its way through the town, they're getting their money's worth. How else could they get to rub shoulders with the cream of the English stage? Which other hooker could bring his client off in such style and extravagance? At this thought our hero cheered up a bit. He liked to see a job well done and as he watched the laughing faces caught from time to time in the flash of a street lamp, he suddenly felt happy and laughed too.

'Rhys is laughing!' squeaked the Waxworks in unison.

'Isn't that great? You're not exactly a great laugher, are you?' said Elida.

'It depends. Sometimes,' replied Rhys. It seemed pointless to explain that normally he did very little else.

'Still, he's laughing now, ain't you, honey? That's the main thing,' said Rikki, smiling. She looked frail and frighteningly skeleton-like, propped against Elida as she was. They both had broad smiles on their faces and even though the image was one that belonged in a horror film, there was still something rather sweet and touching about their general childlike enthusiasm, given the decadent quality of the adventure. Rhys was aware that Thelma was watching him closely. He looked at her and she winked. She's got the whole situation taped, has that one, thought Dorita.

The restaurant was in an old white house through a courtyard. The table of thesps stuck out a mile, billowing as it was with cigarette smoke. In fact it looked as if it had just caught fire. Sir Maurice, at the head of the table, had a large cigar. Rhys could see that Bob Browser already had several Disque Bleus going. 'Pepsi' and 'Shirlee' were avid Marlboro addicts and even Lady Dinah had a fag on, always an ominous sign.

As Dorita and his party approached, the cricket club all rose as one with Sir Maurice at the head. 'Welcome, welcome,' he said with a bow. Rhys took a deep breath and dived into the introductions.

'This is Bob Browser, the cinematographer, Rikki.' Bob Browser suffered from alopecia. He had no hair anywhere and a rather large chin which meant you could more or less turn him upside down and his face would look exactly the same. He had known Dorita for several years. Browser by name and, unfortunately, Browser by nature, he'd been arrested browsing in the toilets at Notting Hill Gate Tube station. In fact, thought Rhys as he went painstakingly round the table introducing every-one, that was really the communal thread of the party. In his earlier days, poor Sir Maurice had had a scrape with a guardsman in a siding and had ended up in the clink. Not to mention Harry Bellows-Forth, who had been handcuffed to a tree on Hampstead Heath by a 'friend' who then lost the key and promptly ran off in panic. He had had a fair bit of explaining to do to the early morning dog walkers and later the local police when he was found, still attached to the tree, with his trousers down. Unfortu-nately for him he was appearing in *Within These Walls* at the time and the press had a field day. His name was also in keeping with his nature. He was a famous theatrical bellower. No chance of missing a word Harry said on an evening at the theatre. Also very little chance of missing an exhibition of his private parts, on that same evening out, since Bellows-Forth was proud of his equipment and displayed it to the public at every possible opportunity.

On round the table to Wally, an ex juve lead in the Steerforth mould. Black hair, black eyelashes and watery blue eyes, Wally was also quite a bellower. He had been dubbed the Duke of Darling-Darling by his agent, Dumpling Hines. He was always shrieking Darling this or Darling that.

The Crazy Waxworks were behaving as if they'd known Dawnford during the war. Rhys's heart was in his mouth as he introduced them to a newly peroxided Lady Dinah who, besides having been under the influence of the entire hair and make-up department of the mini-series, had also, Dorita guessed, been under the influence of several tankloads of alcohol – P and S were never far from a bottle – and she now looked like Bet Lynch, in *Coronation Street*. Her own mother, Rhys's late grandmother, would have had a hard time recognising her, let alone the Waxworks. The introductions over, Sir Maurice stood up.

'I suppose it's up to me to do the placement. What a nuisance Roger isn't here, he's an expert at seating people.' Sir Maurice was famous for his unconscious use of double entendres and there was endless nudging and guffawing from the others at the mention of Roger's seating. Sir Maurice went on unruffled.

'Rhys, dear boy, you are next to me. This dinner is in your honour. We all feel terribly guilty that you are not in *Love in the Desert*. It is the role of an Englishman, after all, and perfect for a performer of your talent.'

Rikki's raucous tones suddenly intruded.

'*My late husband, Herman, was a gilt fetishist.*'

Rhys looked around the table and noticed several pairs of eyebrows shooting up at this revelation. Needless to say the joke flew way above Sir Maurice's head. He pretended to listen intently but it was clear he had no idea what she was talking about. 'He wanted our whole house in Palm Springs covered in gold leaf and I said to him, Herman, this is going to cost you an arm and a leg. . . .'

'Ah, yes,' agreed Sir Maurice, 'but once you get started you just can't stop, can you?'

'No, she can't,' chirped Elida. The Waxworks were beginning to come out of their shells and the dinner party erupted into a hubbub of conversation. Rhys kept an eye out for Lady Dinah who appeared to be rapidly losing her marbles with 'Pepsi' and

'Shirlee' at the other end of the table. They were hysterical with laughter. Dawnford, who as usual was in his black polo neck and trousers, ordered for everyone.

Wine flowed throughout the dinner and tongues loosened as did Rikki's arm which started to play up and down Rhys's leg.

'Are you all right, Rita? you've gone awfully pale,' said Bob Browser.

'He's just tired, that's all, aren't you honey?' said Rikki, leaning her face against his. 'I'm gonna take him home in a minute and put him to bed.'

'Oh, I see,' said Bob, glancing round the table at his colleagues, and then there was one of those silences in which Rikki, running her fingers through Rhys's hair which was standing up on end, said, 'I love this boy. He's really special.'

At the other end of the table Lady Dinah rose to her feet, drunk as a sailor, and shouted, *don't be so stupid!*' She was quickly pulled down again by 'Pepsi' and 'Shirlee' and luckily the Duchess didn't quite realise what was going on. 'You see, darling, women go crazy for you. She couldn't bear not to be with you, that dame, so she had to get up and holler about it. I hear her.'

'So do I,' said Rhys, staring fixedly at his mother, and all the while the Duchess's hand was creeping closer to his private parts which were shrinking rapidly as her trotter advanced. They were just approaching acorn size when there was an uproar at the other end of the table.

There was a political row going on. These were very popular in theatrical circles but normally they were discussions rather than arguments since everyone was a socialist and if they weren't they pretended to be. This evening, however, the party included both the Duke of Darling-Darling and Betty, alias Lady Dinah Waveral. Bob Browser and Harry Bellows-Forth were purple with rage as Betty, slurring her words, pronounced; 'Nobody in our part of the world wants to work.'

Luckily for Rhys, he was too drunk and past caring about those familiar fascist remarks of Lady Dinah. Normally it was down the other end of the table at Waveram and now it was here in Tangiers. So what, a table's a table, thought Rhys, as he felt the trotter squelch around his penis. Suddenly he started laughing silently. It was all too ludicrous. His mother was having a political set-to at one end of the table and he was being squeezed by his new client at the other and all of it was going on right next door to that bastion of the theatrical establishment, Sir Maurice Goodbuns. In fact, thought Rhys, I'm thoroughly enjoying myself. Whatever next?

Whatever next, indeed!

They left the dinner to the raucous strains of Lady Dinah's political views and travelled home in a reflective mood. They had all drunk far too much and Thelma Romanelli had passed out and was snoring by the time they reached the Saunders.

Dorita had to play the next bit quite carefully. He didn't want to Do the Deed two nights running so, as they crossed the lobby, he said, 'I'm dead,' and began to kiss everyone goodnight. As he got to Rikki his heart was once again lurking in his mouth. Maybe she'll just insist, he thought. 'I think I'll call it a day now. Tomorrow is going to be a long day and I didn't sleep a wink last night.'

'All right, angel, I'll go to sleep too. I'll be dreaming of you,' replied the Duchess.

'Me too,' he whispered and they disappeared into separate elevators.

Tucked up in bed, Rhys opened the pamphlet of the new Catholic prophet. First there was a very graphic description of the Last Judgement and then it launched into a section on venereal disease. At this point the hair on the back of Rhys's neck began to rise as he read that it was more or less impossible for anyone who had had the clap to make it through the Day of Judgement. He could still count on his fingers the number of times he had personally been afflicted. Now he read on. The prophet, it seemed, was a healer but it said that if he came upon anyone who had the clap it might kill him and he could never cure anyone who had it. Rhys freaked.

He put down the pamphlet and turned off the light. This was not the time to be reading such literature. On such a mission as this he did not need to know that he was forever barred from the pearly gates in which, despite everything, he held a firm if Gothic belief. Oddly enough he was quite a serious Catholic and he tried as best he could to live within the structure of the Catholic church.

At the same time he had knocked around a bit.

This had always caused him agonising guilt but reading Penny's pamphlet – Chapter 17 began, 'Ye with clap shall not enter the kingdom of heaven' – really sent the shivers down his spine. Luckily he had a sleeping pill that Rikki had given him earlier and he took it.

But he dreamed all night that Lancelot was in a clap clinic and the specialist was the Brigadier.

CHAPTER NINETEEN: in which Rhys comes out of the
closet

Rhys woke up the next morning with a headache and a general
feeling of malaise. The rain was still pouring down outside and
he might just as well have been in some swish hotel in Birming-
ham instead of 'hovering above the Tangiers souk' as the Saunders was described in its brochure.

Depression engulfed him in a thick mist as it so often did and
he lay motionless for several minutes. No matter how hard he
tried, Rhys often thought, he simply wasn't cut out for the type
of life he was trying to live. Locked in some inner closet deep
inside him, blindfolded and gagged, was a gentleman farmer

desperately trying to get out, bashing away with all his force against the cupboard door and screaming with indignant might behind the gag.

Dorhys, who had himself spent many years in the same cupboard, was now skating on the ice rink in his frilly little tutu, smiling at anyone who wanted to be smiled at (and probably a few who didn't), enjoying the liberty that only a former captive can appreciate. Dorhys knew only too well that some day the gentleman farmer would escape, and a compromise would have to be reached. Already the constant friction between the two personalities had made him thin and ill. His stomach, once a staunch, upright hold-all, incapable of being upset, had, over the past two weeks, turned into a flimsy little evening bag which couldn't retain a banana let alone all the food, chemicals and stress that Dorita tried to squeeze into it like some ill-organised debutante. It was constantly overflowing, like an ashtray, causing Dorita to become – among other things – one of the most famous belchers of his time.

The fact of the matter was that neither Dorita – actress, prostitute and general floosie – nor the gentleman farmer – conservative, religious and staid bore – really suited poor Rhys's temperament.

Whatever that was.

As he lay in his bed in the Saunders, with his client next door, his mother down the hall, his wife in spasm on the floor below and, it seemed, everyone else he had ever known in various nooks and crannies around the town – not to mention Jesus, Mary and Joseph in the shape of Penny, the pointed finger – he knew that the compromise must soon be made. This constant battle was getting him nowhere. Worse, it was creating all kinds of explosive karma that would undoubtedly bring him tumbling down into a crisis.

The trouble was, the gentleman farmer bored him to tears, whereas the life he had discovered in the streets, first in London, then later in Paris, glittered for him with a special glamour. It had become an addiction he could not shake off. Somehow it had turned into that old trick of light where you point a camera at a perfectly normal street corner and suddenly that corner becomes a film with more shadows and light in it than it ever had in real life.

Suddenly he knew he was too old for renting. His conscience, like his stomach, had been tightening up on him. He decided there and then that he would not go through with Rikki and all she required of him. He would, he thought, warming to the idea, ring up Peach and tell her to send him a telegram ordering him home immediately. Deep inside himself he felt a hole being smashed through the door of the closet as the gentleman farmer broke through and felt around for the handle.

But Dorita was not about to go down in the first round. 'What about the money?' she shrieked, on the rampage. What indeed?

Rhys got out of bed and stood, staring out of the window at the city below. The cities of the plain. 'All this could be yours,' he whispered to himself. He could not ignore the fact that his bill at the Leicester had to be paid. Nor would the Brigadier ever fork out the funds, even if Rhys wanted him to. Would he get out of Tangiers alive or would he be killed in the proverbial swarm of locusts before he could cross the frontier?

So many questions and so few answers. He sighed and got back into bed. No backbone, he murmured as he put his head under the pillow, no backbone whatsoever. And he went back to sleep.

The gentleman farmer withdrew his hand and settled back into his cupboard with a resigned sigh and, as she wafted off to sleep, Dorita took a quick lap of victory around the skating rink in her spangled tutu, bowing and waving to the screaming crowd of pixie demons gathered to cheer her on.

Peace was not to reign for long, however, within the poor tormented soul battling for salvation, if only because his mother, always an early riser even after an evening of such dramatic alcoholic intake, was at that very moment marching along the hotel corridor towards his room.

Rhys felt the familiar twinge in his stomach button which always heralded her arrival even before her Rat-Tat-Tat sounded smartly on his door. He had risen and was at the door in one split second which showed how hard he found it to relax, even in sleep.

'It's rather early,' he mumbled, opening the door and then returning straight to bed.

'What absolute nonsense, it's half past nine,' bellowed Lady Dinah, tripping on the leg of a chair and hurtling into the room going, 'Whoopsadaisy!' as her handbag went flying.

Rhys peeped out and inspected her from underneath his pillow. 'You're still drunk, Mummy. How late did the party go on?'

'Oh, for hours and hours. Cheroo and I didn't get to bed till half past four. *Poor* darlings! They're already out shooting. They only had two hours' sleep. I *do* call that a bloody good show, don't you?'

'They've always been like that,' replied her son rather crossly.

'She's gone, by the way. I stopped by her room to smother her with a pillow at about six o'clock this morning and she'd gone.'

'Who's gone?' asked Rhys, alarmed. Sticky Rikki and all his money?

'Your ridiculous life,' drawled Lady Dinah.

'I suppose you mean my wife, Mummy,' said Rhys sadly. 'You've chased her away with your vile behaviour.'

'That woman is a hazard.' So saying, Lady Dinah lay back on Rhys's bed, her hair a shock of messy peroxide spread out on the pillow beside him. 'I'm bored with the pair of you,' she went on in a rasping, low voice which Rhys had never heard before. 'Protecting one against the other, making stupid excuses, listening to your wife's ravings. I like Adrienne, don't get me wrong. I always did, but there are limits. You've been a disastrous influence on one another ever since you were children and things have never improved. The day you told me you were getting married . . .' she was silent for a moment, concentrating, trying to remember something . . . 'was the last day I ever took communion.'

'Absolute rubbish!' Rhys's head popped out from under the pillow. 'The last time you went to communion was when you went on the Pill. I know because I remember hearing you discuss it with Daddy at the time. You really are being terribly sentimental, Mummy.'

Lady Dinah looked daggers at her son for a second and resumed staring at the ceiling.

'Absolute rubbish to you, too,' she said finally. 'When I *think* of all the effort I have put in over the years to patch things up between you all, it's suddenly dawned on me I might just as well have sat in a corner and got on with my tapestry.'

'Quite right,' agreed Rhys, 'only you weren't doing tapestry then.'

'Well, what was I doing then?'

'Lampshades,' replied Rhys, smiling in spite of himself.

'Oh, goodness, so I was,' laughed Lady Dinah. 'They were the real Pill, those lampshades. I only started doing them because Dim was too mean to pay poor Miss Polenska to make them. I quite enjoyed them, though, I can't deny it. I always like to keep myself occupied. That's been my saving grace. If I'd been like you two, constantly slumped in great heaps of boredom, I don't know what I'd have done. Caved in, probably. Lucky for you all I didn't. But what have I got for my trouble, I ask you? An alcoholic husband who, given his own way, would shoot me with a twelve-bore, and a homosexual son.'

'*What did you say?*' asked Rhys, popping right out from under his pillow again.

'I said a homosexual son,' replied Lady Dinah simply.

'Oh,' said her son – and popped back underneath.

There was a silence again. The rain continued to batter against the window. A telephone rang in the next room. Lady Dinah lay breathing heavily like a drunken tramp.

'You *are* homosexual, aren't you?' she asked, slightly accusingly. She's going to turn into some sort of crazy queerbasher, thought Rhyssie, the pillow-peeper.

'More or less,' he replied eventually. 'It depends. But since you ask, yes. Mostly yes.' He waited for a reaction but there didn't seem to be one forthcoming. What a strange way to be starting the day, he thought; in bed with one's mother discussing one's sexual preferences.

'I don't blame you,' declared Lady Dinah finally. 'I don't really know whether I can advocate marriage in the end. It's the most terribly . . . lonely business. Now, what I think would be absolute bliss would be to live with a girl friend. Sonia Barker, for example, would be heaven. Never washing up alone. No shoes to clean, except your own. Dressmaking together and all that. So much easier *à deux*, you know, with seams and everything. Not to mention the garden. I've come to the conclusion you thoughtless bastards deserve each other. Daddy would have been much happier married to one of his hunting chums.' She began to laugh at the idea.

'Anyway, I won't be tonight,' said Rhys.

'Won't be what, darling?' Lady Dinah was drifting off.

'Won't be homosexual. I shall be in full swashbuckling macho action tonight.'

'Why is that?' asked an already dreamy voice.

Rhys sighed. 'Rikki. *Idiot*. I told you.'

'Don't call your mother an idiot. I remember quite well. All I can say is that if you weren't before you're bound to be after. . . .' And she chuckled to herself like a chicken on an egg.

'Weren't what?'

'Homosexual, of course, *homosexual*.' As she said it the second time, enunciating every syllable, she tailed off into a loud snore.

Lady Dinah had finally collapsed.

As Rhys put on his uniform – Cerruti trousers, white shirt and Armani jacket – to the strains of Lady Dinah's snuffles and grunts together with the unrelenting rain battering against the window pane, he noticed a letter on the floor beside his mother's handbag. He picked it up.

It was from Adrienne.

Rhys settled down in the armchair by the window to read it. On the first page was just a large drawing in biro of an anguished stick figure with an enormous head, grimacing mouth, and huge, paranoid eyes. Its hair was sticking up on end, there was a long scar down the neck and the character's hand was plugged into the electricity socket in the wall.

A startling self-portrait by Adrienne. '*My state*' was written in shaky, spidery writing at the bottom. Rhys smiled. For a long time the couple had communicated via letters of this nature. Somehow they were much more descriptive and revealing than pages about 'the weather here is simply wonderful, darling you *must. . . .*' Sometimes, even with no accompanying letter, a picture could describe much better the particular state they were in than words ever could.

This time Adrienne had sent a letter as well. It started on the next page in enormous writing.

I HAVE GONE HOME, I'M AFRAID. DONT HAVE A FIT. IF I'D STAYED I WOULD HAVE HAD ONE (A FIT). SEE YOU SOON. COME UP TO SCOTLAND AFTER, AND WE'LL DISCUSS . . .

and on a page on its own, written in huge horror-film writing was

EVERYTHING

Rhys put the letter down. He felt terribly sad. He stared out of the window for a while in a kind of trance then he took a piece of paper and pen and drew a picture of himself as a thin skeleton squeezing an empty tube of Clarins Beauty Flash in one hand, holding a gun pointed to his head in the other. Underneath he wrote:

NO LIFE WITHOUT BEAUTY FLASH

He put it in an envelope and addressed it to his wife.

He was still reeling from the shock of having played the 'coming out of the closet scene' in such peculiar surroundings and here to cap it all was a letter from his wife implying that she was being electrocuted, not to mention that he himself was dressed for the set and about to go on as Lancelot in an all-day extravaganza with the Duchess which would no doubt last way into the night.

Rhys decided there was nothing else to do but take a walk and try to find something to get him through the day. He threw off his hated uniform, put on instead his jeans and baseball cap and a big coat, grabbed his Walkman from beside his bed and walked out. Outside in the rain his spirits lifted a bit. He was a great advocate of walking in the rain. In Paris it was always raining and he was always walking in it, finding little bars here and there where he would sit out the afternoon enjoying what he called 'French spotting'.

And now he set out to discover the souk. One hundred years ago, perhaps, poor Rhyssie would have found his niche as an explorer, forever turning yet another corner, but the first thing he wanted to find on this trip was something to smoke. He wandered down the winding streets and very soon a man came up to him and asked him if he wanted to sell his hat.

'For what?' asked our hero. The little man's eyes glistened under his little red fez.

'Hashish, you want hashish, eh?'

'Yes, but not rubbish,' said Rhys.

'Noooooo rubbish,' replied the little man with a chilling lack of authority. 'Come.'

So off Rhys went, following the man deeper and deeper in the labyrinths, imagining the headlines:

ACTRESS FOUND DEAD, BOUND AND GAGGED IN MOROCCAN SLUM. Lady Beth Fraser, legendary beauty and startling performer, was found with a flagstaff bearing the Union Jack up her. The enquiry is being led by none other than Sir Maurice Goodbuns. . . .

CHAPTER TWENTY: in which nothing much happens

Somehow Rhys had found his way back to the Saunders and was fast asleep. There was a sharp knock on the door. Rhys woke up with a jolt. Imagining for a second that he was still safely tucked up at the Leicester and that this must be Cherubin arriving with his breakfast, he jumped up – as was his wont, such were his nerves – and crashed headlong into the wall by the bed. He came to and realised that this was not the friendly wall that he knew so well beside his bathroom at the Leicester but somewhere quite different. It was dark in the room. He stood stock still for a while, trying to get his bearings, as flashes from the disastrous night before popped in and out of his mind.

There was another knock on the door and it finally dawned on Rhys where he was.

On location.

So who was that knocking on the door? Was it the Duchess? Could Rikki possibly be thinking of a little pre-ball preamble? Well, she wasn't going to get it. But when he opened the door there stood Penny, pink and quivering. She appeared to be more nervous than usual.

'I thought we might do one now,' she said. Rhys went blank. Was she after a bit of pre-ball whatsit as well? 'You know,' she prompted, 'a rosary.'

'Oh, right,' said poor, tired, neurotic Dorita, 'come on in.'

Actually he was rather pleased. He had been feeling distinctly uncertain, to say the least, over the last few days, particularly after reading Penny's prophecies. His own history was as varnished with Catholicism as an old black plank and his guilt-ometer was generally right up on a clear day, not to mention one where heavenly visibility was down to a minimum, smothered in thick smog. Our hero had never felt more like a grounded aeroplane in his life and the idea of a good knees-down very much appealed to him.

'Do you want to do it sitting or standing?' asked Penny, rummaging around in her handbag. Neither of them heard a quickly muffled gasp of horror from the other side of the communicating door.

'I prefer sitting. I always get dizzy if I kneel for too long. I'm afraid I always flunk it during the consecration. I just can't concentrate on anything else but kneeling when I do it.'

'Naughty boy!' giggled Penny. Out of her handbag she produced a rather ornately painted candle.

'*Goodness*, what's that?' said the actress to the bishop.

'You don't mind, do you? I always find a candle lends a bit of an atmosphere. You're laughing at me, aren't you?'

'No, not really. It's just that it's funny how converts always

take everything much more seriously than us jaded old has-
beens.'

Penny lit her candle and suddenly the room seemed much
more friendly. Penny looked to Rhys like Mary in a nativity play
as she leaned into the candle, holding her rosary. Bathed in the
waxy, yellow glow she looked beautiful and innocent. What
would this little sparrow do if she knew I was being paid to service
her employer, wondered Rhys. Probably get out another candle
and perform an exorcism.

They settled into their seats and started.

'*Hail Mary, full of grace, the Lord is with thee. . . .*'

Rhys loved the Hail Mary and was always reminded of the
time when he was about nine and he would go into the woods
near Waveram and say it over and over, hoping against hope for
an apparition. Now here he was, over twenty years later, saying
the same words. Though he had searched for one ever since –
and in the most unlikely places! – still no vision had appeared.
He had almost come to the conclusion that he was simply not
destined to have a vision of anything and certainly not of the
beautiful, sad white lady. Perfection was just going to keep on
eluding him and the search for it would presumbaly continue to
grate against his life like an old gym shoe.

'*Pray for us sinners now and at the hour of our death. . . .*'

Rhys and Penny swung into the second decade and he felt the
words begin to have their magic effect. Shadows danced around
the room and Rhys prayed for Peter Moody and for Jean Luc
who were both dying. Was the Catholic prophet really right?
Did that mean that when Jean Luc finally went down, all he'd
get for his trouble would be St Peter throwing up his arms in
horror and running in the opposite direction for fear of being
zapped like the Yugoslavian priest?

'*Blessed is the fruit of thy womb Jesus. . . .*'

This was just not possible. Jesus was a baby, after all, and
rejoiced with the simplicity of a child at the recovery of each lost
sheep, not to mention any heavyweight sufferer in the vale of
tears.

'*As it was in the beginning, is now, and ever shall be. . . .*'

Penny felt Rhys's attention lapse and paused before the next decade. Dorita gathered his thoughts and they went on. He prayed quite hard for he had been feeling quite fallen, not just because of the Rikki affair but a general malaise from drifting too long and too far.

They were coming to the end of the fifth decade when the door handle on the communicating door turned slightly. Rhys and Penny were so wrapped up in their endeavour that at first they didn't notice a thing. Their voices were now sounding dangerously like Buddhists' as they chanted the two thousand-year-old prayers.

Into the room crept Rikki, followed by Elida and Thelma.

'Hah! Caught ya!' screeched Rikki, pouncing on them like a bat out of the shadows. Elida and Thelma flew out, crooning, flapping about in their dressing gowns like mad witches attacking secretive Christians.

Rhys knew perfectly well that Rikki had imagined she was going to catch them out at something much more interesting than praying. He edged a little closer to Penny.

'Oh, you're too sweet!' shrieked Elida and Thelma quickly.

'Wouldn't you just know it? On top of everything else Rhys is religious. That is *soooo* beautiful,' cried Rikki.

'*Soooo* beautiful praying together,' echoed Elida. 'You should come channelling with us, you'd *love* it.'

'Oh *no*,' said Rhys in horror. 'That's against my religion!'

Penny lifted her head like a startled fawn and looked rather flustered as if they really had been doing something disreputable.

'Penny, Ethan is all alone and wondering if you will go and play with him,' snapped Rikki. Clearly, they had not looked *that* beautiful together. Poor old St Penny got up and shuffled out, murmuring, 'Of course, Mrs Lancaster.'

'Rhys, I am so excited about tonight,' said Mrs Rikki Lancaster, rubbing up against him like a frail old Siamese cat.

'So am I, Duchess,' Rhys told her, rather harshly for him, actually, as he snuffed out the candle and cleared it away. Penny's retreat had been so hasty that she had left everything all over the place.

'We came to tell you that your costume has arrived from

Ashby and we're all just dying to get a look at you in it. So come on, now, get in the tub. . . .'

'Get in the tub,' repeated Elida, 'rubadubtub. . . .'

'Yeah, yeah, yeah, get in the tub, get dressed and we'll all meet for cocktails in the lobby. Elida, where exactly did you put Rhys's costume?'

'Oh, it's right here, Rikki.'

'Into our costumes, then. Come on, girls, let's get looo. .oow,' and with that the Waxworks squawked off through the communicating door, chattering away as they went through one room, then another, finally reaching the stick hive, their voices echoing back to Rhys like exotic jungle animals, their laughter reaching hyena level.

Rhys took one look at the mound of parcels which constituted his costume and decided the time had come to take a rain check on his entire drug supply. He went to the bathroom and rummaged around in his sponge bag – 'his face' as Lady Dinah called it – until he found his La Prairie eye cream in which he had stashed the four Ecstasy capsules. Clutching his 'face' to him, he swaggered back to the bedroom with confidence, dumping it down on the table next to his lump of hash which was masquerading as a matchbox. Next stop was the minibar, patron saint of all indulgent travellers, where he poured himself a large vodka. Tonight, he whispered to himself, I am going on a complete bender. No-one will notice since, God knows, my costume is going to create enough of a disturbance without any outside help.

Setting down his drink beside the drugs department he started planning his agenda. It was now six-thirty. He would be washed and dressed by seven, in the bar downstairs by seven-fifteen. The party started with dinner at eight followed by the competition. So it would be a joint and a vodka before bathtime followed at nine minutes past seven precisely by the first Ecstasy which would begin to take effect just as they were finishing the first course at dinner.

Perfect.

Ideal.

The rest of dinner would pass in a fair state of tranquillity and with coffee he would embark on his second Ecstasy plus a quiet joint in the courtyard to help him prepare for the fruit trolley fiasco. By this time he hoped to be sufficiently projected into the upper stratosphere so as not to notice the ghastly humiliation. For all he knew, by that stage, he might even feel quite like being a Fruit Plate.

I wish Peach could be here, he thought to himself as he set about rolling five joints, laying out a production line of papers, filling each one with tobacco from a cigarette, beginning really rather to enjoy himself. Who knows what my earning capacity might go up to considering the hit I have already made with old Budleigh Salterton – I mean Ashby de la Zouche – or both. There must be pushovers like him all over the place. They'll be mine for the asking. That is if I'm in a fit state to be receiving. I wish Hennie were here. I could just send them over to her.

How like the Brigadier he looked as he organised his joints with military precision and prepared his kit-bag. He ran his bath, downed the vodka and lit the first joint in the tub, relaxing for a few minutes. He pictured the inevitable *Women's Wear Daily* coverage.

Rhys Waveral, who has been absent from our screens for some time, appeared as a bowl of fruit and danced with his fiancée, the slender Mrs Lancaster, who came as a . . . VERY LONG THIN WINDY CARROT.

Rhys shaved with care, rose from the bath and reeled towards the basin. A vodka at bathtime could be quite effective.

As he looked in the mirror, donning his new Rikki-style underwear, he started singing his version of his favourite bit from *Gypsy*.

'I thought you did it for me, Mother. I thought you did it for me! I thought you made a no-talent slob into a star because you liked doing things the hard way . . . *and you have no talent*, not what I call talent. . . .' and so on.

Thoroughly roused by this rendition – rather a good impersonation of Rosalind Russell, actually – he swanned over to the costume department with the joint in one hand and a freshly poured vodka splashing about in the other.

'What I got inside of me . . .' he sang away in his *lully* new boxers, 'WHAT I GOT INSIDE OF ME . . . there wouldn't be lights bright enough, there wouldn't be signs high enough. . . .'

He tore away at Ashby's brown paper packages like a spoiled brat on the rampage under the Christmas tree, desperate to find the key to the new Porsche parked outside.

Instead of a Porsche he found his silver tights and his Fruit Plate tutu and clumsily clambered into them. *Whoops*, and the joint burned a hole in the tighties!

Actually the Plate was painted rather prettily with bunches of grapes and oranges and there was a marvellous concealed pocket for him to hide everything in. He walked tentatively towards the bathroom – to practise walking – feeling a bit like an ice-cream girl sauntering down the aisle of a cinema before the main feature.

The telephone disturbed his reverie. He tried to sit down as he picked up the receiver and discovered that he had to make a vertical descent rather like a flying saucer which was quite exhausting for his wimpy little calves and thighs. God, he thought, they'll be a shaking wreck by the end of the evening.

'Hellooo!' he trilled into the phone, forgetting to stop being the choc-ice girl.

'Rhysling bitch, *c'est moi*, Peach Delight. I have something to tell you. . . .'

And then the line went dead. He lurched off back to the bathroom. He wondered what could be the matter with Peach. She was probably in trouble. Damn! He always knew she'd end up floating face down in the Seine. Oh dear! Back to Gypsy.

'Here she comes, boys, here she comes, world,' he sang.

Five minutes past seven. Four minutes to zero hour. What could Peach want? Why had she been cut off?

He strapped on the fruit jacket – peaches, pears, pineapples

185

and oranges – not very exotic. Still, he'd make up for that himself.

'Mamma's doing fine . . . mamma's doing fine. . . .' he sang as he fitted on the banana hat. He grappled with the bow and squeezed into his silver pumps. 'My dear, you've got the legs of a very old showgirl,' he whined to himself, but he didn't really care. With everything assembled, he took one brief look in the mirror. 'What a way to make a living!' he grumbled, feeling the sooner he was semi-conscious the better.

All he could think of was the La Prairie eye cream and its hidden secrets. Getting through the bathroom door in his costume was extremely hazardous. He had to bend this way and that and frequently lost his balance. The flying saucer landed vertically on the sofa. He opened the La Prairie eye cream with shaking hands and promptly had a heart attack. The pills, all in time-release capsules, had melted and the normally white cream was yellow with toxic . . . *waste*!

What a waste!

Oh no, thought poor Rhys as he plunged his fingers in and started to suck the cream off them, there's bound to be something fatal in La Prairie eye cream that's going to kill me. Nevertheless, he consumed what he reckoned to be a quarter of the jar and then slipped the rest between the two sides of the Fruit Plate. His mouth and throat immediately felt like an oil slick.

Poor Dorita felt sick. And also very stupid.

Why didn't I think of this, he thought, as he squeezed through the door into the corridor.

It was seven-thirteen.

He checked his hidey hole for the evening's special effects. Everything was in place and Lady Beth Fraser, holder of the Fruit Plate, minced off to the lift, and her future.

Not to mention the outstanding fifty thousand dollars.

Or maybe all sorts of other exciting bonuses she'd never even dreamed of.

CHAPTER TWENTY-ONE: in which nothing much
   happens again

The lobby of the Saunders Hotel was awash with fruit. Hordes
of international trash revellers were converging, all dressed as
pineapples and peaches, Fruit Punches and Banana Splits.
   Rhys suddenly experienced a rush of drug-induced paranoia
and nearly fainted coming down the rather grand staircase into
the old-style Moroccan colonial hall. To top it all he slightly lost
his balance and went out of control like a car with a burst tyre.
He accelerated and for one hideous moment it looked as if he
would collide headlong into the fruity revellers. At the last
moment he managed to swerve and hurtled round the corner

behind the stairs to collapse in a chair. All his fruit was concertinaed as the Fruit Plate rose to chin level. Rather slowly he recovered from his anxiety attack.

After ten minutes – ten minutes late on his precious agenda – he lifted off in his flying saucer and made his way to the bar.

Rikki and Elida were dressed as wild vines growing on a wall. Their bodies were the twiggy branches and out of the branches shot leaves and grapes. On her head she wore a turban clustered with grapes. At their feet the vine turned to roots disappearing into the ground. Their hairstyles looked as if two potted plants had fallen on them from a first-floor window. Underneath the Bacchanalian forest of leaves he could just discern their eyes and mouths.

Having seen Rhys, they were now waving madly. Two poor old vines in a force eight gale, branches and leaves everywhere. Poor old Thelma was dressed relatively simply by comparison, as a strawberry. Since he was three feet in diameter a path cleared automatically for Rhys to make his way through the crowd.

'Look at that fruit salad. Bravo! Bravo!'

By the time he reached them his anxiety attack had returned but he took a firm grip on himself and pushed it firmly down.

'Whaddya drinkin', Dolrita?' slurped Thelma with a friendly wink.

'Give him a small port!' screamed Rikki and Elida in unison, just as they done all those years ago (for so it seemed) in the Voltaire Restaurant in Paris. To Rhys's horror they then continued with their pagan ritual.

'Gimme five,' screamed Rikki, shaking her heavily jewelled branch.

'Gimme ten,' screamed Elida, and then together, their peals of laughter soaring above the noise of the crowd causing other fruit to turn and stare at them, they rose to, 'Gimme fifteen!'

'And gimme a break!' said Thelma, sliding off her bar stool on to the floor.

'So how are we getting there?' she asked from her resting place. 'Hand me down my drink, Rhys honey.'

'On Ecstasy and several large spliffs, my dear, how else?' Rhys turned to Rikki. 'How are we getting there, darling?' putting his arm casually, yet intimately around her wall. She responded by leaning over his plate – three feet wide on either side – and trying to snuggle up to him. In her own pathetic effort at intimacy she promptly lost her balance and leaned heavily on poor Dorita who lost his as well.

'I've rented a minibus for us all. You don't need to worry, Elida, I've thought of everything. Darling, would you get me a gin fizz please? Just one before blast off.'

'Gin fizz? All right, darling,' said Rhys softly into Rikki's ear. He had decided to turn on his seductometer. Strangely enough it was much easier for him to imagine being with her when she was dressed as a vine. Maybe it was because he was stoned, but Rhys warmed to the idea of making love with a wood nymph, a mad tree spirit from an Arthur Rackham drawing.

He bought everyone another round and sensibly drank a Perrier himself. He was feeling warm all over with not a care in the world. He was looking forward to everything. Rikki was looking more enticing by the minute and Rhys was arriving at that part in his 'E' trip where he definitely needed to hold hands. Touch flesh. He would have preferred someone else's but Rikki's was going to have to do. His favourite thing was kneading and pummelling someone's hand while he was high. He took Rikki's hand gently in his and felt her shiver up and down like a xylophone. He started massaging her fingers and he must have got carried away because she began to look at him with worried concern all over her face.

'Gently, dear, gently,' and then she turned to him and whispered seductively, 'I can see I'm gonna have to teach you a thing, or two, rough guy.'

'Everything!' said Rhys dramatically. He put his arm around her and promptly got caught up in the foliage. Rikki tensed.

Mercifully she was distracted by the arrival of Penny and Ethan. Rhys observed that Penny had not exactly made an effort. She was dressed in a mauve silk dress. Ethan, however, for reasons best known to himself, had dressed up as a Roman centurion.

'Mom,' he whined, 'can I have a gin fizz too?'

'OK, honey, but only one so you'd better make it last. Rhys, dear, get Ethan a gin fizz, would ya?'

'Sure,' said Roger Moore and he stroked her back, right down to her nibbly little buttocks where there was a branch sticking out. He was just about to start stroking Ethan's head, his need for physical contact growing rather alarmingly by the minute. He thought better of that one, however, when Ethie landed him one in the stomach.

'Ethan, you're going to have to drink that down very fast 'cause we're leaving in like five minutes,' said his ever-vigilant mother as Rhys handed superbrat the glass into which he would have been very tempted to slip an Ecstasy (if he'd had one) to see what would happen.

The hall was beginning to empty as all the fruit dispersed into buses and taxis to set forth up the mountain. Rather like a curtain going up, the crowd disappeared to reveal the entire cricket club sitting in a row like wallflowers.

None of them wore fancy dress. Goodbuns was immaculate in white tie while the rest of them sported black tie. The women all appeared to be in black, too, including Little Beige Riding Hood who was dressed as Anastasia, the missing Tsarina, except that her version was chillingly Frinton Rep, thought Rhys. Bellows-Forth looked just like a hit man.

She must have slaved for years over a hot mirror to pluck, tweak and blow-dry that act into position. One breath of wind and she'll be completely undone. Rhys raised his glass at his peer group across the hall.

'Hello darlings,' he mouthed. They in turn, with great restraint and queenly dignity, raised their champagne glasses.

Thelma the strawberry was trying to get up off the floor and making the most extraordinary noise in the process.

'Thelma, what in hell are you doing?' enquired the Sticks.

'Thelma, what on earth are you doing?' enquired Rhys.

'I'm doin' a raspberry in both places,' rasped Thelma.

'Well, kindly stop,' warned Rikki, 'please try to remember that we are ambassadresses for our country.'

'Shambassadresses, ya mean,' replied Thelma with an evil

cackle. Rhys could see that she was out for a scrappy evening. It was clearly a friendship fraught with much hidden jealousy and unspoken rebukes. Elida's face was deeply agitated as she looked from one to the other as if to see who would crack whose jaw first.

But the two women just stared at each other like two dogs. For about fifty seconds. Then eventually the Duchess, looking daggers, said, 'Not tonight, Thelma, not tonight.'

And Thelma, with great difficulty, pulled herself up to full strawberry position.

Waving *au revoir* to the cricket club, they bumped out to the minibus with the strawberry, the Fruit Plate, the Roman centurion and the mauve silk nanny following behind.

CHAPTER TWENTY-TWO: in which Rhys goes to the
   Exotic Fruit Ball

Tangiers had never seen the like – a minibus trundling through
the town with rows of grinning faces pressed to the windows.
And as the bus climbed higher the suburban hills were alive to
the sound of caterwauling from inside.

Dorita was flying. He looked around him at Thelma and
Penny and Ethan, and his heart, pumping away, overflowed
with joy. He burst into song.

'How do you solve a problem like Maria?' he chanted from
his favourite musical as the bus lurched over potholes on its way
up the old mountain.

'How do you catch a cloud and pin it down?' Thelma joined in. 'How do you solve a problem like Maria?' they both sang and looked blank. Neither of them knew the next line.

Moroccan cyclists swerved in desperation to avoid collision with the singing fruit. The passing scenery seemed to Rhys like back projection upon which the others had been superimposed. In his delirium everyone seemed to be floating outside of reality. He blinked to make sure he wasn't dreaming. He wasn't. He went on singing.

'But how do you make her stay – and listen to what you say?'

Soon the Lancaster minibus turned off the main road and infiltrated itself into a traffic jam of other cars on their way to the de la Zouche party. Rhys lay back for a moment, breathing deeply, and closed his eyes. The air from outside was fresh and cold and the other voices faded away as if they were coming from the other end of a long corridor.

'Doesn't Paris seem ages away,' he murmured to himself. He could feel little beads of sweat foraging their way through his pores and gurgling their way out on to his skin. He could feel light breezes across his nerve endings that made the little blond hairs on his arms wave around like corn in the changing wind. He could even feel the beginning of a mammoth hangover brewing like a distant storm somewhere at the back of his mind and he liked that.

Suddenly a little slice of strawberry shortcake was winging her way back from the other end of the corridor in his dream to blast in his ear.

'Wake up, honey, we're here.' Thelma!

The little Moroccan driver opened the sliding door and the torrent of festive fruit poured out into the crowd of party-goers, their faces filled with anticipation, eyes darting here and there looking for the first friend to whom they could show off their costumes. Rhys had considerable difficulty negotiating his plate through the door of the minibus but then a push from Thelma Romanelli sent him flying into the fruit salad.

At that point he noticed the rather frisky Moroccan slave he had met on his last visit to Ashby beckoning to him.

'Excuse me a minute, darlings,' he murmured.

The boy was rather hard to reach since by this stage they were separated by a river of swimming fruit as more and more guests arrived. He was going to need a new Fruit Plate before the party had even begun at this rate. His own had become severely crumpled. But the frisky slave beckoned again and said, 'Please, come this way. Mr de la Zouche would like to see you. Your friends will be looked after.' He took Rhys's hand and led him through the little door in the wall and on and on until Rhys found himself in the same long, narrow passage. Inside Ashby's passage, he mused as he strained to get his Fruit Plate through the narrow door. Frisky was skipping on ahead and Rhys nearly fell over in his endeavour to keep up since he had to run sideways like a crab to accommodate his plate. They went through the door at the end of the passage and there, standing in front of a blazing fire, resplendent in purple, was Frutta di Bosca de la Zouche and . . .

Dumpling Hines.

Rhys gasped.

'Y'all simply have to do something, Dumpling,' Frutta di Bosca was whining as he paced up and down in front of the fire, a mountain of blueberries and blackberries.

'I don't really know what I can do,' replied the typically despondent voice of Dumpling Hines.

'Well, he's your client, isn't he?' screeched Ashby, turning on poor Dumpling and waving his Peter Stuyvesant perilously close to Rhys's agent's face.

'Yes, I know he's my client, but this is not a strictly professional appearance,' replied the deferential Dump.

'Hah!' snorted Ashby, flicking his ash on to the floor. 'You said it, not me.'

Rhys could see that the two men were so involved in whatever drama they were discussing that neither of them had noticed him. Quietly, he slipped over to a sixteenth-century prayer stool in a darkened corner and knelt down. In the hearth the enormous fire crackled and spat just as they did in old movies about the Normans in their giant halls, shooting light and shadow about the room like a huge hose. Or so it appeared to Dorita, closet

Knight of the Round Table. He was dumbstruck as the scene between his agent and Frutta di Bosca played in front of the fire. Their silhouettes threw huge shadows across the room like a mad puppet show. God only knew what spanner had been thrown into the works to provide a reason for Dumpling being there in the first place.

'Wilbur is *your* client,' repeated Ashby madly.

Wilbur?

'I'm well aware that he's my client, Ashby darling, but I was not aware that he was being brought out here in his professional capacity.' Rhys could see that Dumpling was furious. Whenever his speech became really slow it meant he was in a very bad mood. 'But if he is here in his professional capacity . . .' Dumpling went on . . . 'then I would remind you that his stage name, to which he responds on all professional . . .' and by now good old Dumpling was almost spitting out the words . . . 'engagements is . . .'

Then something terrible happened. Dumpling couldn't remember the name of his client. He took on so many in the course of a week – his motto being 'Many hams make light work' – that without the help of his assistant, the Flower Fairy, he was hard-pushed to remember the names of even his old faithfuls when he saw them at funerals. He hummed and hah'ed for a few moments, mumbling, 'Where are you, Flower Fairy, when I need you?'

'I thought we had agreed on Lewis for this particular engagement,' snapped Ashby through his snake lips.

'Was that it?' said Dumpling, as if he couldn't have cared less. He took a bunch of capsules from his pocket and proceeded to pop them into his mouth.

'That ulcer again,' breathed Saint Dorita of the prayer stool as she knelt in her corner.

Then someone new walked into the room. He was young and blond and strong and preppy. He had on a white shirt and a pair of flannel trousers. For some reason the boy's appearance provoked the most extraordinary reaction in Ashby. He began to hop up and down in rage. His berries threatened to burst and send blueberry and blackberry juice spurting all over poor Dumpling. Ashby pointed at the boy and screamed, 'Look at you! *Just look at you!*'

'I'm not going to do it, I'm sorry,' said the poor young man, in a shaky voice with an American accent.

'But you must,' shrieked Ashby, waving his arms in the air.

Rhys felt as though he'd stumbled on a voodoo mass in the middle of the jungle. I think this is the bit where I make my entrance, he thought. He rose from the prayer stool, arranged his Plate and moved on to the stage.

'NOW LOOK HERE, EVERYONE . . .' he bellowed in his best Girl Guide's voice.

The three actors on stage froze.

'Anyway,' said Dorita, suddenly at a loss. 'I've arrived. I'm Rhys Waveral,' he said to the young blond, shaking hands, 'otherwise known as Miss Fruit Plate.' He moved over to Ashby. 'Frutta, my dear, you are looking simply marvellous. Accept the gracious homage from your sister Fruit Plate,' and Rhys threw out his arms over his Plate and hugged the bewildered Ashby before turning to Dumpling.

'Why did you tell me *Love in the Desert* had been cancelled, you ridiculous man, when here it is going on right underneath my very nose?' Once an actor always an actor.

'Oh, you know, I was *Reelin' and Rockin', Reelin' and Rockin',*' said a now severely crushed Dumpling. 'Can't you even say hello?'

Rhys considered this for a moment. 'No,' he said sharply, 'I can't. You're just too stupid. Now,' he continued turning on the group as a whole, 'what *is* going on?'

The Fruit Plate costume seemed to have turned him into Mary Poppins. The three men gaped at Rhys, still in shock at his arrival, and even more so at his manner. 'What's the matter? Cat got your tongues?' In the silence that followed they could hear the party going on in the distance. From their inner sanctum it sounded like a palace revolution.

'Wilbur refuses to put on his costume,' said Ashby finally. He threw his cigarette into the fire and stalked out of the room, slamming the door behind him as he went. Dumpling wailed inanities, rushing out after him. 'Don't go.'

197

'It's like a Greek tragedy in here every day,' said the well-spoken preppy after a short pause.

'Well, my dear, the one thing to remember about Greek tragedy is that almost all the dramatic scenes happen off stage,' giggled the Fruit Plate.

As if on cue, the voices of Ashby and Dumpling could be heard screaming at each other from the floor above.

'To be honest, I don't really understand what's going on,' said Rhys.

'Well, nor do I,' mumbled the young man.

'What's your name, anyway?'

'Like he said. Wilbur. They want me to dress up as a fruit salad or something but I said to them, "I'm just not like that, I couldn't do it, that kind of thing really embarrasses me."'

'Oh, I'm used to it,' laughed Dorita cheerfully. 'I was cross-dressing at the age of two. I could dress up before I could stand up. But I know what you mean. It can be very embarrassing. Were you paid to come here?'

'Of course not,' blustered Wilbur.

'I'm only asking because, you know, I was and I thought if you were too it would have been more fun. That's all.' Rhys shrugged hopefully. 'Would you like half an Ecstasy?' He produced the La Prairie eye cream and offered a fingerful to Wilbur.

''Scuse my fingers,' he said, sticking his pinkie into Wilbur's mouth.

'Isn't this face cream or something?' spluttered Wilbur, trying to push Rhys's hand away.

'Was, my dear, was. Don't ask questions. Eat!'

'Oh, yes please,' said Rhys's new little chum. 'Who's paying you then,' he asked rather slyly, 'and for what?'

'A fiendish old woman dressed as a vine. She's at the party now. I was with her at the entrance and then suddenly I was swept away and found myself here. Still, it's been frightfully educational and the bliss of a moment away from one's client to put one's feet up! It's the endless talking that gets to one, listening to them all hammering on, driving their hideous knife-like voices and opinions into the centre of one's brain so that instead of going "Oooooh!" and "Oh, really?" one just wants to reach for one's handbag, take out one's revolver and shoot one's client dead. Right in the middle of the forehead. In cold blood. Self-preservation.'

Wilbur laughed nervously. 'This guy's a crank,' Rhys could hear him thinking. 'I don't normally act this way,' Rhys went on, 'it's just that my personality, such as it is, seems to have been profoundly influenced by this costume. That is to say, I have become Fruit Plate. When you see me again, you will not recognise me. So, I ask you again, how much are you getting paid?'

'Five thousand dollars,' replied the preppy.

'Hmmm. Not bad. Cash?'

'Cash.'

'In advance?'

'Fifty per cent up front. Fifty per cent after the weekend.'

'Hmmm. It sounds suspiciously like we have the same agent.' They both laughed. If Hines was a pimp, it would certainly account for why he was never in his office and yet still seemed to be very rich even though hardly any of his clients ever worked.

'Dumpling isn't my pimp, you know.'

'Oh, really! He's not your older sister up-from-the-country either.'

'What are you like?' asked Wilbur, not sure whether to be amused or annoyed by this interfering stranger.

'What are you like? What are you like?' Rhys mimicked. Wilbur laughed.

'Now, come on,' said Rhys, 'go and get changed. I'm fucked if I'm going to be the only one on the fucking float with the old boiler. So put on your costume. Go on. You'll be stoned now that you've had your little "E", you won't notice what a cunt you're making of yourself.'

'Are you aware that you are talking about a part of my body?' a slurred voice suddenly echoed out of the shadows.

The two boys strained their eyes through the gloom to see who was there. A large strawberry blob emerged. Thelma Romanelli, dangerously drunk. She was clearly out for a fight. Her eyes had a 'Confront me' look.

'My dear, I didn't know you had one,' said Dorita.

'I got one, all right, but it's healed over.' Thelma sat down on the floor and rolled over on her side.

'All for the best, I'd say, Thel darling. Where are the others?'

'The others? Nowhere. They're . . . nowhere.' She giggled and the giggle became a groan which in turn drifted into a snore.

'What a relief. Alcohol to the rescue again. Now let's go and get you into your costume.'

And Rhys and Wilbur escaped the great hall, leaving a huge, beached strawberry lying in front of the fire.

CHAPTER TWENTY-THREE: in which Rhys discovers there's no such thing as Never Again

Wilbur's costume turned out to be identical to Rhys's except that it was covered in rubber cream.

'So we're nothing more than glorified bookends,' commented Rhys as he strapped his new friend into his fruit jacket.

'Obviously he wouldn't want to share centre stage,' sneered Wilbur. 'He is, after all, the most egocentric person in the entire world.'

'The second most, actually,' said Rhys. 'Rikki Lancaster is the unqualified winner in that category, my dear, I can assure you.'

'Whoooo,' said Wilbur, exhaling deeply, 'I think it's kickin' in.'

'So much the better,' laughed Dorita. 'Now you might get your wits about you and not be a disgrace to your profession as you were, I'm afraid to say, earlier on. One thing you must remember: the punter is always right. Anyway, I think this outfit brings out a whole new side to you.'

The two new friends looked at themselves in the large mirror across the room.

'The worst side!' they sang in unison, and laughed.

'If only being a page-boy at weddings had been this much fun,' sighed Dorita, who had thoroughly enjoyed being one in his day.

'Page-boys on acid,' said Wilbur and curtseyed. 'I suppose we should go and find the others.'

'I suppose you're right. I really ought to find Rikki.'

'Wait a second . . . we can't,' said Wil. 'Ashby doesn't want anyone to see him or the fruit trolley before the grand entrance. So, forget your own life for a while and come and eat.'

They walked out into the corridor and caught a glimpse of the party going on through a half-open window.

'They all look so frenzied, don't they?' said Wilbur.

'Ridiculous,' agreed Rhys, noticing that the Waxworks were still paralytic with laughter. 'There's mine,' he said, pointing out the Duchess who just happened, at that very moment, to be examining a large bogey she had just picked out of her nose.

'Gee!' exclaimed Wilbur, 'Is she eating bogeys? I don't know which one of us has the worst job.'

'My dear, six of one and half a dozen of the other, I should say. They are both more or less unspeakable. Mind you, I did see Ashby in a pair of very tight briefs and he looked as though he was hung like a donkey.'

'Yeah, tell me about it,' said Wilbur. 'He's always trying to take me by surprise with it but I say "No way". It's not on the menu. He'll have to move on to the *à la carte* section before he gets that.'

'Before *you* get it, you mean . . . You'd better put in for danger money.'

'Still, if the price is right . . .' said Wilb, loosening up by the minute.

'What are you like?' whined Dorita, like a London queen.

'What's this party like, you mean?' replied Wilbur.

The entire courtyard, some fifty yards square, had been covered by white tents, all swathed in Moroccan fabrics. There were white poles to hold up the tents smothered in clusters of psychedelic fake fruit. Down the sides under Ashby's cloisters were large round tables. In the middle was a huge dance floor with a curtain at the back through which the fruit trolley would undoubtedly be wheeled. A Moroccan band in white pyjamas and red sashes played for the international fruit salad dancing away. There seemed to be thousands of them and the two boys couldn't help noticing that there seemed to be very few people under forty in the room.

'It looks like we're the youngest – by at least fifteen years,' said Rhys as they slipped back inside the harem area.

Dinner for the Fruit Plate contingent and their agent was to take place in a small room off Ashby's bedroom.

It was a fairly tense affair. Ashby was drunk. The strain of the day was beginning to show and he was morose and catty during the meal.

'You have bathed in mah admiration for too long, young man,' he told Wilbur, 'like a naked man under a sun-ray lamp. But now that lamp is bein' switched off. Snapped off, if you please. Maybe you will live to regret the pain you have caused me today. Dignitaries the world over have gathered here tonight to witness this occasion – the cream of international society.'

'Dairy products. Frightfully bad for one,' said Rhys in defence of his new friend who appeared to be speechless in the presence of his patron.

'Don't y'all try to joke around with me. Remember y'all are a guest in my house.'

'Guest or prisoner,' continued Rhys, whose dislike for Ashby was growing by the second. 'And frankly, my dear Ashby, I would never try to joke around with you. Any joke that I could tell would fall flat on its face in the shadow of your own deep and global sense of humour.'

'Ashby can be frightfully funny, I can vouch for that,' mumbled Dumpling.

'Shut up, you stupid pimp,' snapped Rhys. 'Anyway, when is the fateful fruit trolley being launched on the party?'

Ashby cheered up at the mention of his precious ball and became quite animated again. While he droned on about the interminable arrangements for the horror show he had planned, Rhys dived into his Fruit Plate hidey hole and extracted a dollop of Ecstasy from his treasure chest.

'Have you ever had a heart condition, Ashby?' he murmured.

'What? Oh, no, no, never. Anyway, what we do next is. . . .'

'Good,' said our hero and the next time Ashby wasn't looking he smeared the cream into the great decorator's dessert glass.

Suddenly he was aware of Dumpling watching him.

'Fuck off!' Dorita said simply.

'What language your client uses, Dumpling,' Ashby snorted.

'I am no longer his client, Ashby. A mortician would make a better agent than Dumpling.'

'Certainly a more appropriate one for you, Rhys dear, since, after all, you are dead,' said Dumpling in a rare flare up. 'Dead all over.'

Rhys ignored him. 'Ashby, the thing is, I really need a new Fruit Plate, mine's dead, as my former agent was quite rightly pointed out, and one doesn't want to let you down. I know how important all this is to you.'

'There's another Plate in the bedroom. C'mon, ah'll show you.'

In Ashby's giant Cecil B. de Mille bedroom another Plate lay propped up in the corner.

'I'm so enjoying myself,' said Rhys, jumping with verve into his new Plate. 'What time is showtime?'

'In about fifteen minutes,' said Ashby and left the room.

Half an hour later Ashby, Rhys and Wilbur were standing on a huge trolley about six feet high. On the other side of the enormous curtain that divided the courtyard the party roared like the noise of a railway station. It appeared to be going terribly well. Rhys peeped through a tear in the curtain and spied practically everyone he knew. His mother, 'Pepsi', 'Shirlee', Sir Maurice talking animatedly with Rikki, Bob Browser chatting with a

Moroccan slave like a hawk swooping on a poor, succulent young rabbit and over in a corner, Ethan and Nanny-Penny.

'What a life,' thought Rhys.

Someone had put up a ladder to the trolley and Ashby started to climb. Now he was completely out of his head.

'Once more unto the breach, dear friends,' he hollered, grabbing Wilbur in the crotch at the same time.

'I'm quite sure Henry V never did anything like that,' said Rhys.

'Come on, you rascals, get up here and show me what you've got.' Ashby was unstoppable now.

Getting up a ladder in a Fruit Plate was no easy job. No amount of training in beauty school had prepared him for this particular speciality but Dorita, a seasoned pro, managed to carry it off with reasonable aplomb.

Wilbur, on the other hand, had much more difficulty. Pumped up with the other half of the Ecstasy, he was all over the place – including Rhys's tights. Finally they all managed to position themselves on the trolley. Ashby in the middle, of course, and the two hustlers on either side. Ashby put his arms around his two boys.

'Ah have never been surrounded bah such beauty, y'all. Ah do declare, ah want to touch y'all all night.' He was looking from one to the other waiting to see who would scream 'Me first!' His face, an astonishing sight, covered in purple make-up, came close to Dorita's. Then he leaned over to Wilbur and, horror of horrors, started to kiss him.

As luck would – or would not – have it, at this point the lights on either side went down and the sinister hiss of dry ice machines anounced to anyone in a reasonably organised frame of mind that the show was about to begin. Sure enough the curtain opened and the trolley wobbled out. The pilgrim's theme from *Tannhauser* blared from the loudspeakers and the stage area was suddenly flooded with light. Ashby, however, seemed completely unaware of the fact that he had made his grand entrance and continued in his ghoulish embrace.

Poor preppy Wilbur looked absolutely horrified, his eyes bulging in panic, his face red with indignation and embarrassment.

Ashby had all but swallowed his whole face like a phython starting on his breakfast. Dorita tapped Ashby sharply on the shoulder. To no avail. Ashby was off. The crowd, who had emitted a collective 'Ooooooo' when they saw the smoke enshrouded trolley arrive, began to shrink away in horror. This was not the tasteful, discreet Ashby de la Zouche, decorator to the rich and tasteless, that they all knew. Mercifully, the music form *Tannhauser* saved them from the sound show, which consisted of slurps and 'Aaaarghs!' from Wilbur and '*I wanna eat y'all's face*' from De la Zouche. As the lights became stronger Rhys too became a little self-conscious, wallflower that he had turned out to be.

Then everything started to happen at once. Wilbur managed to extricate himself from Ashby and hurled back his arm to punch his patron in the stomach. Luckily Dorita saw it coming and picked up Ashby just in time to save him from the blow – only to receive it himself. Wilbur's punch landed square in poor Fruit Plate's abdomen, sending his breath flying. His brain, already crowded with so many substances, went into freeze-frame and he remembered something he had not thought about for a very long time. It was New Year's Eve, 1979. . . .

He was dancing with Dorinda Carr Smiley at the Embassy Club. By now she was up to her eyeballs in drugs and it would not be long before she handed herself in – rather like a walking piece of lost property – to Alcoholics Anonymous, and began the upward struggle back into daylight. In fact, although the two friends didn't know it, the evening was to be a kind of adieu, the final gory scene before the curtain fell on that rather louche production – their youth.

At this point, however, they were blissfully unaware of what was to come and were dancing like zombies, shiny with sweat, eyes pinned like cats'. On the way to the bathroom, decked out in his new white satin skin-tight trousers, Rhys bumped into a client. He was a rather sleazy type called Derek in a black suit and a white shirt open to the waist.

'What you doin' later, Rex?' asked the client.

'Don't know,' answered 'Rex', wondering what on earth had induced him to choose that name and what accent was meant to go with it. He hadn't much liked this client when he had been with him before so he moved on. But there was more to come.

'I'm with my wife and her girlfriend. We fancied a foursome. We've got some good coke, too. What d'you say?'

'Well, if you've got forty quid. . . .' said Rhys, hoping to outprice himself. The man sniffed a bit and Rhys noticed that his nose was rather red.

'Prices gone up a bit, have they, eh?' he said, rubbing his red honker.

'Well, you know how it is, group bookings. . . .' answered 'Rex'. 'Think about it. I'll be on the dance floor,' and he continued on his way.

Half an hour later, back on the floor with Dorinda Carr Smiley, Rhys felt a tap on his shoulder.

'We're leaving. You coming?' said the sleazy man. Dorinda looked at him as if he were a bit of smelly old fish.

'OK,' said Rhys. 'See you outside in three minutes.'

'Who on *earth* is that?' asked Dorinda as they left the dance floor.

'Friends,' said young Rhys evasively.'

'Acting people?'

'Yes, acting people, Dorinda. We're going to discuss a project. So goodnight, darling, I'll call you tomorrow.'

Derek was waiting outside in his car, one of those snazzy penis extension types. There were two girls in the back and introductions were made. One girl was called Beverly and the other Karen. Apart from their names they were more or less indistinguishable from each other, both sporting long frazzled blonde hair, mascara-caked eyelashes, noses like little King Charles spaniels' and quivering pink lips. They were also steaming drunk and giggled all the way to Derek's 'pad' in cosmopolitan Swiss Cottage.

'You won't recognise my pad. It's been done over since the last time you were there,' said Derek as they zoomed past the

Centrale Kontiki Drama School, from which Rhys had only recently been expelled.

'Oh, right,' said Rhys in his 'Rex' voice rather meaninglessly.

In the flat drinks were fixed, Barry White was shoved on the record player and the lights were dimmed. The flat was now a festival of brown suede and beige rugs and frosted wall-to-ceiling mirrors. Things had obviously been going rather well for Derek and as if to celebrate this he produced a large packet of coke which he proceeded to empty on to his mirror-topped coffee table. 'Oh, no, not more!' squeaked the girls as they held back their long hair and snorted their way through one of Derek's crisp new fifty pound notes.

'Where's the toilet?' asked Rhys.

'Oh, I'll just show you,' said Beverly, whom Rhys imagined to be the wife. She took him into the bedroom where Barry White was still crooning from hidden speakers. The decor was much the same as the lounge. Rhys disappeared into the bathroom and Beverly sat on the bed.

'Did you enjoy yourself this evening, then?' she asked. Rhys looked down at his cock, unable to piss with a stranger at such close quarters. When he emerged from the bathroom, Beverly was still there but now she was down to her bra and pants. Her stomach bulged out over her undies and her rather large tits overflowed out of her tiny black bra.

'Come over here, sweetie,' she purred. So over he went. They kissed for a moment and then without further ado she shoved his head down past the quivering jellies to the heart of the matter, and kept it there for what seemed like hours.

It was in this position that they were discovered by Derek and Karen who appeared in the doorway, clutching one another as if they could no longer walk on their own. Derek was brandishing a bottle of Scotch in one hand. Beverly gasped when she saw them. Rhys looked up and Beverly pushed him off, screaming, 'My husband! He's home.' She ran over to him, terrified.

'So you couldn't wait, could you, you fucking hustler. Is this how you repay my hospitality? As soon as I'm not looking you're down there eating my wife's pussy, you dirty little wanker.'

'Listen, I don't understand, I thought I was meant. . . .' began

Rhys but, before he knew what was happening, Derek was striding over and picking him up by his hair. He hurled Rhys against a chest of drawers where he landed with a resounding thump. Rhys felt blood running down his cheek.

'OW!' Panic was suddenly coursing through his veins.

'I'll teach you to eat my wife's pussy,' Derek shouted as he lunged again and started systematically to kick Rhys towards the door where by now the two women were huddled together, sniggering.

'All right, rent boy, eat pussy. . . .' and he slapped poor Beverly square on the chops, picking up Rhys at the same time and jamming his face into Bev's stomach.

Oh dear, thought Rhys, this is all way over my head, and he tried to speak. 'I thought you wanted . . . aaaargh!'

'I'll tell you what I want, cunt, I want to see you lick my wife's cunt, that's what I want.'

Rhys tried to get up and make a run for it which was a fatal move because Derek suddenly went completely mad and smashed the bottle in his hand. There was blood on Beverly's stomach from the cut on Rhys's head and she started to scream when she saw it. Derek was clearly right out of control. Rhys abandoned his favourite leather jacket which was lying on the bed and barged past the two women. At the front door, as he fumbled with the complicated Banham locks, he turned and glimpsed the three of them standing in the doorway, eerily backlit from the bedroom, the man in black with the two courtesans. Over the strains of Barry White singing 'You're the one that I love,' they were laughing.

Laughing!

This is it, he thought, I'm going to be killed.

'Call yourself Rex, you wanker,' Derek was screaming. 'I know all about you, you snotty nosed git, Sir fucking Lancelot. Yeah, that's what you are, Sir nancy-fancy fuckin' bleedin' Lancelot. Want to rough it a bit, do yer? Well, you've come to the right place,' and he started to move towards the front door.

With one final effort Rhys managed to unlock the door and burst from the flat like the proverbial bat out of hell, leaping down the stairs two at a time.

It was to be his last professional engagement. On New Year's Day 1980, he had been fired from his drama school, which he passed once again, and now he had chucked in his evening job. In the freezing night air he walked all the way from Swiss Cottage to his home, past honking cars full of festive passengers. He was utterly crushed and frozen and miserable in his T-shirt and satin trousers.

'Never again,' he said he himself. 'I'll never be hit again.'

So much for 'Never again'. Poor Dorita was reeling but Ashby, delirious, seemed not to notice.

'Rhys, dahlin',' he leered, moving in for the kill.

'We should start the competition, shouldn't we?'

'Oh, I suppose you're right. We can pet later. Ladies and gentlemen. . . .' Ashby turned to the assembled company and the music cut out. 'Ladies and gentlemen,' he repeated.

Ah, here is the good old Ashby that we know and love, they all thought. There was a thunderous round of applause. Forgotten and forgiven were the recent indiscretions. A spotlight searched the room and landed jerkily on Ashby, leaving Rhys and Wilb completely in the shadows. In the cold remorseless tungsten, Ashby looked even madder than ever. The applause continued. He raised his arms. A mircrophone on a stand was handed up to him. Ashby grabbed it and suddenly his voice was a thousand times louder, reverberating round the hall.

'Ladies and gentlemen,' he said a third time. Now the applause had reached hysterical proportions, 'we have all gathered here to celebrate the Fruit Ball. . . .' Endless whoops and 'Attaboys' from the Lancaster party, which in turn set off the English contingent. From his perch on the trolley, Rhys watched everyone out of the corner of his eye.

Bob Broswer was laughing so much at Rhys's appearance it looked as if he was going to die and the Moroccan slave took this opportunity to escape.

'Pepsi' and 'Shirlee' began to scream, 'Go for it, Dorhys!' whereupon Lady Dinah joined the chorus in thick Hooray brogue with, 'Go for it, Dorita, show us some leg!' Resplendent in her long tartan skirt and her new peroxide hairdo, Rhys thought he had rarely seen her look so contented and he was happy to see the three women laughing away, waving their drinks, whispering to each other.

Ecstasy had rather played havoc with Ashby's timing and he droned on for what seemed like hours with his interminable speech. 'All the competitors should line up and they will be given numbers by the organisers. We, the fruit trolley, will cast our vote and the winners will take a round of victory with us on the trolley.'

Back came *Tannhauser* and all the various contenders rushed to the side of the room to queue up as if awaiting to be given their presents at a children's party. Ashby remained in his spotlight watching over the proceedings like Toad of Toad Hall. Rhys and Wilbur slipped away to smoke a well-earned joint in the other courtyard. It was peaceful underneath the sickle moon and the two boys were silent as they heaved away on the spliff, sitting on their haunches, surrounded by their Fruit Plates, like two giants astride flying saucers. The noise of the competition, the bursts of applause, the laughter and the chatter all seemed to disappear and as the moon shone over the little courtyard with its fountain in the middle, Rhys sensed for the first time that he was actually in another country and not just waiting in some mammoth first-class airport lounge.

'How long have you been on the game?' asked Wilbur, who looked solemn and beautiful in the moonlight.

'It feels like forever but actually since I was sixteen. What about you?'

'I'm not really on it. I just seem to have fallen into it this last year.'

'Just a gifted amateur, is that it?' asked Rhys, amused. The boy was a kind of innocent.

'I guess,' said Wilbur, a little sadly. 'It doesn't make me feel that good.'

'No, it never does in the end, but when you fall into something it's hard to fall out of it again. Unless you have enormous luck which, actually, I did have. I managed to grab a career as an actor which, of course, is just another form of prostitution. But then here I am again. Life seems to move in a series of extremely irritating circles.'

'If it was such a mistake, why do you do it again?' asked the naive boy, resting his head on the rim of Rhys's Plate. Rhys stroked his golden hair.

'My dear, the only thing one learns from one's mistakes is that one is surely going to repeat them. And, anyway, I always hope for the best. Maybe, just maybe, one will be able to withdraw oneself from the rat race at the last moment and settle down to something else. No low life, no hustling. No drugs. But to be honest, I don't feel that hopeful right now and anyway it would be so boring. You, on the other hand, have time on your side. You could stop. You haven't gone very far yet. There's still time. My life is catching up with me and it's a horrible feeling.'

'Hmmmm. . . .' said Wilbur, looking up into Rhys's solemn face.

'Hmmm. . . .' said Rhys, looking down into his new friend's. And so they went on.

Half an hour later they returned to the fruit trolley looking as if their Fruit Plates had been through a dishwasher. Ashby was even more hysterical than ever, dancing about on the trolley, waving his arms. He didn't seem to have noticed their absence.

'Now we must select the winner,' he said into his microphone, bopping about and grinding his pelvis. They seemed to have got down to some sort of semi-final since a row of ten hopefuls was lined up with their numbers pinned to them. Among the finalists were Rikki and Elida but Thelma Romanelli was arguing with an organiser, brandishing her number as if it were proof of something.

'I'm a finalist, you arsehole, I'm a finalist!' she was screaming.

'You are not,' screamed back Ashby from the trolley. 'Thelma Romanelli, leave the stage, y'all.'

'Y'all, y'all, y'all. . . .' slurped Thelma as she went back to the table.

The finalists were in line. A recorded drum-roll blasted from all the speakers. The spotlights flew from one contender to another like Tinkerbell and came to rest on a little podium erected by the fruit trolley. A scuffling could be heard behind the curtain and as the drum-roll grew deafeningly loud, a hand could be seen groping its way through the opening.

A very familiar hand, thought Rhys, as who should appear, still decked out in his overcoat, brolly and briefcase, but the Brigadier.

CHAPTER TWENTY-FOUR: in which who should appear
but the Brigadier

The crowd gasped. The Brigadier squinted into the spotlight.
Then Peach Delight appeared, immaculate in her little cocktail
dress, and the audience broke into thunderous applause.

So did Ashby de la Zouche.

'The winner, the winner!' he screamed demoniacally, jumping down from the fruit trolley with all his prizewinning medals
and hurrying past the ten finalists to the poor, bewildered Brigadier. Ashby ran up the steps to the podium, kissed first the
Brigadier and then the Peach on both cheeks, and proceeded to
hang around their necks the first and second prize ribbons.

'I hereby announce that the winner of the 1988 Fruit Ball is Blackberry and his companion, Crumpet.' He handed the Brig the microphone to say a few words.

Dim Waveral hadn't a clue what was going on. He appeared to have won something but he was blowed if he knew what it was. Still, it didn't do to let the side down and he was obviously requried to make some sort of speech. Luckily, he was never short of a few words and, indeed, travelled with a ready-made speech written out for just such an occasion. He groped in his pockets for it now as he cleared his throat and began to speak to the cheering fruits.

'Thank you, ladies and gentlemen, for this marvellous gesture. I have just arrived from Paris, don't y'know? The weather is much colder there, I can tell you. I'm actually looking for my son, Rhys Waveral. You've probably all seen him on the box. He's a simply marvellous actor and I'm here with his closest friend, Mademoiselle Peach Delight, to tell him that all will be well. . . . Ah,' and he withdrew an envelope from his coat pocket, 'my speech!'

'Oh no!' groaned Rhys as he recognised the letter he had left for his father at the Leicester.

'Dear Father,' read out the Brigadier as Rhys tried to crawl inside his Plate in embarrassment, 'I have searched deeply to find words of comfort for you in your predicament. When I am feeling a trifle blue I always say these words to myself. The prayer written below has always given me great strength. Kneel down and say it three times. . . .'

The Brigadier, helped by Peach, descended to his knees, bones cracking all over the place. The spotlight moved down to focus on him and he knelt, praying, like some stock-market knight about to embark upon a crusade. As he began to read, Rhys realised to his horror that instead of a prayer he had enclosed in his father's letter one of the last remnants of his training at the Centrale Kontiki.

'All I want . . .' began the Brigadier,
'All I want is a proper cup of coffee,
Made with a proper copper coffee pot.

I may be off my dot,
But I want a cup of coffee from a proper coffee pot.
Tin coffee pots and iron coffee pots,
They're no use to me,
If I can't have a proper cup of coffee,
In a proper coffee pot,
Then I'll have a cup of tea.
Now, I'm supposed to say this three times . . .
All I want . . .'

'No, Dim, once is enough. . . .' Gently Peach extracted the piece of paper from the Brigaider's clutches, to Rhys's intense relief, and helped the old man to his feet. The Brig was quite overcome with emotion.

'What a wonderful prayer my son has given me. Where is he?'

'Over here,' said Dorita, waving.

The Brigadier and Peach linked arms and shielded their eyes with their hands, looking for their wayward friend. They looked like a double act in a musical comedy about sailors.

'Hi, bitch!' said Peach when she found him.

'Hi, darlings. What are you both doing here?'

'We came to see you.'

'Are *you* his Daddy?' asked Ashby.

'Yes, isn't it marvellous?' sang the Brigadier.

'Yes, well, ah think we should start the dancing, don't you?' said Ashby.

'Certainly,' answered the Brigadier and held out his arms to Ashby. The couple waltzed off together.

Peach, accompanied by Rhys and Wilbur, went over to Rikki's table.

'I don't have any more drugs. I can't give you anything,' apologised Rhys.

'Bitch! Don't worry. We've got plenty. Dim, where are you?'

'Here, little girl,' called the Brigadier as he swept by in the arms of Ashby de la Zouche.

'Where is my little packet, darling?'

'In my briefcase, darling thing.'

217

'What is going on?' asked Rhys. 'Has Daddy been smuggling drugs? What has happened to him?'

'He discover Peach Delight. He change a lot.'

And slowly but surely the entire cast of characters assembled – Sir Maurice Goodbuns, Bob Browser, Harry Bellows-Forth, 'Pepsi' and 'Shirlee', Lady Dinah and even Little Beige Riding Hood. Only the Brigadier was missing and that was because he was off doing the twist with Ashby de la Zouche.

Rhys endeavoured to explain everything to Rikki but luckily she was so drunk she wouldn't have understood even if her own family had arrived.

'You very professional with your client.' Peach smiled at her friend.

'Well, we have a living to make.'

'You don't have to worry. I sort everything with Dim. He give you the money.'

'You're joking?'

'No, I serious. It no good for you in the marketplace, honey.'

'Why on earth not? It's good enough for you.'

'Is different. I have no choice. You do.'

'That's rubbish, Peach. You have a choice as well.'

'Yes, honey. I have choice. But what do I do? Become secretary? I prefer hooker on the street than booker in model agency. And the money. . . . You understand?'

The two friends sighed in unison.

'So what do we do?' asked Rhys.

'We enjoy,' she replied. She pointed to Wilbur who was now talking earnestly with Ashby. There seemed to have been a reconciliation. 'I go dance with him. He cute.' And before Rhys could object – this was all Ashby needed at this point – she was off. He watched his exquisite friend squeeze her way round the table to Wilbur. She wriggled between him and Ashby and sat down on Wilbur's lap, flirting wildly all the time. Wilbur smiled at her, entranced. She put her arms around his neck so that her enormous, perfect tits came up to his nose and she looked down on him so that her long dark hair splayed out all over his face.

A cat with a mouse.

Ashby began to look a bit peeved and, sensing this, Peach

turned to include him, putting one arm around his shoulder too.

Very professional, thought Rhys, smiling. Peach caught Dorita's eye and laughed. A sweet, innocent laugh. The one she hated laughing and she immediately covered her mouth with her hand.

'*Vas parler avec ton michton,*' she said. '*Sois professionel, cheri.*' Be professional, darling, go and see to your client.

'*Jes suis defonsé,*' he replied. I'm stoned.

'*Moi aussi. Allez!*'

Rhys moved over to Rikki who was laughing all by herself.

'What are you laughing at, darling?'

'My costume, it's so kooky.'

'Yes, it's terribly kooky, isn't it? Would you like to dance, darling?'

'I'd love to, Lancelot,' she breathed.

As they got up from the table, Lady Dinah screeched, 'Rhys is going to dance with that Duchess. What fun! Come on 'Pepsi', let's dance too.'

Rhys and Rikki waltzed together. Rikki put her head on Rhys's shoulder. The Fruit Plate had long since been discarded and Rhys was down to his silver tights.

'Oh, Lancelot. . . .' she murmured.

'Yes, Rikki, my own wild vine . . . ?'

'I just love you. That's all. . . .'

Aaaaargh! thought Rhys. But, 'I love you too,' he said.

'Can we meet again after this weekend?' she slurped in his ear.

'As often as you want, my darling,' he said carefully, meaning, 'As often as you can afford'.

'I want you to meet all my friends back home.'

'I'd love to,' he said, inwardly quaking.

Back at the table they all drank more champagne and Rhys took another Ecstasy slipped to him by Peach. The final act was at hand and, unlike Greek tragedy, it was unfortunately going to be played out on stage.

The Brigadier came and sat next to his son. They had not really spoken since he had arrived.

'They really are the most frightful bitches, the French, aren't they?'

'In what sense, Daddy?'

'Well, they say the most frightful things. Do you know someone actually told me that our darling Peach was in fact a man masquerading as a girl. Have you ever *heard* such a ridiculous story?'

'Seldom,' smiled Rhys.

'When I mentioned it later to the divine creature, do you know what she said? "We don't care." She's an absolute cracker, isn't she?'

'Yes, that too,' laughed the prodigal son. 'Did you have a good time in Paris?'

'Oh, yes, rather. Splendid people, your friends. *Splendid!*'

'I'm glad you liked them.'

'I misjudged you all, I'm afraid. For that, I apologise. Of course, you are all utterly without discipline but that's our fault, really, just as much as yours. When are you going back?'

'First thing tomorrow. And you?'

'I'm going to take P up in the Atlas Mountains. Raleighe-Smith and I were holed up there for months during the war. Want to revisit some old spots.'

'Good idea, Daddy. Well, I'll see you soon, then.'

'You needn't worry about that. I shall certainly be up in your neck of the woods more often, old boy. I want to lead a totally new life while I've still got something left in me.'

'So does Mummy, by the looks of things. She says she's going to stay here until the end of the *Love in the Desert* shoot to help out "Pepsi" and "Shirlee". Then she says she might go with them on this shoot in Colombia. Mummy a hairdresser, would you credit it, Daddy?'

'*Goodness!*' chortled the Brigadier. 'Whatever next?'

'Whatever next indeed,' said Rhys, watching Sticky Rikki edge her way towards him round the table.

'Now, where's my briefcase? I feel like another half an "E". Will you excuse me?'

'I'll see you later, Daddy. Glad you came,' said the son, slightly shocked.

'So am I, old boy, so am I. I think I might get a house here. Property's terribly good value, y'know?'

'Good!' said Dorita, and father and son parted.

For the first time in his life Rhys was sorry to see his father go as he turned to face Rikki, heaving in anticipation beside him.

It was nearly time to Do the Deed.

CHAPTER TWENTY-FIVE: in which Rhys and Rikki do the deed

Rikki's room, which had seemed so banal in daylight, took on a whole new character as Rhys crept through the communicating door that night. The windows were open and the thick dirty net curtains were blowing into the room.

Outside the new moon hung over the white city. Rikki was lying in her bed, propped up against a mound of pillows. She was wearing a honey-coloured negligée and towelling turban and she looked younger in the blue moonlight. She had had the good sense to turn off the lights.

'Darling. . . .' she said simply, as her knight in shining armour stood by the door.

Rhys was in another world. He had pushed himself to the limit with countless drugs and he now imagined himself to be a hero in a trashy novel. He looked at Rikki and in his eyes she was completely transformed. A young, frail girl, lost in the desert, miles away from home, was lying on the bed waiting for him. He was so far gone that he really had made the leap into fairyland. And while he did not even know who he himself was in this cheap story he had written, he knew that he too was lost.

'I've waited for this moment for so long,' he said, leaning against the half open door.

'Ooooooh, so have I,' wailed Rikki, lost in her own personal drama.

He walked over to the bed and suddenly, for a split second, he saw his mother, Lady Dinah, lying there. He blinked. 'Three hundred spastics. Rather a good show!' he heard someone say from far away. His confused computer jammed on the image.

He lay down on top of Rikki. Her bones snapped and crackled like a blazing log fire. His face approached hers and her face changed from his mother's to his wife's and then, quite suddenly, disappeared altogether. 'You *are* awful . . .' the voice from afar continued. 'Now here are some sweet peas from home. . . .'

'What's the matter, honey?' whispered Rikki, breathless with desire.

'I feel lonely,' said the boy, truthfully. Her face came back like the picture on the TV screen and he smiled. 'There you are,' he said, stroking her head. He took her jaw in his hand and kissed her hard with his eyes tight shut. Her little old tongue, rather like a parrot's, responded eagerly to his own. Dorita was a very good kisser and he knew it.

Even if he didn't exactly know who it was he was kissing.

Rikki moaned. He opened his eyes and for a moment remembered where he was and with whom. His heart suddenly began to thump.

'Is that you, Rikki?' he said in a far-away voice.

'Yes, my darling. It's me. Come to me.'

Hurtled back into reality, Rhys fought off the desire to giggle and tried to push his racing mind back into the picture he had enjoyed before. His mother flashed back. Then Wilbur. Then nothing. He felt himself being rolled over and his shorts being pulled down and then, as a mouth with sharp little teeth enveloped his (luckily) hard cock, he remembered where he was again. It was certainly a toothy blow job but, while he'd had better, he'd certainly had worse. He smiled at his situation and looked dreamily out of the window.

'Nobody could find me here. Not even me,' he whispered.

'What, honey?' said Rikki with her mouth full. He removed her head and laid her back on the pillows. He was lucid, back in the present, but it didn't seem to matter. He wanted her. In fact he found he was rather excited and without further ado Rhys Waveral made love to Mrs Rikki Lancaster.

The net curtains blew in accompaniment and Rikki's cries resounded into the Moroccan night like a cockatoo's. When the act was over she fell straight away into a deep sleep. Rhys lay there on top of her for ten minutes, reflecting on life and art in general.

This is my new career, he thought. Then, carefully, he got off and left the room and went to his own to prepare for the mammoth hangover he could already feel arriving with the approaching dawn.

The telephone was ringing in his room. Oh no, he thought, she's woken up and wants an action replay. Well, it's just not on. He picked up the receiver and, trying to sound as tired as he could, he said hello.

'Rita, it's Bob. What are you doing?'

'I was just going to bed. I've had the most harrowing day.'

'I can imagine. I'm downstairs. Shall we have a drink?'

'All right. Come on up.'

Rhys took a shower and decided not to go to bed. After all, escape to Paris was at hand. The flight was at 10.45, and it was now 5.30. The dawn was rising and the sky was streaked with red. Bob knocked on the door and as he came in, as if in salute to the meeting of the two foreign queens, the high priests on all the mosque towers broke out. 'Aaaahhooooowaya!' they sang. Bob and Rhys looked out of the window. Pigeons and gulls were circling the city. It was very beautiful.

'It feels like the end of the world,' said Rhys.

'My dear, it probably is,' said Bob.

'Well, the end of the one we know at any rate. It's funny to feel old at thirty.'

'It's because we're outmoded machines, my dear. The world has moved on so fast and one suddenly finds that all the things that one was brought up to do and think are completely obsolete in the modern world. My dear, when you think about it, I used to get up at about one, hit the street at about three, bring some-body home, fuck them, then drink half a bottle of wine before starting the whole delightful process again. Work was something one did if it didn't interfere too much with one's life. And one did it well with no compromise to what other people would think. And now. . . .' Bob left off half way through his sentence and stared gloomily out of the window. They were silent again for several minutes.

'Your problem is that you made the fatal mistake of giving up sex and taking up money. There was a half-way house, you know?' said Rhys.

'You mean safe sex? I couldn't, my dear. You see, that's what I mean, condoms, fumbling, no fluids, or whatever it is they say. It's all too much. For my money it's better to do nothing.'

'So you don't drink, you don't fuck, you're just wasting away in a bitter obsession over money which doesn't suit you at all.'

'In your opinion. And anyway, look at you. You look com-pletely wasted as well. You can't possibly think it's good for you to carry on the way you do. You looked positively grey this evening. Even Goodbuns noticed. That Ecstasy is no good.'

'I know,' sighed Rhys. 'I suppose I'm just holding out. I can't bear the idea of giving up being young and becoming an old theatrical codger like the rest of you.'

'Better an old codger than an old cripple, my dear.'

'It used to be so much more fun when we didn't know any-thing, that's for sure.'

'We still don't know anything, that's the trouble.'

Rhys began packing his clothes into his new suitcase.

'When did you start dressing like this, may one ask?'

'She bought them for me,' said Rhys.

'Who, the old boiler?'

226

'Yes, she wanted me to look presentable. The result is that I look more like a gigolo than ever.'

'Are you back on the game then?' asked Bob, laughing.

'I'm afraid I am rather. I'm broke, you see.'

'How you can lecture me on my life when yours is clearly in such a state of chaos is beyond me.'

'Well, just don't think about it then, Bob. Anyway, I must ask you to excuse me. I must sit down and write a letter and sort myself out. I'm leaving in a few hours.' Rhys was a little bit peeved by now, if the truth were known.

Alone again, he settled down to write a farewell note to his bride.

Darling Rikki,

I didn't want to wake you. And my plane is at ten. So I'll see you in Paris. I had a wonderful weekend. I hope we can spend another soon.

Love Rhys

He sealed the envelope and slipped back through the communicating door. Rikki was snoring like an elephant. Her turban had slipped off and underneath she had the hair of a new-born baby. He left the letter by her sleeping face. She looked old and haggard again in the cold morning light. Rhys moved on into the next room.

Elida and Thelma were asleep on the sofa. Rhys had to get the other half of the money and he wondered if Wilbur was in the middle of doing the same up at the de la Zouche mansion. He shook Elida Schumann and she woke up.

'Hi, honey,' she said, launching straight into the speaking clock routine.

'Hi, darling, I'm leaving. My flight is at ten. I thought you might . . . you know . . . be able to give me the cheque.'

Elida looked coarse for a moment. She got up and trotted into the other room to have a look.

'We had a marvellous night,' he said, hoping to make the situation clear.

'Good,' said Elida, yawning. She staggered back to the sofa and reached for her bag. 'Here it is, all prepared. I think we're going to all meet again. She likes you.'

'I like her, too,' lied Dorita.
'Good,' said Elida again. 'So aren't you going to say goodbye?'
'I already did,' he said – and left.

CHAPTER TWENTY-SIX: in which Rhys discovers that
 boots are not necessarily made for walking

The taxi taking Rhys to the airport was falling to pieces. Every
one of his nerves was frazzled and raw. He was beginning to feel
seriously ill and the usual self-reproaches emerged. In fact, he
could feel himself working his way into a major panic. To make
matters worse, the taxi driver was chatty.

'You like Earth, Wind and Fire?' he asked, brandishing a
dog-eared tape.

'Not terribly,' answered Rhys as coldly as possible. He was
going to be sick if he had to talk.

'Me too,' enthused the driver and put on the tape. So to the tune of *Sequins and Pearls*, Rhys jogged and lurched across the green plains towards the airport. Luckily for him he had a bottle of 10 mg Valium. He took one and began to feel better, so he took another.

To distract himself he started to read the mail that Lady Dinah had brought out to him from London. It was mostly bills and invitations which he promptly threw out the window. Then he came across one from Peter Moody's friend who had been looking after him. It read:

Peter Moody has been ill with cancer for six months now. Unfortunately he has never had any medical insurance and now his resources have been completely depleted. We, his friends, are trying to raise fifty thousand pounds for him so that he is able to pay his mortgage and his nurse. We hope you will be able to make a donation.

It was signed by three names Rhys did not recognise. He put down the letter and felt the familiar panic seethe through his body. He closed his eyes and said a Hail Mary, thinking of the Catholic prophet all the while.

Then suddenly everything started to move very quickly and before he knew it he was taxiing down the runway, strapped into his first-class seat, on the way to Paris. His nerves, insufficiently quelled by the two Valium, demanded a third to which he foolishly succumbed, washing it down with a very strong vodka. The plane roared into take-off and Rhys passed out into a dreamless slumber.

It is a well-known fact that drug mixing can be fatally dangerous and Rhys's body was doing all it could to retain the contents of his sloshing stomach as he slept. His breathing was irregular and gasping. He woke suddenly and, through filmy eyes, became aware of some disorder in the first-class cabin. Air hostesses were running about and little 'Fasten Your Seat Belt' signs were flashing and pinging. The passengers were all 'Ooooohing' and 'Aaaahing' because outside a gigantic electric storm was raging. The plane swooped and rose again. Bags were falling out of the overhead lockers. In short, there was pandemonium.

Dorita regarded all this through half-closed lids and the fuzz of his drug-raddled brain. Then he thought he heard someone say the fatal words, 'We've lost an engine.'

So we're going to crash, he thought calmly. Suddenly oxygen masks were dropping down, at which point the entire plane screamed.

'Just like a children's party when the crackers are pulled,' thought Rhys.

Then the lights went out and there was further screaming. Rhys thought he'd better have a shot at it too but he couldn't seem to move his mouth and nothing came out.

'Oh, well,' he thought, 'this seems to be it. Just after I've slogged my guts out to pay my hotel bill. . . .'

Lightning flashed and crashed against the side of the plane.

What am I going to do with all my money? What a waste!

Then he remembered the letter from Peter Moody's friends.

I'll give it to Peter Moody. That's what I'll do.

In the dark he managed to find Rikki's cheque and then he searched for his pen with an arm that would hardly move – the brand new Waterman that had come with Rikki's outfits. He crossed out his own name on the cheque and wrote in Peter's. He stopped a hysterical hostess as she passed and asked politely: 'Do you have an envelope, please?'

She just looked at him in horror so he put the cheque in the envelope Peter Moody's letter had arrived in and readdressed it, writing on the top: URGENT. PLEASE SEND.

Then he laid it on his lap and searched for his Valium bottle.

If the plane's going down I'm not going to wait up for it. He emptied the remaining Valium – eight in all – into his hand and swallowed them. Then he said a Hail Mary and lay back as the plane continued to fall and, with his hands clasped to the letter, our hero passed out into a coma.

Suddenly he was Lancelot again. Running as always. As in life, in fact. Exhausted, coming apart and sweating. There they were, as usual just out of reach, the black knight and the two barge ladies. Why was everything in life too far away to grab? They were talking and looking at him and he knew suddenly that he was going to die and that if he didn't find out what it was they were saying this time, he never would and he would be committed to an eternity of running. With a huge effort he girded his body into overdrive and began to run faster than he had ever run before. The blood surged through his muscles and he prayed deep, wordless prayers of supplication. The rocks sped by, his feet barely seeming to touch them. The sea crashed against him, knocking him sideways, but he sped on regardless. He could feel his breath going and he knew he couldn't hold on much longer. Then suddenly, out of the sky from behind, a giant oxygen mask swooped down. It hissed at him and with one final effort, Lancelot jumped and caught it as it went by. Just as he could breathe no longer, he put it to his face and then he was floating in the air, totally weightless.

There they were, the black knight and the barge ladies, right beside him and he could hear them laughing.

'Now I'm going to find out,' he gasped. 'I'm saved, they will teach me the secret of existence, the most profound truth of the Round Table,' and he hovered over them, listening.

''Ere, I reely like your boots,' said one of the barge ladies in a surprise Cockney accent. Maybe they were Bond girls after all?

'Yeah, they're really nice!' agreed the second.

'Where did you get them?' asked the first. The black knight didn't answer. He seemed a bit nonplussed, as indeed was Lancelot. This wasn't what they were meant to be talking about. Or was it? 'Are they theatrical boots?' ventured the second barge girl.

'Yes,' answered the black knight finally. 'When you open the box, they say, "Hello darling, are you working?"'

To Be Continued?